I'LL BE THERE FOR YOU

I'LL BE THERE FOR YOU

BRIEANNA WILKOFF

NEW YORK   LOS ANGELES

Jacket design by Rejenne Pavon
Jacket Copyright 2022 by Winding Road Stories
Interior book design by A Raven Design
Reverse Burn Book design by Susan Albert

ISBN#: 979-8-9850815-5-8 (pbk)
ISBN#: 979-8-9850815-6-5 (ebook)

Published by Winding Road Stories

www.windingroadstories.com

To my family, my "Heart and Soul,"
most especially:

My parents—I am so grateful for "The Love in Your Eyes"

My daughter—I adore you, "Sweet Child O' Mine"

My husband—my best friend—"Thank You for Loving Me"

"NEVER SAY GOODBYE"

I like to pretend my father's mortician was Jon Bon Jovi's grandfather. Granted, we didn't go to Bongiovi Funeral Home because we don't live in Raritan, New Jersey, and Bon Jovi's grandpop is probably dead too, but if somehow Mr. Bongiovi had buried my dad, it would have made him happy.

He loved '80s rock. (My dad—I don't know about Mr. Bongiovi. But I figure if your grandson is the front man of a famous rock band, the music can't help but grow on you.) Journey, Def Leppard, Mötley Crüe, Guns N' Roses, AC/DC—their songs were all regular fixtures in my house growing up, but none more than Bon Jovi. They were Dad's favorite.

Shamelessly, he took every opportunity to tell people about the 23 times he'd seen them in concert. My mom and I would roll our eyes at each other whenever he started in. But it was an eye roll of loving indulgence, which is why I stop outside Mom's room at the sight of a Bon Jovi shirt on top of a pile of clothes on her bed.

"What are you doing?"

She doesn't answer. When I step through the doorway, I see the earbuds. I move closer and wave my hand to get her attention as she drops another shirt—the Slippery When Wet Tour—onto the stack.

Startled when she finally notices me, my mother wipes quickly at her eyes and then stops whatever she's listening to.

"What are you doing?" I ask again, an edge to my voice.

With a sigh, she sits on the bed, her shoulders hunched forward. "Going through your dad's stuff. I figured it was time."

Arms folded across my chest, I demand, "What are you doing with it?"

"Donating what I can, pitching the rest."

I note a hole at the collar of the SWWT shirt and stare at the pile in horror. "Is this the trash?"

Mom sticks her finger through the seam. "Does this look like something I can donate?"

Maybe not. I dig through the rejects—countless (*okay, exactly* 23) Bon Jovi shirts, along with a bunch paying homage to other rock gods. "How can you get rid of these? They're Dad's Bon Jovi shirts."

"I know what they are, Rae." She shrugs. "What would you have me do with them?"

My heart beats faster. "I don't know. But you can't throw them away—Dad loved these."

"We can't keep them forever. It's been a year since—"

"No, it hasn't! Not till Tuesday."

"You're right," Mom says as she rubs her forehead.

Once she meets my gaze again, I dare her with my eyes to pick up the trash bag on the floor. Instead, she brushes her fingers over the shirt, no fight left in her. I grab the pile from under her hand and storm out.

♪

MY DAD DIED ON MONDAY, October 22. I tried really hard to not remember the date. For weeks after the accident, every time the date would pop into my head, I'd say other numbers to fuddle my brain. *October 22...25...20...27.* I hate the idea of a death-iversary. But despite my best efforts, the date was insistent, and now I'll never forget it.

The day before the one-year milestone (*death-iversary*), I try unsuccessfully to focus on other dates teachers deem worthy of my attention, but none of them can drown out *October 22* muttering in the background.

After last period, I look at one more date: October 24. Above it is a single word: AUDITIONS. I've stood before this poster every day since it went up two weeks ago. The theatre department is putting on *It's a Wonderful Life: A Live Radio Play.* Last fall they did *Peter and the Starcatcher.* I had signed up to audition. Then my world fell apart.

By the time *Little Shop of Horrors* rolled around in March, I could have auditioned, theoretically. But I wasn't ready to sing again. I don't know if I'll ever be.

"You signing up?" A voice intrudes on my thoughts, and I turn to find a boy whose most striking feature—despite nice eyes and invitingly tousled hair—is his shoes, which sport a collage of Playbills.

"Um...I haven't decided yet." I refocus my attention on the wall.

"You should. It'll be fun."

I hesitate before I turn to him again. "Are you auditioning?"

The look he gives me refutes the "There are no stupid questions" credo. "I don't act. I'm the student director. Name's Mac."

He stares at me expectantly until I say, "I'm Raina—Rae."

"You a freshman, Raina-Rae? I haven't seen you in our theatrical environs before."

"I'm a sophomore."

"Same. Why didn't you try out last year?"

I study the *Les Mis* waif on his foot. "It didn't work with my schedule."

"Then now's your chance. And come on, who doesn't like *It's a Wonderful Life?*"

"It's not at the top of my list." I'm not trying to be difficult, but seeing George give up so much throughout the movie makes me sad.

"No? Watch it again. I'll admit the first couple viewings are painful—the situation looks so bleak. But once you're one hundred percent positive things will turn out all right in the end, it wins hands down for feel-goodness."

I'm rusty at this talking to new people thing, so I don't know how to end the conversation. I go back to the poster, hoping Mac will disappear as suddenly as he materialized, but I can tell he's still here, waiting. "Do I have to prepare a monologue or something?" I ask.

"Nope, just read from the script." He raises his eyebrow. "So, I'll see you Thursday?"

"Maybe." I start walking away.

"I'll give you the moon, Raina-Rae!" he calls after me.

THAT EVENING, I descend to the basement to watch the Frank Capra classic. Forgoing the couch, which faces the TV, I sit in Dad's recliner, pulling his knobbly fleece blanket over me as the black and white title sequence appears on the screen. I don't mind the old movies—I grew up watching Julie Andrews in *The Sound of Music* and Frank Sinatra in *Guys and Dolls*. My grandma died before I was born, but my grandpa lives right down the street, meaning movie nights are a regular occurrence, so the simple filmmaking fills me with comforting nostalgia.

During the scene when Harry returns home from college, Mom comes down the stairs carrying a laundry basket. "A little early for Christmas movies, isn't it?"

Given that she continues past me into the laundry room, I don't feel the need to respond. I turn up the volume to mute the rhythmic *swish* of the washing machine.

She returns empty-handed and sits on the couch, perched on the edge of the cushion. "Can you pause it a minute?"

I turn toward her with a sigh, swinging my legs over the side of the chair.

She rubs her hands together and looks at her lap. "So, we haven't talked about tomorrow."

And just like that, it's ten degrees warmer in here. "What about it?"

"I understand it will be a hard day for you, for us. What can I do to help?"

Squirming, I look at the floor. "I don't know."

"Do you want to skip school?"

"And do what?" Like it matters. School, home, freakin' Disney World—tomorrow, any of them will be the unhappiest place on earth.

"Whatever you need—talk, cry."

"Haven't we done enough of that?" You could fill a bathtub with the tears I've shed.

Mom reaches her hand out, but I stand, the blanket falling to the ground and burying my feet. "I know you're hurting," she says. "I wish I knew how to help you."

"You can't help me because nobody can fix this." I move toward the stairs, but Mom blocks my path.

"I'm not saying I can make everything okay, but sometimes... sometimes I'm afraid you're not really processing what you're feeling. Of course, you're struggling. But you have to work through those emotions."

I cross my arms. "Oh really? Is that what I need to do?"

Mom's face takes on a pinched look that's equal parts exasperated and wounded. "I don't have all the answers. But if you would talk to me, share what you're going through, tell me what you want—"

"What I want?" The heat that flashes through me must melt my filter because words spew out. "What I want is to go to school tomorrow and come home and have dinner with my parents. I want to go to bed and know they'll both be here in the morning. What I *want* is to not be having this conversation. I want to rewind time and pretend the last year didn't happen. And no matter what I do tomorrow, or the next day, or the day after that, it won't be the tiniest bit okay because I won't see my dad, and I hate that he's gone!"

Rushing past Mom before she can stop me, I race up the stairs and slam my door. I sit on the floor, reach for Dad's New Jersey Tour shirt, and hold it close to my heart as I sob.

For the past 364 days, I've woken up and missed the smell of coffee, which I don't even like, because Dad was always the first one up. At night, I've longed for him to raise his hand, pinky and index finger up, and say, "Rock those dreams." I'd give anything to hear him ask about the most interesting part of my day or, if I was being snarky, the least interesting part. Every time I've heard one of his favorite songs on the radio, my heart has ached to not see his excitement, and it hurts to imagine all the Bon Jovi concerts he'll never attend. I miss the smile in his eyes and his one crooked tooth and the ridiculous high-pitched sound he made when he was laughing so hard he could barely breathe.

The past 364 days have been the worst days of my life.

And the very worst part of all is knowing my father died because of me.

"BROKENPROMISELAND"

Twenty-four hours. That's all I have to get through before this year from hell is over. I'll have survived all the firsts—the first Thanksgiving *without Dad*. Our first Christmas *without Dad*. The first last day of school, the first first day of school, the first birthday, fireworks, and snowfall. The first death-iversary.

I emerge from my room with only minutes to spare so I can avoid talking to Mom. To further discourage conversation, I put in my earbuds, then grab a banana and give her a noncommittal wave as I leave.

But sitting through algebra makes me question my decision to come to school. It's impossible to pay attention to quadratic equations when I'm staring at the clock and thinking about this day last year, and how at 7:55 in the morning, I had no idea what was coming. Twenty-four hours is too damn long—how am I going to get through this day?

Teachers stop taking attendance after second period, so instead of going to my third class, I slip outside to my car. I don't leave the parking lot, just pull out my phone, shuffle Bon Jovi, and close my eyes.

For the first month, I couldn't listen to them. No matter the song, the first few notes were enough to undo me. It was problematic—I couldn't listen to the radio; it made driving more dangerous. TV shows or movies unexpectedly turned tragic with a single line of Jon's vocals. During a trip to the mall, a familiar Bon Jovi guitar riff playing overhead in a clothing store could send me searching desperately for a corner to cower in.

After an embarrassing incident at Kroger (*clean up—mess of a human, aisle four*), I resorted to at-home DIY exposure therapy, grabbing a box of tissues and pressing play. I listened to song after song, crying loud, animalistic, body-racking tears. With song after song, I sunk deeper into the pain, sobbing so hard there were moments when I literally couldn't breathe. Rending open the wound, I didn't stop until, finally, the torrent of tears slowed to a stream and then, after a few more tracks, a trickle.

Now the songs are like an old teddy bear, a link between Dad and me. I wish I could have gone to a concert with him. They were here in Columbus two years ago, but we were in Florida for spring break. And Dad tried to take me to the Rock and Roll Hall of Fame induction, but tickets sold out in minutes. He and Mom fought about buying tickets from a third-party seller—she wouldn't agree to the exorbitant price.

He was so miffed about missing the ceremony that he didn't even see the exhibit after the fact. It was the longest I ever saw him hold a grudge. But Mom made a peace offering by planning for us to drive to Cleveland and spend a day at the museum, then fly to New Jersey and retrace Jon's footsteps (an excursion that probably cost more than the tickets would have). She scheduled it for the week of Dad's birthday. In November. Three weeks too late.

I know where I'm going today.

My heart thumps as I pull up Google Maps and type "Rock and Roll Hall of Fame." Two hours. Mom would be a basket case if she knew. I've barely had my license a month, and it took some serious coaxing for her to let me behind the wheel in the first place.

We have a strict to-and-from-school-only agreement. In her mind, every time I move out of Park is an opportunity for disaster, so the less my gearshift moves, the better. And driving across the state? I might never see my keys again.

Still, I put the Jetta in reverse.

Of course, I catch the tail end of rush hour traffic, so I white-knuckle it as I merge onto the freeway. Soon I'm cruising at high speed along I-71 North, focusing on "Bells of Freedom" and willing my hands to relax. I'm sure Mom would have something to say about me listening to music while operating a motor vehicle, but Bon Jovi gets me there unscathed.

I've seen pictures of the iconic pyramidal building but seeing it in person—my breath hitches. I stare at it for a minute, trying to regain control over my body. Once I'm ready, I cross the street and stand before the giant red letters proclaiming "LONG LIVE ROCK."

It's probably only fifty degrees, so I don't think I'm shaking from the cold. Since Dad can't be here himself, I have to be his eyes and ears, and I have to do it right.

He would have wanted to see more than the terrace, though, so I draw in a determined breath and make my way to the revolving door. On the other side, I stop and stare up at the metallic car suspended from the ceiling, wondering what Dad would have done first.

Tickets, genius. The smiling woman under the welcome sign directs me down the escalator and to the right. A minute later, armed with my purple wristband, I enter.

A bearded guy taking souvenir photos mobs me. "Grab a guitar and let's get a picture of you rockin' out."

I wasn't prepared to acknowledge the existence of anyone other than the two-dimensional gods of rock, and my armpits shove sweat through my pores. With Camera Guy staring at me, I have no desire to pick up a guitar, but we would have done it with Dad. He would have stuck out his tongue or faked the splits, and he would have demanded we take the grossly overpriced evidence home with us. But I could never bear to look at such a picture without him in it. Shaking my head, I rush past without making eye contact.

My nerves settle a bit in the dimness of the museum. I could spend hours here but know I have to be home before Mom is, so I imagine this like a scavenger hunt—find as many items as possible from the bands Dad loved. It doesn't take long before I come across several, and I get a little misty-eyed. I don't know what he would have liked best. Would it have been the outfits—the jacket and red-striped tie of Angus Young, from AC/DC? Or the instruments— the bass guitar of Michael Anthony from Van Halen, or Slash's electric one from Guns N' Roses? Alice Cooper's thigh-high leopard boots, Axl Rose's suspenders? Or my personal favorite, the handwritten (and largely illegible, but still badass) original draft of "Highway to Hell"?

Although I'm a little disappointed there's nothing of Bon Jovi's, I turn the corner and find "Legends of Rock and Roll." Surely, they'll be in there. I wind my way up and down the aisles, looking for the names that soundtracked my childhood. My heart dances when I see Guns N' Roses and the Slash pinball machine. *How cool is that?* Like it can read my mind, the insistent voice overhead reminds me not to touch the artifacts. The placard says the song "Ain't Goin' Down" can be heard exclusively in the machine. Knowing about an undiscovered GNR song would have driven Dad crazy, and I can picture him reaching his hand in, nagging voice be damned. If it weren't covered by a clear lid, he probably would have tried to get his fingers on Slash's top hat too.

Quick time check reminds me I better move, so I take the escalator up to the Hall of Fame. I know the most recent inductees will be featured, but I still feel a pang at the sight of the gallery with the new class, mourning the absence of all the Bon Jovi stuff we could have seen last year.

Running my finger down the *B*s on the wall of past inductees, I linger on Bon Jovi before tracing the letters of their signatures:

David Bryan, with his oversize "D" and "B"; Hugh McDonald, with not much more than a "D" and a line; Alec John Such, with the overlapping "S" and "h"; Tico Torres, whose handwriting is surprisingly pretty; Richie Sambora, whose name is the only one I can read clearly; and finally, Jon Bon Jovi, with his circles around each initial letter.

Next, I don a pair of headphones and cycle through video clips until I get to Bon Jovi. It's only three minutes of the induction ceremony, but it's three minutes more than my dad got to see.

My heart swells when the band starts performing, and my head floods with thoughts of all the concerts my dad saw, of all the ones he won't. I try to watch through my blurry vision, but eventually, I close my eyes and just listen. When it cuts to Jon's speech, I lose my shit because what he says hits too close to home: "Time is the most precious commodity we have. I thank my lucky stars for the time that I got to spend with each one of you."

How do I feel lucky for the time I got with my dad when what I got was monumentally less than I should have had?

I dig a tissue from my purse, smush it up to my face, and try to breathe without blubbering. When the video ends, I swallow the lump in my throat and twist the dial to the beginning. As I go through the alphabet—AC/DC, Aerosmith, Guns N' Roses, Journey, Queen—I remember all the times we listened to these songs together. All the times Dad turned up the volume when one of his favorites came on the car radio. All the times he shook his head in admonition when I started to talk during a killer guitar solo. And all the times we rocked out while he made dinner.

By the time I get to Van Halen, my tissue is a soggy, shredded mess. I place the headphones back on their hook, then squeeze my eyes shut and wipe my face with my sleeve.

There's a light touch on my shoulder, and I turn to find the worried face of a museum volunteer. "Are you okay, honey?"

Normally, I'd say, "I'm fine." This stranger doesn't need to know my story. But today my head shakes no. I'm so far from fine it's a speck in the distance.

The woman, short and stooped, takes my hand and gently pulls me to a bench. "What's making you so upset?" She has grandma eyes, full of concern and caring.

"My dad loved rock music. Bon Jovi most of all." I take a shuddery breath. "He didn't get to see their induction exhibit.... He died last year...a year ago today."

Saying these words out loud sucks. It's not like they're news to me, but every time I say them, they unleash a new flood of tears. I cover my face with my hands and try to hide the red, scrunchy pain I am helpless to contain.

Marlene, according to her name tag, pulls a fresh tissue from her pocket and gives it to me. "Thank you," I choke out as I attempt to wipe away the tears and snot and sadness.

I ball up the tissue in my fist and place my hands in my lap, but Marlene reaches out and takes them in hers.

"You poor thing." She gives me a squeeze. "What an awful loss. Your heart must be broken."

Sympathy. Another surefire way to open the floodgates. "I'm sorry," I say once I can talk.

"Honey, don't apologize. You need to let these feelings out. If you don't, they'll eat you up inside." After a moment, she says softly, "Are you here alone?" When I nod, she continues. "Grief will do you in if you keep it bottled up, but it's too hard to manage without some folks by your side."

Not sure what to say, I look at the Hall of Fame gallery. "I wish my dad could have seen Bon Jovi's stuff. Is any of it still here?"

"Most of what the museum gets is on loan from the musicians or their families. We don't actually own very much of what's in the exhibits. Oh, wait." Marlene takes out her phone, tapping and scrolling as she says, "It's not much, but I can show you what was on the display."

I look at the photo she shows me—blurbs about Bon Jovi's top hits, their influence on young bands, and Jon's philanthropic efforts for housing and hunger. "Do you have any pictures of the artifacts?" I hold my breath, angry at myself for hoping.

Marlene furrows her brow. "You know what?" Without waiting for me to respond, she stands. "Come with me."

We take the escalator to the lowest level. As we start down a dark corridor, she whispers, "If anyone asks, you're my granddaughter."

At the end of the hall, she looks over her shoulder, then unlocks a door and ushers me inside. The room has a distinct attic vibe. Boxes are stacked chest-high, and mysterious objects are shrouded by sheets. Marlene picks her way through the labyrinth until she eventually kneels before a box and pulls open the flaps. "I thought I remembered...there are a few things we haven't shipped back yet."

Gently lifting out the contents, she sets a pile of clothing on a table, and I cautiously approach. In reference to the item on top, she says, "They wore that suit for the *100,000,000 Bon Jovi Fans Can't Be Wrong* boxed set."

I know it well—the shimmery gold from top to bottom. Instinctively, my hand reaches out, but I pause and look at Marlene, who nods. The material is cool and smooth and so gloriously *Bon Jovi* that I hold my breath and try not to cry.

Next is a black velvet jacket. I run my fingers over the gold buttons as Marlene says, "Richie Sambora wore that on tour."

Slowly, I set the jacket aside and inhale sharply at the sight of the last piece. "The *New Jersey* coat?"

"Yes, ma'am."

My shaky fingers need a moment before they can pick up the long garment. I turn it over and caress the red letters: BON JOVI and NEW JERSEY. Jon wore this. It touched him. And now I'm touching it. What Dad would have given....

"Thank you," I whisper.

Marlene takes my hand into her warm grasp and stares into my eyes. "Music feeds the soul. You keep listening to Bon Jovi and the rest, and you'll keep your father alive in your heart. And don't mourn him alone. In our darkest hour is when we need others the most."

As the tears threaten again, I nod. "How can I repay you for this?"

She smiles kindly. "No need to repay me. Just pay it forward."

♪

I PULL up to the house and see two things I'm not expecting: Grandpa's Buick LaCrosse in the driveway and Mom's Camry in the garage. *Shit.*

If Mom came home early and saw I wasn't here after school, I would expect several frantic voicemails and ALL CAPS texts. But I check my phone, and—nothing.

Muted voices drift from the family room when I walk in, and Mom and Grandpa look up from the couch. Mom wipes her eyes and says, "I lost track of time," then glances at the clock. "Wait. You're late. Where were you?"

So, good news: Mom wasn't panicking because I was gone; calling neighbors, friends, and hospitals; and picturing me dead in a ditch, the ramifications of which I shudder to imagine. Bad news: I need an excuse, stat.

"I'm thinking of auditioning for the school play. I stayed to prepare with a friend."

What friend? she'll ask—I curse myself for dragging nonexistent supporting players into my production of throwing her off the scent. An audition workshop! That's what I should have said.

But Mom only looks surprised. "That's great."

"What's the show?" Grandpa asks.

"*It's a Wonderful Life.* But done as a radio play."

"Ah, a classic." He leans back and puts his arm around Mom. "We're looking at old pictures. Got room for one more." With his other hand, he pats the empty space next to him.

I've already met my tear quota for the day. "Thanks, but I'd rather not," I say as I move toward the stairs.

An hour later, there's a knock on my door. "I wanted to say goodbye before I head out," Grandpa says. He sits on the bed and gives me a hug, wrapping his strong arms around me. "Where were you really?"

Startled, I pull back. "What?"

He tilts his head and raises an eyebrow. "You're not the only Leahy woman to lie to me over the years."

I look at my lap. "The Rock and Roll Hall of Fame."

When I glance up, Grandpa nods knowingly. "What would he have thought?"

"Mom should have let him get tickets for the induction. All their stuff is gone.... But they had the music. Dad would have loved the clips from the ceremony."

"I'm sure he would have." He kisses the top of my head. "Are you okay?"

"I made it through the first year. That's something, right?"

Before he gets up, he gives me a squeeze. "That's something, all right, kiddo."

"HUNGRY LIKE THE WOLF"

Certain things will brand you in the public-school caste system. Ezra Klein will forever be the kid who threw up onstage during the third-grade play. Alina Ullman is memorable to many because she peed her pants in first grade. Marisol Jez is known for sending a wildly inappropriate picture of herself to our seventh-grade science teacher, Mr. Hilmer. And thanks to stupid Mrs. Keating, who made us read stupid *Of Mice and Men* in freshman English, I'm the girl who ugly cried so hard she passed out.

It's not that *Of Mice and Men* is like my life. Lennie isn't a father. His death is a mercy killing. But in my fragile emotional state, reading about any guy who died was way more than I could handle.

So, as I stand before the *Wonderful Life* poster for the dozenth time, I contemplate my fraternization of late with the likes of Judy Garland, Gene Kelly, and other titans of the silver screen and can't help but admit I could use some new friends.

But auditioning would require me to talk to other humans, IRL, and teenage humans at that. I'm staring at the pen hanging from the wall when a colorful pair of shoes stops next to mine.

"I don't see your name up there—yet."

Glancing at Mac, I take a small step back. "I've never been in a play before."

"Everyone's in their first sometime. What's your last name?"

Without thinking about why he's asking, I answer. "Ballester."

Mac picks up the pen and writes on the audition sign-up sheet: *Raina-Rae Ballester*.

"Just Rae is fine." I cross out the first several letters and consider letting my scribbles continue until my whole name is buried beneath black ink, but Mac puts a hand on my wrist. I drop the pen and let him guide me toward the auditorium.

Twenty, maybe thirty, kids are waiting. Mac waves to a girl as he moves down one of the rows. I follow him, sit with an empty seat between us, and stare at the stage, my foot tapping nervously.

An older man with longish gray hair who's wearing jeans and a sport coat walks out from the wings. He consults a clipboard, then pushes his glasses on top of his head and looks out at us. Not everyone has noticed his arrival, so he waves his non-clipboard hand to get the group's attention. "Hello. Welcome. For those of you who don't know me, my name is Jay Hockenberry, and I'm the director of *It's a Wonderful Life: A Live Radio Play*."

Mac leans across the chasm and whispers, "Jay's my neighbor. Great guy."

"This show has a cast of five—actors who have gathered in a radio station on Christmas Eve, 1946, to perform, live, the radio play version of *It's a Wonderful Life*. Three males and two females who each portray multiple roles in the radio play.

"Before we talk about how auditions will work, I want to introduce you to a few more people. Dave?"

The lights over the stage flash off and on.

"Dave Rardin is our technical director."

Several kids turn and wave to a man in a booth at the back of the auditorium.

"And Janice Ehrenbach."

I swivel my head to see the woman who stands at the other end of our row.

"She's the costume queen. And Mac? Where are you?" When Mac raises his arm, Jay says, "Mac Reddington is our student director.

"I've chosen three scenes to use for auditions." While he talks, Jay walks to a table at the side of the stage, picks up a packet of papers, and holds it up. "Everybody will get a copy of the scenes. The lines are highlighted in five different colors. These denote all the roles each actor plays. Let's take ten minutes, then I'll call various groups and we'll have some fun."

The other kids stand, so I do the same.

"Break a leg." Mac smiles at me before I force my feet to move.

Even though some people have gathered in groups and are reading out loud, I sequester myself to review the scenes, but lose my focus when I recognize one of the girls sitting in front of me. After my ugly-crying incident last year, this girl told her lunch table, very clearly within my earshot, that she thought my "performance" in English was a ruse to get attention.

I manage to finish the first scene but only make it halfway through the second before Jay claps. "Okay, everybody, let's get started."

Mine isn't among the five names he calls, and I breathe a sigh of relief. I don't know most of the group, but one girl, Joss, is in my English class. Also, despite not attempting to lend my talents to last year's shows, I did see *Little Shop*, and I'm pretty sure she played Audrey. Her hair is blond like in the show, but longer, and I wonder if it's grown out since then or if she was wearing a wig.

She's the first of us Jay calls up a second time. As she reads lines for Mary, I study how she makes the role distinct from those she read initially. I hear "Joss" in all the parts, but it's clear they're different characters.

Her alteration is nothing, though, compared with this one guy, Arlo, in the next group. He plays *four* people in the same scene, having an extended conversation with himself, and if I closed my eyes, I would bet there were four different guys reading.

I'm still clapping when I hear my name, and my stomach does a somersault. Jay assigns me the pink lines—Mary and Young Mary— and I try to channel my inner Donna Reed, from the movie. My cheeks burn when I say George is "making violent love to me," but at least Jay stops us before Mary cries and she and George say, "I love you."

The next time I'm called, I play Young Violet opposite Joss as Young Mary. After we finish, she smiles at me, making her cheeks dimple.

"Okay, everybody, nice work." Jay runs up onto the stage. "Thanks for coming out. I'll post the cast list by end of day tomorrow."

While I'm putting on my coat, Joss appears at my side. "You were good up there."

I feel myself blush. "Not as good as you."

She waves her hand dismissively as Mac joins us. "You're not scaring her off, are you?"

"Please. I was telling her how great she did."

Mac leans forward. "I shouldn't be saying this, but I agree."

Joss feigns offense. "Hello?"

"You know you're the next Idina," he says before being summoned by Jay.

On my way out of the auditorium, I look wistfully at the stage. *It was nice being someone else for a change.*

♪

I TRY NOT to be obvious when I walk by the poster the next morning—barely even stop on the way to my locker—but nothing is posted yet.

The wall is still empty after first period.

After second period: nothing.

Each time I check, I feel a little bubble of anger. Why am I getting my hopes up?

Don't check after lunch, I tell myself. And I don't—but ten minutes into fifth period, I "go to the bathroom": nada.

Despite my increasing self-annoyance, I check three more times before the end of the day. At the end of last period, my palms are sweating because I know this time, it will be there.

Tearing out of the room, I clip my shoulder on the door frame and massage it as I run toward The List. I pause and take a deep breath before going close enough to read it.

FREDDIE FILMORE (Potter/Others)......................... Arlo Curtis
JAKE LAURENTS (George/Young George)........Casey Sammons
SALLY APPLEWHITE (Mary/Young Mary)............Rae Ballester
HARRY HEYWOOD (Clarence/Others)..................Rory Niemiec
LANA SHERWOOD (Violet/Others)...........................Joss Cohen

Holy shit.

Classes are letting out, kids are stampeding down the stairs, and lockers are opening and slamming shut. I hurriedly turn away, not ready to process this in public, but don't get far.

"Congratulations." Mac—I know his voice now.

"Thanks." I can't tell if I want to squeal or puke. Oddly similar sensations.

"You in that role was a no-brainer."

Maybe for him. My brain is still very much conflicted about this whole group-activity thing. I start walking, ready for some solitude to think things through, but Mac keeps pace with me, so I offer, "I guess I owe you a thank-you for convincing me to audition."

He shakes his head. "I didn't do anything. You wanted to audition."

♪

WE HAVE CHIPOTLE FOR DINNER, a sign that Mom's day was too busy or stressful for her to cook. Maybe she won't be in the best frame of mind to talk about me doing the show.

I decide to wait until tomorrow to tell her, but she brings it up. "When will you hear about the play?"

"Um...I found out today, actually." I lick guacamole off my finger and meet her gaze. "I got a part."

"That's wonderful." She comes over for a hug, which I return with one arm. "I'm so happy for you."

"Thanks."

"Congratulations, Rae. You should be proud of yourself." She keeps beaming at me, and it gets a little intense, so I take a bite of my barbacoa bowl; she takes the hint and her seat.

Around a mouthful of burrito, she asks, "I assume rehearsals will be after school?"

"Yeah. Mostly weekdays, with some weekends once we get closer to the performances."

"What time?"

"Till 5:30, I think. I don't remember when on the weekends."

Her burrito hovers in the air, and her eyes narrow. Alarm bells go off in my head, and my body tenses. "It'll be dark before then," she says.

The spice flavors disappear from my food, and I set down my fork. "*Around* then."

"You don't drive at night."

My shoulders droop. "Because you only let me drive to school, and that's not a nocturnal activity."

Mom wrings her napkin, the poor paper quickly turning to shreds. "I don't want you driving at night. I'm sure you can understand why."

This meat is not sitting well. I swallow and fiddle with a strand of hair that has slipped out of my messy bun to focus on something other than the roiling of my stomach. Neither of my parents were redheads, but I'm proof they both carried the gene. Dad made me a list once of the reasons why I was special, and this was number four.

I push my bowl away. "I know. But it's not exactly night. We live in Ohio—it gets dark at five o'clock."

"Could you leave rehearsal a little early?"

"Come on, Mom. That's ridiculous."

She nods slowly and drops what used to be her napkin. "Okay. But if you're going to be home a minute after 5:40, you text me."

This is the least satisfying win ever. My mother has gotten in my head, and she's right, I don't drive at night. The last time I did, it was a nightmare.

We were in the car together; I had my learner's permit and had almost completed the requisite number of hours. It was my last hour of night driving. And of course it started raining.

I'd driven in the rain once, during the day. Everything was different in the dark—lights reflected off the pavement, and I couldn't see well even with the windshield wipers whipping back and forth at top speed. Mom warned that the roads might be slippery and said if I did feel the car sliding, I should take my foot off the gas. She kept yelling at me to go slow and leave more space between us and the next car.

"Stop!" I finally yelled back. "I can't concentrate."

"I'm sorry, I didn't know it was going to open up like this. The forecast said showers."

My knuckles hurt from gripping the steering wheel so hard. I couldn't stop looking back and forth from the front windshield to the rearview mirror, equally afraid I would crash into someone and that someone would crash into me.

"Keep your eyes on the road."

"I am."

"Raina, slow down."

"I'm going forty-three!"

"That's too fast—you have to slow down when it's wet!"

And that's when the brake lights up ahead screamed at me too, their menacing red glow filling the darkness.

"Raina!"

"I see it!"

I slammed on my brakes, without really needing to—I came to a stop with a full car length to spare. Still, the adrenaline from lurching forward was the final straw. My hands shook and I started crying, and it took everything I had to swing the car onto the shoulder.

"You can't stop here!" Mom yelled, even as a tear slid down her cheek.

"Then you fix it!" I got out and hurried to the passenger side. We stared at each other through the window as rain drenched me, my clothes sticking to my skin in a matter of seconds. Shaking her head, Mom opened her door and ran around to take the spot I had vacated. Neither of us said another word.

Me driving at night is a recipe for anger, sadness, and more anger—the worst conceivable sandwich cookie of emotion.

Maybe I shouldn't do the show.

"WELCOME TO WHEREVER YOU ARE"

In the Starbucks drive-thru, I take my vanilla steamer from the barista, the smell of flavored milk wafting into the Jetta. I consider buying coffee for the car behind me to pay off my debt to Marlene after what she did for me at the Rock and Roll Hall of Fame, but a four-dollar latte hardly seems commensurate with her act of charity on arguably the second-worst day of my life.

The red Volkswagen follows me, though, and for a second, I'm afraid it somehow knows what I was thinking and is pissed I didn't comp its driver a drink. After making a right turn, I glance in my rearview mirror and still see it. When I pull into the school parking lot, so does the VW, and then Sadie Haddix gets out.

If she recognizes my car, she doesn't let on, and I bow my head as she walks past. Sadie and I don't run in the same circles, but I've heard things. The word (in middle school) was that she was the first girl to lose her virginity. People say she got high once with Mr. D'Arezzo, the guidance counselor who lectured us about bullying freshman year and who didn't return sophomore year. She has a reputation for being a subpar student and, frankly, a bitch.

I've only had a single conversation with her—at the one party I went to last year, the weekend after school ended, and only because Mom "thought it would be good for me" and I was argument-fatigued.

As I was pouring Coke into a cup at the kitchen counter, Sadie slid gracefully, like a cat, onto a bar stool across from me. "Raina."

I was surprised she knew my name.

"I heard about your dad."

Like a mouse, I put up my guard. Even well-intentioned words of sympathy were a threat, so easily did they crumble my resolve, but I had no idea what kind of intentions were harbored by Sadie Haddix. So, I looked for an escape—a familiar face, a crowd I could glom onto, or a trash can to busy myself with—but wasn't quick enough.

"Bet you caught a lot of breaks this year."

Her eyes were bright, hungry, like she wanted me to say the wrong thing. Yes, I was granted extensions. Yes, teachers called on me less, leaving me to my cocoon of sadness. Yes, I was given space to try to figure out what I needed and how the world could possibly make sense anymore.

"I guess," I finally said.

"You're not the only one whose home life is shitty, you know." She slipped off the stool and cornered me by the stove. "Was he a good guy, your dad? Did you love him? Did you *like* him?"

Afraid to speak, I nodded.

"So, he didn't hit you then?" Her voice rose, catching the attention of people nearby. "He didn't come home drunk and decide he wasn't in the mood for teenage bullshit and think a belt across your ass would shut you up?"

I looked at our audience, pleading with them to intervene, but we were the entertainment, and no one was willing to make it stop.

"Everyone feels so sorry for you, but do you know what they feel about me? Annoyed. Disappointed. Impatient, hopeless, disgusted."

She used so many adjectives I didn't see how she could be failing English.

Standing so close she could touch my chest with her finger, she jabbed emphatically into my rib cage. "You think your life sucks? It could be So. Much. Worse."

Over seven months, I'd grown accustomed to sorrow, to regret, to shame, anger, and loneliness. I'd never before felt guilty for having a dad who was dead.

♪

I FEEL like shit all day as I figure out how to decline the part Jay has offered me.

Before I compose my email, he sends us a link to a promo video for some other production of the play to give us a feel for the show.

The woman who plays Mary sounds just like Donna Reed in the movie, and my heart flutters. *Could I be that good?* I know there's only one way to find out, but the cast is small, necessitating a good bit of interpersonal communication, which I generally prefer to avoid. And I haven't spent nearly enough time stressing about what happens if I forget my lines or otherwise give the student body another reason to make me the butt of their jokes.

Still, I *did* get a part. Jay wants me to play Mary. Me! I hit "Reply" and stare at the screen.

Even though I'll have to drive in the dark, at least Mom won't be in the car. Spending less time at home is a bonus. Plus, pretending to be somebody else stopped me from thinking about all of my problems.

And all of Mary's problems get fixed in the end.

Okay, yes—I type, *Thanks*, and hit "Send" before I chicken out.

♪

AT OUR FIRST REHEARSAL, we take our seats around a table in the middle of the stage. Jay pushes his glasses up on his head and claps his hands together. "Hello, magic-makers. I've got to tell you: I've wanted to do this play for a long time. I'm excited to be here with you.

"Let's go around—introduce yourselves. Share one of your favorite holiday memories or traditions. Has everybody seen the movie?" We all nod. "Good. At the end, Clarence tells George that no man is a failure who has friends. What do you think defines a successful life? Mac, will you go first?"

"Sure. My favorite tradition is seeing *A Christmas Carol* at the Ohio Theatre. And staying involved in theatre would mean success for me."

"Excellent. Thanks, Mac. Next?"

Sitting to Mac's right is Casey, one of the guys I auditioned with. He brushes a mop of brown curls out of his eyes and smiles. "I guess what I like best about Christmas is dressing up as Santa for my little brother and sister. They're four. And I think helping other people makes for a successful life." When Jay nods, Casey relaxes into his chair.

"Hi, I'm Joss. My favorite Hanukkah memory is when I finally beat my three stepbrothers at our dreidel tournament two years ago, and I like what Clarence says—friends and family are what matter most."

I forget the next guy's name, so I'm relieved he says it. "My name's Rory, and I think if you're true to who you are, you're winning at life. Oh, and I'm a dancer, so my favorite tradition is seeing *The Nutcracker*."

The dancing explains his lean build. I'm still staring at the muscles in his forearm when I realize everyone else is staring at me. "Um, hi. I'm Rae." Memories hurt, and *tradition* has lost its meaning. "Well...I love watching *White Christmas* with my grandpa." I exhale, then remember I'm not done. "And..." My pulse quickens. *Say something*, I command myself. "I think...kindness is what we should be judged on."

Marlene pops into my head, but then so does my dad. Before my tear ducts can get any ideas, I point my eyes at Arlo, visually begging him to start speaking.

He clears his throat. "Uh, my grandma loves *It's a Wonderful Life*. We watch it every year." He looks up at the ceiling, thinking, and the stage lights highlight his freckles, an even darker shade of brown than his skin. "I guess family is my answer." His tone makes it sound like a question, and Arlo watches Jay until he nods.

"That was great, everybody. Thanks."

"What about you?" Joss asks.

"Fair enough. I lived in New York for a few years as a child, and there is nothing more wondrous than the tree at Rockefeller Center. More than fifty years later, it still holds a top spot in my memory. As for success, for me personally, it's living a life with purpose, which I'm lucky enough to do here. So, let's get started."

WHEN WE FINISH, Jay says, "Hard not to feel good at the end of that one."

Minus the awkward crying/I love you scene between Mary and George, I think the read-through went well. We're all grinning at each other, which helps dispel some of the heat that has risen to my cheeks.

"One more thing before we wrap up." Jay raises his book. "If you look at the last few pages of your script, you'll see some suggestions for the sound effects. Mac and I will be responsible for these, but you might have some items lying around your house. Take a look and let us know if there's anything you could bring in."

As I sling my backpack onto my shoulder, Mac sidles up to me. "We're going to Romano's."

It's unclear whether an invitation is implied.

He starts walking backward toward the door, but before he turns, he says, "You coming?"

"Um, sure." My lips return his smile, but my heart clenches. Despite my need for new friends, I wasn't prepared to acquire them instantaneously.

A text argument with Mom ensues. I win by pointing out that it will be equally dark, not dark*er*, an hour from now.

Because of its proximity to Rickenbacker High, I bet every RHS student has been to Romano's. The last time I was here was the last time my friends—my old friends—managed to convince me to voluntarily leave the house.

I tried to pretend I was okay. For a while. But it's hard to laugh when jokes aren't funny, hard to say what's new when every day's sadness is the same, hard to truthfully answer how you are without bringing everyone else down.

Still, stepping out of the cold air and into the warm lighting, the heat moves past skin, muscle, and bone and infuses my soul. The music is the same Italian songs they've always played, the tablecloths are the same checked red and white, and the board at the back is the same ode to the elite group of diners who've managed to devour the four-pound meatball bigger than a baby's head.

The hostess shows us to two tables, and Mac and Rory drag them together. It doesn't look like our waitress remembers me, but I smile at her name tag like I always did—German Greta in the Italian restaurant.

No need for me to look at the menu. I'll get my favorite, spaghetti and meatballs. Not the four-pound variety, but normal-sized balls that are equally delicious. (My—former—friends and I polished off the Monster Meatball once. Didn't make it onto the board since it was a group effort, but we were proud of ourselves.)

Mac closes his menu and crosses his arms. "Okay, question time."

Joss rolls her eyes. "Really? Already?"

"What? I'm inquisitive." He looks around the table. "What was everyone's first Broadway cast album?"

Picking up a straw, Joss partially removes the wrapper and blows it at Mac.

Batting it away, he says, "Mine was *A Year With Frog and Toad*."

"That's a musical?" Casey asks. "My brother and sister love those books."

"A great and underrated musical." Mac lifts his foot above the table and points to two men dressed like a frog and a toad on his shoe. "What was yours?"

"Mmm...something Disney, probably. Maybe *Beauty and the Beast*? But I think it was the movie soundtrack."

"Close enough. Joselyn?"

"*Fiddler*. Cliché, I know."

"It's a classic."

Joss nods at Arlo. "What about you? Are you a musical theatre guy?"

Arlo fiddles with the paper around his napkin, staring at the table. "Nah. I've never seen a Broadway show, like, when they come through town or anything."

After a pause, Mac taps his knuckles on Rory's shoulder. "You're up."

"It wasn't a cast album, but the music of *Oklahoma* is the first I can remember. I watched the movie all the time because of the dream ballet."

"Ugh, the dream ballet is the worst!" Mac cries. "No offense."

"Mac!" Joss glares at him.

"What? I said, 'No offense.'"

"Ignore him," she says to Rory. "He was raised by wolves."

"How dare you call my mother a canine."

Joss shakes her head as Mac turns to me. "And last but not least. Your introduction to the auditory glories of the boards, Raina-Rae?"

My cheeks flush. "Just Rae is good. It was a movie musical for me too—*Meet Me in St. Louis*."

"Isn't that the one with 'Have Yourself a Merry Little Christmas'?" Joss asks.

"Yeah. That song almost didn't make it into the movie. Judy Garland thought the first draft was too sad and refused to sing it."

Greta comes by to refill our water glasses. As she pours, I remember the debates we used to have about how she came to work here. One of my friends, Carolyn, said Greta wanted to leave Germany and go to Italy, but her parents made her go to school in the US, and that's why she took a job here. Maya argued that she was born here, but her love affair with Italy stemmed from the food. Shelby's theory was that she was engaged to an Italian guy, and I held that she did it to be ironic.

Interrupting my memories, Rory asks, "Has anybody seen *Once*?"

"It's one of my favorites," I say softly. A heartbreakingly beautiful romance between two Irish musicians. One of the few movie musicals I didn't see with Grandpa. But when I stumbled across it last year, I watched it three times in one weekend.

Mac lifts his other foot and points to the guitar from the Playbill. "It's so sweet and sad."

"I watched it a lot—" I almost say, *after my dad died*, but manage to stop talking.

Apparently immune to embarrassment, Mac leans toward me and sings—badly—"Broken Hearted Hoover Fixer Sucker Guy," a funny song from the movie, but one I doubt the rest of the Romano's patrons want to hear right now.

Greta, though, claps after she sets down our tray of food, and Mac gives a little bow in his seat.

We all dig in, eating in silence until Rory looks from Mac to Joss and says, "So, tell us newbies some good backstage stories."

Mac grins. "Tell him about *Little Shop*."

"Do you know what this asshole did our last night? When I climbed into Audrey II, there wasn't supposed to be anything else inside the plant. But for the final performance, Mac stuffed it full of severed limbs. You know, the plastic kind with blood dripping down the sides? But that wasn't 'realistic' enough." She makes angry air quotes. "He covered them in fake blood that was still wet and sticky when I got in. I was a mess, and I had to do the rest of the show like that."

His dinner momentarily forgotten, Mac leans forward. "It washed out. And come on, you know that was our best show."

"It was gross!"

"It was funny!"

Joss doesn't meet Mac's eyes as she scrapes her fork against her plate.

"Did you get back at him?" Arlo asks.

"No. Not *yet*."

"Please," Mac scoffs. "Like you'd do anything to me."

"I'm biding my time."

Rory looks back and forth between them, then says, "In one of my dance recitals, a guy dropped a girl in a lift and broke her nose."

"No way!" Mac says around a mouthful of fettucine.

Arlo shakes his head. "It'd suck to be that dude."

I feel sorry for him too, because now he's branded as "the guy who dropped a girl and broke her nose." He's a story, just like me, "the girl who cried so hard she passed out."

As the others finish and set down their forks, I take one last bite, savoring the herby oregano in the sauce, the slight spice from the sausage in the meatball, and the fresh Parmesan sprinkled on top. Greta brings a bunch of mints along with our checks, and we're like pigs at a trough trying to get our share of the candy. When she returns after we pay, she drops so many mints on the table, it's like we busted open a piñata.

That definitely deserves a thank-you, so when we leave, instead of tagging along with Joss to the bathroom, I veer off toward the kitchen and tap a waiter. "Excuse me. Hi. Is there a manager I could talk to?"

He sets down the drinks he was carrying. "Is something wrong?"

"No, sorry. I wanted to say something nice, actually."

"Sure. One second."

I wait while he disappears behind a swinging door. A moment later, he comes back leading a guy in a crisp white button-down. Manager Man offers me his hand. "I'm Mark. What can I do for you?"

"Our waitress, Greta, was great, super friendly. She gave us excellent service, and I thought you should know."

Mark smiles. "Thank you for taking the time to tell me. I'll be sure to pass along the compliment."

When I turn around, I nearly bump into Mac, who says, "What was that about?"

"What?"

"You talking to the manager."

I pick up my pace to catch up to the others, who are milling about at the front. "I...just wanted to tell him something."

"What did you want to tell him?"

"Why do you want to know?"

"Why won't you tell me?" Hurrying ahead, Mac blocks my path.

With a sigh, I say, "I wanted to tell him our waitress did a great job."

He nods slowly, like he's trying to comprehend. "Do you do this regularly? Bestow compliments on strangers?"

"It feels nice to make someone else happy."

We lock eyes for several seconds, then he steps aside, sweeping his hand in an arc. "Proceed, kind madam."

I tip an imaginary cap. "Thank you, good sir."

On the drive home, I imagine Greta's face when she heard the compliment. It's not enough to repay Marlene, but maybe it's a start.

"REBEL YELL"

I'm listening to an '80s rock mix on Spotify when I sit at the table. Mom points to her ear, and I reluctantly pull out my earbuds.

"How was rehearsal?"

"Good." Tonight's dinner is my mother's definition of "cooking": Costco rotisserie chicken and microwavable rice and veggies. "We worked on the kid scenes today."

"That sounds fun."

I nod, and we both fill our mouths rather than try to think of something else to say. *Clink, clink.*

"Oh, I forgot." When I rise, Mom tilts her head, ready to scold, but I wave away the reprimand. "I just have to get something." A second later, I return with my script and flip to the back. "Can I have a baking sheet for the show?"

"Sure. When do you need it?"

"I'll take it in tomorrow."

"Well, hang on. Do you need it so soon? I might use it between now and December."

"We have more than one."

"I use them all when I make Christmas cookies for the neighbors."

"So, make do with one less." It comes out snippier than I mean for it to, and my stomach clenches, waiting for Mom's reaction, but she just sighs.

"Okay."

A moment passes. I now understand the phrase "companionable silence"—this is not that. "What about one of Dad's belts?" I move the mushy peas to one side of the plate.

"What about it?"

"Can I use it in the show?"

"Uh, yeah. You'll have to look in the Goodwill bags."

"And I need plates."

"What?"

"Dinner plates."

Mom sets down her fork and sighs with her whole body. "Can't other people bring in some of these things?"

"There's a lot I'm not asking to take, but I want to do my part. We have an extra set."

"That's our nice holiday set. I'd rather not risk one of the pieces getting broken."

"Fine." I stuff another bite in my mouth, the chicken somewhat compensating for the rice, which is dry. Who knew you could screw up instant rice? "The last thing I need is wind chimes."

Although Mom has picked up her fork again, it hovers in midair. "We only have the one set."

"Right, but we have some, so can I use them?"

Lowering the utensil, she looks at her dinner like it's making her sad, which it very well may be. "You know your dad gave them to me."

Heat rises to my ears. "It's not like we're going to use them as a piñata."

"But accidents happen."

I bristle at the word. "Not to wind chimes."

She long-blinks and swallows. "Something could."

"Like what?"

"The strings could get tangled, or the top could get damaged."

I roll my eyes. "They're going to sit in a box on the stage. Stop being paranoid."

"*Excuse* me—wanting to protect something that's important to me is not paranoia. It would be nice if you'd be a little more sensitive."

"And it would be nice if you'd help me out. I'll take good care of them. Unless you don't trust me." I push back my chair and stand.

"Hey, watch the tone and sit back down."

We stare at each other as I remain on my feet.

"Raina." She doesn't blink. After several seconds, I roll my eyes again and sit, loudly scooting my chair forward, then shovel in another forkful.

"Let me think about the chimes."

"Think fast. I need to know by tomorrow." Probably not true, but close enough.

She grits her teeth before speaking. "You could do with a little gratitude."

"You want me to do the show, don't you? Have friends again? Stop being such a loser?"

Mom's expression wavers between frustration and pity. "Don't say that. Of course, I'm glad you're doing the show. But we're both struggling here."

I snort. "I think losing all your friends is worse than worrying about—but not even—losing a set of wind chimes."

"That's not what I mean."

"Then why don't you say what you mean." I slide my plate away.

"I want to help you, Rae. But I can't if you won't let me."

"You had the chance," I say quietly.

Her brow furrows. "What are you talking about?"

The shift in her tone signals a change of direction toward

emotional connection; I stand to avoid the detour. "You deal with this in your way, and I'll deal with it in mine."

"Hiding your emotions is not dealing with it."

"You're one to talk about hiding things!"

Now Mom stands too, facing off against me across the table. "Raina, stop being cryptic. If there's something on your mind, then say it."

I head for the stairs. "I'm done having this conversation."

"Hey! I'm not."

Without responding, I run up to my room and slam the door.

ON HALLOWEEN MORNING, I drop a handful of fun-size candy bars in my backpack. Dad used to buy full-size. I wonder if Mom will want (expect) me to help pass them out tonight when what I want is to take my own bowl of chocolate down to the basement and watch *Sweeney Todd*.

At the end of rehearsal, Mac doesn't pack up his stuff.

"Aren't you leaving?" I ask.

He shoves his hands in his pockets and shrugs. "I thought I'd check out the prop room."

"No Halloween plans?"

"Nobody but me likes haunted houses."

Jay tosses his keys to Mac, then salutes as he walks down the aisle toward the door.

"He isn't staying?"

"Nah. Since I live next door, he lets me lock up sometimes."

In the middle of zipping my coat, I stop. "Do you need help?"

"Raina-Rae, that would be delightful." His shoes may have been the first thing that caught my eye, but his smile has my attention now. My heart flutters when he directs it at me.

After I shrug off my coat, Mac sweeps his arm toward the stage. "Shall we?"

I follow him up the stairs and into the wings, through a door at the back, and down the hall. We walk past a few doors before he stops and puts a key in the lock. "I should warn you: it's crowded in here."

He's not kidding. There's barely room for us both to stand in between floor-to-ceiling shelves crammed with boxes and furniture. Clothing racks are set three-deep at the other end.

While Mac checks a list on his phone, I lean down, careful my butt doesn't bump the shelf behind me, and run my finger along the edge of a picnic basket.

"Okay, keep your eyes out for old telephones, a fake cigar, buckets or tubs, a cash register, and bells." He crouches next to me and pulls a box off the shelf. Maneuvering in the tight space seems relatively easy for him, and I realize how small he is, even though I'm a little below average, height-wise. Granted, when dealing with sixteen-year-old boys, some stand a head above me and others barely come up to my chin, but even among the short ones, Mac would stick out.

He sits cross-legged on the floor and rummages inside his box. I grab another and kneel before it. Nestled inside are all kinds of baskets—some empty, one holding waxy red and green apples, another overflowing with bunches of grapes hanging over the sides. At the bottom are vases and candy dishes, candelabras and fake jewelry, and dice that make me think of *Guys and Dolls*.

Something nudges my shoulder and I jump, then whirl around to find myself face-to-face with a fake lobster, which Mac waves in front of me.

"What did you use that for?"

"They did *Little Mermaid* a few years ago."

Inside Mac's box is a chef's hat just begging to be placed on his head. He twirls the ends of his pretend mustache and picks up a plastic cleaver. "Les Poissons!"

Despite the phony props, my heartbeat actually quickens at the sight of the cleaver in the air. I grab the poor lobster and hug it to my chest. "Not Sebastian!"

Once Mac abandons the crustacean killer, I lift up a Magic 8-Ball. "They had these in the '40s, right?"

He reaches for it, then gives it a shake. "Will my parents let me get a dog?" He turns it over. "'My sources say no.' Hells bells."

"You don't have any pets?"

"Not since our dog died."

I hold Mac's gaze. "I'm sorry."

"Yeah, thanks." He looks away. "My folks have their reasons. They say it's nice not having the work of a pet, and they're so expensive, and training a puppy is like having a baby...." He leans back on his hands. "But really, they just don't want to lose another one."

My chest tightens at the mention of loss. "It's hard...opening yourself up again after losing something you love."

"But having no pet feels empty. Getting a new dog would make it easier."

"It wouldn't replace your old one."

"Of course not." Mac cocks his head. "Whose side are you on here?"

Heat fills my face. "Sorry, I'm not really a dog person." I flip up the clasps on a briefcase with a satisfying *click*. "Cats are the superior pet."

Mac withdraws a pillow and proceeds to whack me with it. Laughing, I use the briefcase as a shield until he ceases fire.

"Cats...." He shakes his head.

We're quiet for a while. Finally, I find something promising. "Would this work?" I show him an old rotary-style phone.

"Nice, stick it by the door."

Over the next hour, we make a small pile. Then Mac decides we've exhausted the possibilities of the prop closet, so we gather the things we found. "Next, we hit Goodwill."

I smile as I follow him out. He said *we*.

After we deposit our stash in the wings, Mac turns off the lights and drags a stand with a single lightbulb to the center of the stage.

"What's that?"

He stops dragging and stares at me. "Do you not know what a ghost light is?"

His tone makes it clear he thinks I should, but I shake my head and approach the stand, the only source of illumination in the auditorium. Mac finishes moving it, then walks to the front of the stage and sits with his legs hanging off the edge. He looks over his shoulder at me and points at the spot next to him. Slowly, I make my way downstage in the dark, my footsteps echoing in the silence.

"Raina-Rae...I will grant you allowances because this is your first show, but there are certain things you must understand."

I shift so my body is angled toward his, and my shadow swings across the stage.

"Whenever you leave the theatre for the night, you must always leave a light on to appease the ghosts."

"The ghosts?"

"That's correct."

I demand further explanation by raising my eyebrows.

Scooting sideways, Mac leans toward me. "All theatres have ghosts. And they yearn to perform. We leave a light on so they can take to the stage when no one is around."

"What happens if you don't?"

He looks over both shoulders, then whispers, "Don't tempt fate, Raina-Rae. Darkness riles 'em up. They'll wreak havoc."

"So, who are the supposed ghosts here?"

"We have two. Annette is the ghost of a girl who went missing in the '60s. And Melvin was a stagehand who died on opening night a few years after that."

I wish I believed in ghosts. I'd be A-OK with my dad haunting me for a while.

Mac squints at me, presumably trying to read my expression in the dimness. "You scoff. Don't believe it?"

"Do you?"

"I don't *not* believe it."

"Meaning what?"

"Meaning no one knows for sure, and it makes for a good story. Especially on Hallowe-e-e-n." He wiggles his fingers in front of my face. "Speaking of, I should probably get home before the hordes of tykes descend. I'm on candy duty this year."

Nodding, I stand and step cautiously down the stairs to where I left my bag. *Thud.* I whip around. "Mac?" He's not behind me, and his form is no longer visible at the front of the stage. "Mac? Where are you?"

My heart beats faster. Surely, he didn't fall off...I have to assume the ghost light also serves a practical function. *Maybe he beat me out of the auditorium*, I tell myself because it's creepy in here, then hurry toward the side door. At the end of the row, someone jumps up and grabs my arm.

First, I scream, then I hit him with my bag. He laughs as I make my way into the light, obviously proud of himself. My pulse is still racing, but less from the scare and more from the feeling of his touch.

"NOTHIN' BUT A GOOD TIME"

The next day after rehearsal, Mac loiters. "I'm going to Goodwill. Want to come?"

"I don't know. What's in it for me?" Of course, I'll go, but it's fun watching him squirm.

"Starbucks? On me?"

"Deal."

We drive together, Mac behind the wheel of his blue Ford Fusion, which, he informs me, is named Dinah.

"Because...?" I ask.

"*Starlight Express.*"

As if that answers the question.

"Andrew Lloyd Webber musical? She's the sweet and lovable dining car."

In the drive-thru, he orders a cappuccino, then turns expectantly to me.

"Tall raspberry steamer...and a birthday cake pop, since we're in a dining car."

Cups in hand, we pull open the doors to Goodwill and escape from the sleety drizzle that started a few minutes ago. I brush the wetness from my forehead while I wait for Mac to check his list. So many people despise the Ohio winter trifecta of cold, clouds, and crappy precipitation, but it doesn't bother me. If the weather is going to be lousy, I'd rather Mother Nature commit. November sunlight is misleading. It tricks me into thinking it's warm, then freezes my nose hairs when I walk outside.

"I really want to find a tub for George's jump in the water," Mac says. "We need time to figure out how to make it sound right."

"Tub: check."

"And keep your eyes peeled for a metronome and a cuckoo clock. I'll be over the moon if we snag a wind machine, but I don't think we'll get that lucky."

I purse my lips and do my best wind impression. Mac looks over as we walk, and I switch to *ticks* and *tocks*, which makes him smile, so I stick my neck out, then in, then out. "Cuckoo...cuckoo!"

He stops in the middle of the aisle and turns to me. "Why are we even here?"

Being able to make sound effects probably isn't a skill I can put on a college application, but Mac's playful pride dispels any remaining chill from my cheeks.

Once we spot a promising collection, I walk immediately to a cat clock with a tail that swings back and forth.

"That one eats the one we're looking for," Mac reminds me. I leave the kitty and help him scour the aisle, but no cuckoo. Maybe online.

"Those birds are expensive," I say after checking Amazon. "Does your budget have $400 for a cuckoo clock?"

"Nuh uh." Mac grabs my phone. "They can't be that much." He scrolls through the search results. "Most aren't that high. Here's one for seventeen."

"No bird, though."

"Yes, there is."

"'Bird is only for decoration,'" I read.

"Damn."

"This one for thirty bucks has a bird that 'comes out to sing.'"

"Save it. We'll check some other places first."

A few aisles over, we find an assortment of vessels that appeal to Mac's vision of George diving into the river. He pulls a few onto the floor and crouches next to them. "We need something big enough to drop something in."

"Like what?"

He looks up at me, his brown eyes earnest. "I'm not sure yet. We get the tub, then we experiment."

"So, how do you know what size tub to get?"

"What? I'm supposed to have all the answers?"

"You usually do." I smirk, then kneel beside the options, ranging in depth and diameter, and point to the medium-est one. "Not too big, not too small."

"Goldilocks would approve." Before lifting the tub, Mac hands his phone to me. "You're now in charge of the list."

When I take it, the cover flips open and reveals his driver's license, which shows his name—his full name. "Your name is Macmillan?!"

His head falls back so he's staring at the ceiling, and he makes a sound between a sigh and a cough. "I beg you to forget you ever saw that."

"Not a fan, huh?"

"Please. They might as well have tattooed 'pretentious' on my forehead."

"It *is* pretty bad. Especially as a prelude to 'Reddington.'"

"No shit. It's a wonder I'm not in boarding school."

"With boys named Whitaker."

"Or Bradford."

"Thatcher—no, Thad," I say.

"Kingsley."

"Darcy!"

"God, at least mine has a nickname that's not atrocious."

"How many people know your real name?" I waggle the phone at Mac, and he narrows his eyes at me.

"Full name. Mac *is* my real name. And one more now. But hopefully no more than that come tomorrow."

I eye him, a small smile dancing on my lips. "I'll make you a deal: I'll forget I saw your regal appellation if you stop calling me Raina-Rae."

Mac pouts. "What about in private?"

My cheeks flush at the word *private*. To divert that train of thought, I say, "Are you willing to roll the dice? One slipup and I let the cat out of the bag."

"I'll take my chances."

We've made it to the music section. I'm surprised to find a metronome right away. "Score." Mac, oblivious of his pun, holds out the tub, and I set the metronome inside. "This thing's heavy. Are we done yet?"

"Wind machine."

He shakes his head and starts toward the front. "We can ask when we check out, but I'm not holding my breath."

An idea pops into my head. "You go. I'll be there in a minute."

He glances at his phone in my hand. "You're not going to do something crazy, are you?"

"No." I offer it to him, but he shrugs—no way to take it. He shifts sideways and I wonder if he wants me to put it in his pocket, but that's way too intimate, so I drop it gently in the tub and walk away.

Halfway down an aisle, I reach into my purse and pull out all the cash I have: three fives and a couple of ones. I dig around for a notepad and pen, write, *I hope you're having a great day*, and tuck the note and a five under a ceramic vase. Quickly, I write two more notes and leave them with the rest of the money under a dish towel and a plush baby quilt.

♪

Before I go to bed, I open the drawer of my nightstand and find a journal Mom gave me after Dad died. It was one of many things she tried to "help me cope," along with counseling (more talking about Dad—no, thank you) and meditation (thinking about nothing —easier said than done). I wrote in it once so I could tell Mom I did, and it's been buried beneath a stack of old T-shirts since.

I rip out the entry from before. At the top of a fresh page, I write "Kindness ideas," then start making a list.

"SAY IT ISN'T SO"

I've been dreading the scene we're rehearsing today—George and Mary saying, "I love you." Both characters are so vulnerable, and saying these lines is like being emotionally naked onstage. Before we start, I ask Casey, "Are you ready for this?"

He gives me a nervous smile. "No. Are you?"

I shake my head.

Jay claps as he ascends onto the stage. "Okay, everybody. Let's start on page 31 after the train whistle. Casey, start us off, sir."

Casey clears his throat. "'Thar she blows....'"

We get to Joss's entrance as Ruth, then Jay puts up his hand. "A lot of people are talking over each other here. Casey, you start talking when Uncle Billy says 'dinner.' Rory, you come in when George says 'professor.' And you cut him off again when you remember Ruth. From the top."

The second go-around is better. Jay nods, and we keep going. Joss and Casey go back and forth, and Casey's ears turn red when he talks about doing "a little passionate necking."

Then I'm up. This was my audition scene, so the first part is easy. Even telling Joss that George is making violent love to me is less awkward this time. I yell out the line, and people laugh.

When George and Mary get on the phone together, I take a step closer to Casey. My palms start to sweat. After George hangs up, Casey puts his hands on my shoulders, but his touch is so light, I can barely feel him holding onto me. He glances at his script, then the book jabs me in the back.

I try to sound like I'm crying. Then we say our lines—our "I love you's"—and turn to Jay.

"Okay, good," he says. Casey and I glance at each other doubtfully. Jay continues, "That's a tough scene. And now you've done it once. Joss, Rory, move upstage a bit with Arlo." Jay puts a hand on my and Casey's shoulders. "You two come downstage so you don't see the others. This is a private moment between George and Mary. Yes, people are around them, but when George drops the phone, the world falls away and it's just the two of them, looking into each other's eyes."

Jay looks straight at Casey. "George has a lot of pent-up emotions. Don't be afraid to be more physical. This is the moment he lets go of his dreams of traveling and building things and chooses a life with Mary in Bedford Falls."

At the ringing telephone cue, Joss begins. This time, Casey grabs me hard enough that it startles me. He shakes me as he speaks, then pulls me close and whispers, "'Oh, Mary...I love you....'"

I'm jealous of George's speech. Casey has a runway to get emotional; I have to flip a switch.

"Good, *good*." Jay comes over to us again. "Much better." Now he faces me. "You've got the hardest part. Mary has loved George since they were children, and he finally understands. While you're listening to him, your heart is bursting. This time, before you speak, I want you to be thinking about something you've felt, here." He points to his chest. "Remember that feeling and let it out when George breaks down, okay?"

My heart is hammering. If anything will make me cry, it's the memory of hearing my father had died.

♪

October 22—our first choir concert of the year, and I had a solo. That was a big deal, me being a freshman and all. Dad tried to get out of showing houses, but with properties flying off the market the day they were listed, his clients were insistent. They had four showings lined up, starting at 3:30, so he should have been done in plenty of time.

Mom got a text while we were eating dinner. The clients—Jasper and Janie (I thought their names sounded stupid even before I hated them)—were dragging their feet, but he was trying to hurry them along.

The second text came around 5:45. They had finished at the last house, but the couple wanted to make an offer, so they were driving back to Dad's office. He would get through the paperwork as fast as he could, and did Mom know what time my solo would be? My shining moment wouldn't come until the third song from the end, so he could still make it.

The letter-writing process that should have taken an hour, max, hit a snag because Dad had to wait on disclosures from the listing agent. Mom checked in with me just before seven to say Dad's last text had said he'd gotten what he needed and would do everything he could to get there by 7:45.

From the stage, I couldn't make out faces in the audience, but I kept watching for someone to enter from one of the side doors. I saw a mom leave with a crying baby and then return, but no one Dad-shaped ever came in.

After the concert, Mom hugged me extra tight.

"He didn't make it?" I asked.

"I'm sorry, sweetheart."

I expected him to be waiting for us at the house, but his side of the garage was empty. "Why isn't he home yet?"

Mom checked her phone. "He said he was wrapping up a while ago...." She shook her head. "I'll let him know we're here." It was 8:30.

Even after I removed my makeup, changed into pajamas, and brushed my teeth, there was still no Dad.

In the living room, Mom sat on the couch, staring at the phone in her hand.

"Do you think he's okay?"

Because she didn't make eye contact with me right away, I didn't believe her answer. "I'm sure he's fine."

I returned to my room and tried to read. After the third time I failed to translate the black letters on the page into something meaningful, I gave up and went downstairs again.

Mom's eyes were closed, but her grip on her phone was far from relaxed.

"What do you think is keeping him?"

"I don't know, Rae. Maybe he didn't leave when he said he was going to."

"Why wouldn't—"

"I don't know. Maybe the seller countered quickly. Maybe he ran out of gas."

"But why—"

"I don't know, Raina, okay?" Mom stared me down. My heart raced and my hands were clammy and cold.

She sighed, stood, and came over to me, putting her hands on my shoulders. "I don't know why your dad is late, but I'm sure there's a reasonable explanation, and I'm sure everything is fine." Her eyes held my gaze until I nodded. "Why don't you go to bed? I'll have Dad wake you in the morning." She gave me a smile—the last one I would see for a while.

Lying under the covers, I stared at the ceiling and listened.

Many minutes passed with no sound. And the sound that came at 11:47 was not the garage door. Like a stake through my heart, someone pounded on the front door.

I crept into the dark hallway, crouched at the top of the stairs, and watched my mother open the door. Her hands were shaking.

Two police officers, a man and a woman, stood on the front porch.

The woman spoke. "Hello. I'm Officer Petty, and this is Officer Monroe." Flash of badges. "Are you Patrice Ballester?"

Mom nodded.

"May we come in?"

Although she nodded again, she didn't move aside. Only when the cops squeezed past her did she take a small step back and let go of the door. Officer Monroe closed it behind him.

"Will you sit down?" Officer Petty walked toward the living room and Mom followed. As quietly as I could, I hurried down the stairs, avoiding the step that creaks. Flat against the outside of the living room wall, I strained to hear.

"I'm very sorry to tell you this, but your husband was in a car accident tonight. He didn't survive."

For a surreal moment, everything stopped, including, it seemed, my heart. It couldn't have been more than a second or two before Officer Petty spoke again, but it felt like the silence stretched out for eternity, smothering me.

"He hit a deer. The tire marks on the pavement indicate he swerved to avoid it, but he was speeding, and there wasn't enough time. The force of the impact caused the vehicle to roll. We believe he died on impact."

More suffocating silence.

"Do you understand what I've told you?" Pause. "Do you have any questions?"

Four people were sharing this moment, but only one voice punctured the empty air.

"Is there someone we can call? Someone who can stay with you tonight?"

Mom's answer was barely audible. "My dad."

A wave of emotion rose within me. I covered my mouth to stifle the sob threatening to escape and rushed back to my room. In bed with the pillow stuffed over my face, I let the tears come.

♪

JAY'S ADVICE WORKS—A little too well. "'George, I love you, too...,'" I say with Casey's arms around me, but when he pulls away, I can't stop the tears, and I sink to the floor. *Pull it together*, I command myself. I do *not* need another Lennie moment.

Casey bends down, close to my ear. "Rae? Are you okay?" Before I can answer, a hand is on my back and Jay says, "Give us a minute," and gently guides me toward the stairs. "Mac, take everybody through the next scene."

We sit several rows back from the stage, and I wipe my eyes as everyone picks up their scripts. Sniffling, I glance at Jay.

"Take your time."

The palms of my hands are wet by the time I take a deep, shuddery breath. "I'm sorry."

"Don't apologize. What you did up there was great."

"It didn't feel great."

"No. Raw emotion usually doesn't. But a lot of actors find this process very cathartic. If you can embrace your pain and turn it into something useful, it loses some of its power."

I nod slowly, staring at the others as they work.

"If it's too much, though, tell me. We can come at the scene another way."

Sometimes I wonder how many times I've cried since Dad died. I imagine a workplace safety sign proclaiming the number of days without accident, only the number of days without tears is abysmally low.

Jay watches me. "Are you ready to go back, or do you need another minute?"

"I'm okay."

When we walk onstage, everyone looks up, but they keep going until Jay holds up his hand. "Good, everybody. Thanks, Mac. Let's do something fun to finish. Who wants to sell some hair tonic?"

Because it's a radio play, the actors we're playing perform commercials between scenes. All five of us sing a jingle for Bremel Hair Tonic to the melody of "Rudolph, the Red-Nosed Reindeer."

We break for the day, and Jay gives my shoulder a squeeze as he walks past. Joss is next in line. "You were amazing."

"Thanks." I don't know that I deserve credit. I'm sure I couldn't have done what Joss thinks is so impressive before Dad died.

"I mean it. You've got serious natural talent." She hesitates like she wants to say more. *Maybe I'm not receiving her praise properly.* I force a smile. After a moment passes, I take a step toward the stairs, but she shoots out her hand. "Are you okay, though? Whatever you thought about—is everything okay?"

As I flounder, Mac inserts himself between us. Joss puts her hand on her hip. "Dude. We're in the middle of a conversation here."

"Don't mind me. Converse." But after Joss rolls her eyes, he addresses me. "I'm gonna stick around and look for period props online. Want to help?"

Joss shakes her head and starts to leave. "Yeah, one sec," I say to Mac, then hurry to catch up with her. "Thanks for your concern. I'm okay."

People struggle with "not okay." They can deal with mad. Take Maya—her parents got divorced because her dad cheated on her mom. Carolyn, Shelby, and I were all there when Maya's mom found out about the affair, and her parents seemed not to care that we could hear their whole argument. Maya was so upset, I seriously feared we would suffer bodily harm. She started throwing things across her bedroom—breakable things: a ceramic figurine that splintered into heavy pieces; a compact mirror that shattered when it hit the wall; and framed pictures that rained tiny shards of glass over the carpet. But she got it out of her system, and then we cleaned up together. The white-hot rage was temporary, and eventually, we could even laugh about it.

People can deal with sadness too—the normal teenage kind. During the summer after eighth grade, Shelby thought she'd found love. Okay, maybe not love, but a nice guy who seemed to care about her. They'd met at church camp, and by the end of the three weeks, they were spending every spare second together. But he lived in California. She moped for the rest of the summer, but then school started and there was a new cute boy and we stopped hearing so much about Evan. You move on.

I know people mean well. They want me to be okay because they don't know what to say if I'm not. For a few months, what I felt was understandable. After half a year, they'd said "I'm sorry" so many times, it seemed pointless to keep saying it. So, finally, if people asked how I was, I told them I was okay, because I, too, was tired of it not being true.

Once everyone leaves, Mac and I settle into auditorium seats and open our laptops. I'm searching for "1940s Corn Flakes" on eBay when Mac says, "So...what did you think about to make yourself cry?"

With a loud exhale, I glare at him. "Nosy much?"

"Sorry." He gives me a sheepish grin. "You're right. Not my business."

I go back to my screen, and we scroll in silence.

"If it were me, I'd think about my dog. You know, if I acted."

Losing my place again, I give him a hard stare. I will not be manipulated into sharing.

"No, really. He was this furry mutt named Finn...Finnegan Reddington Fuzzypaws the Third."

Despite myself, I smile. "Was there a Finnegan Reddington Fuzzypaws the First and Second?"

"No. He was the third because there were already me and my sister." He shrugs. "Five-year-old logic."

"Well, his name fits with yours." I close my laptop and set it on the seat next to me.

"He loved everyone, but he really was *my* dog. If I was home, he had to be in the same room with me. He slept on my bed—was a serious cover hog. And he was the worst alarm clock ever—who wants to wake up to dog tongue? But he was a good boy."

Mac has a faraway look. "We had an electric fence. He'd never broken through it before. Well, maybe when he was a puppy; not once he was older. I was walking home from school one day, like I always did, and he was in the yard waiting for me. Maybe there were too many distractions at once, I don't know. Or maybe he just forgot about the fence. But he took off running for me and there was a truck coming and...he got hit, and that was the end."

After a moment, he sniffs, then glances at me before turning back to his computer. "That's what I would think about. I just wondered if it was something like that for you. But you don't have to tell me. I—"

"It was my dad."

"What?"

"My dad died in a car accident last year."

His eyes widen. "Shit, Raina."

I look up and study the ceiling, like that can stop my tear ducts from functioning.

"I feel like an asshole for comparing my dog to your *dad*."

"You didn't know. And that's really sad about Finn."

"Still...." He moves his laptop aside and faces me. "I'm really sorry, Rae. I can't even imagine...."

His sympathy overwhelms my ability to hold it together. I whisper, "Thanks," as I wipe my face with my sleeve. Once I get tenuous control of my emotions, I say, "That's why I didn't do theatre last year. It happened two days before *Starcatcher* auditions."

He runs his hand through his hair and shakes his head. "That's awful."

The next wave of sadness spills over the rims of my eyelids, and I hide behind my hands. Mac puts his arm across my shoulders and pulls me toward him. We sit awkwardly, the top of my head pressed against his sternum, in companionably sad silence.

"SOCIAL DISEASE"

The day after I cried and fainted thanks to *Of Mice and Men*, it took Herculean willpower to make eye contact with anyone. I couldn't bring myself to do it as I hurried into the classroom and folded myself into my chair. Once my ears stopped feeling like they were on fire and Mrs. Keating began her lecture, I chanced a look around. Not everyone was staring at me, admittedly, but not *no one* was. And every person I caught with my eyes immediately directed theirs elsewhere.

Nobody said anything to me, though. And thankfully, we were at the end of the *Of Mice and Men* unit. Days passed, and I naïvely settled back into my inwardly suffering new normal.

Then I learned about the memes.

Shelby didn't want to show me. She pulled me aside at the end of the day but was vague about why, trying to figure out whether I'd seen them. "I'm really sorry," she said at last, holding out her phone.

Someone had captured the moment my eyes rolled back in my head, tears still streaming down my face, as my body slumped sideways.

The first caption read, **I CAN STILL TEND THE RABBITS, GEORGE?** Obviously from someone in the class. But as the picture traveled the Internet, the memes lost the *Of Mice and Men* reference, ranging from the misguided (**I DON'T HAVE A DATE FOR PROM!**) to the obnoxiously boy-like (**DO YOU SMELL THAT?**). There was **I CAN'T EVEN**, followed by **THIS IS HOW INTERESTED I AM IN WHAT YOU HAVE TO SAY**, and **THE MOON LANDING WAS *REAL*?!** There were a lot, and scrolling through them all was like shackling my heart to a block of cement and throwing it off a bridge. They had infiltrated RHS, a social virus I might never rid myself of.

So, the day after my crying spell in rehearsal, I'm in no hurry to walk into the auditorium, afraid of the fallout from breakdown 2.0.

Casey approaches as I'm pulling my script from my bag, and my body tenses.

"Hey. I wanted to catch you before we started."

He hesitates, like he's trying to figure out how to say what he's thinking: *Yesterday freaked me out. I can't do the show with you now.* I brace myself but am surprised by what he says next.

"I know that scene was hard. If you want to work on it again before the next time we do it here, just let me know."

My mouth hangs open a little as my brain processes Casey's compassion. I'm still staring, dumbfounded, when he smiles, then takes the stairs two at a time and jumps onstage.

I take a breath and climb slowly up the steps. Joss meets me at the top. "I was thinking about making the commercials four-part harmonies. Arlo's a base, and Casey and Rory are tenors. What part do you sing?"

An image of the choir room pops into my head and pinches my heart. "Soprano."

"Great, I'm an alto. I'll see if Jay wants to arrange something."

Mac enters from the door in the wings. The magnetic pull of the boards beneath my feet becomes exponentially stronger, but my eyes resist. He gives me a little wave as he hurries to put down his stuff.

Jay claps his hands together. "All righty, magic-makers. Today George and Mary get married, and George keeps his head to save the Building and Loan."

We open our scripts, and I lose myself in the play, getting so wrapped up in watching Arlo transform into different characters that Casey has to nudge me twice because I'm not paying attention to my lines.

When George comes home to the old Granville house, my exchange with Casey is easy, even when I talk about wanting my baby to look like him. I stifle a giggle when he stutters and asks if I'm "on the nest."

At the end of rehearsal, someone taps my shoulder as I'm picking up my coat. Mac holds out a yellow piece of paper, and my brain leaves the comfort of the radio station and hightails it back to the awkwardness of yesterday. My inner voice says what I'm afraid is in his head: *You made things so weird I can't even talk to you anymore.*

Instead, he says, "I don't know if it helps you to be sad or if the feel-good stuff is better, but I made a list of albums for both. Not that any musical can help, really. I just thought, if you haven't heard these soundtracks before, maybe you'll like them." Fidgeting, he meets my eyes for a second, then walks away.

The front of the sticky note reads:

For a good cry:

1. *Les Mis*
2. *Miss Saigon*
3. *Fun Home*

And the back says:

To feel better:

1. *Mamma Mia*
2. *Hairspray*
3. *Something Rotten*

I grab my bag and run to catch up to him, but as I emerge into the main hall, he leaves through the doors at the end.

Before bed, I prop my pillow up against the headboard, tuck my comforter around me, and review the lists again. Grandpa and I have watched the *Hairspray* and *Mamma Mia* movies. I don't know any of the music from *Something Rotten*. *Les Mis* is classic, and the same people wrote *Miss Saigon*, but I haven't listened to it. I've never heard of *Fun Home*.

That's the one I pull up. I tap "It All Comes Back (Opening)" and close my eyes. I'm drawn in right away, but I don't immediately understand why Mac put this on his list. Not until "Telephone Wire." After the main character, Alison, discovers she's gay and then learns her father secretly was too, I can't turn it off. I don't stop listening even though it's late and I should be trying to sleep.

I'm gutted by Alison's longing to have a conversation with her father that she never got to have, her desperation as she remembers her last night with him and how it wasn't—it could never be—what she wanted, what she needed.

No matter how many times I go over it, I can't remember the last thing I said to my dad, the last thing he said to me. It would have been that morning before school—"Have a good day" or "See you later." Maybe even "I love you," said out of habit.

But as much as I struggle to remember my final exchange with him, I'm crystal clear on how things ended with my friends. That conversation is seared into my memory.

It was the day before my birthday. At lunch, Shelby asked what I wanted to do to "celebrate," like I was capable of such a thing.

"Nothing." I happened to look up from my sandwich in time to catch Shelby's meaningful glance at Maya.

Maya crossed her arms on the table and leaned forward. "Rae. We need to talk."

Mid-bite, I put down my ham and cheese.

"We know you're still...dealing with your dad's death." She looked at the others, but their eyes were glued to the table. "And it's hard. We get it."

Do you?

"But sometimes...it seems like maybe...you enjoy the suffering."

Shelby's eyes shot up to Maya, who shook her head and tried to backpedal. "Not that you *enjoy* it. But that it's...maybe easier to do nothing than to put yourself out there again."

By this point, I'd gotten pretty used to feeling numb, so the heat rising within me was foreign and off-putting. "You think this is easy?"

Maya reached for my hand, but I pulled it away. "Of course not. But they say, 'Fake it till you make it,' right? Maybe you need to act like you're happy and then eventually you will be."

"What if I can't?" I whispered.

No one said anything. Maya looked at Shelby and Carolyn, then sighed. "We just don't know what else we can do for you."

My heart thudded in my chest. "Meaning what?"

Shelby's discomfort was painfully obvious. She was twisted so far to the side that one butt cheek was practically hanging off the chair, like she wanted nothing more than to escape from this conversation. Carolyn was still, hands in her lap, eyes trained on a blob of ketchup.

Maya held my gaze. "Meaning...that if you aren't willing to try to feel better—and we'll help you, if you'll let us—maybe we should take a break for a while."

That was the last thing my friends said to me. And I said nothing, just got up and walked out of the cafeteria, out of their lives.

So, listening to *Fun Home*, when Alison tries to convince her past self to say something else, something different, my heart breaks open to reveal a sobbing, snotty mess.

The rest of the soundtrack only makes me cry harder. When Bruce, Alison's father, sings his final song as he tries to figure out who he is, how to deal with his sexuality, and ultimately decides it's too impossible and steps in front of a truck, it's like my father is dying all over again.

After the album ends, I wait until I can breathe normally and text Mac, hoping he's still awake. **I listened to *Fun Home*. Damn.**

A minute later, he writes back, **Good damn or bad damn?**

This is what my friends didn't understand; maybe I should have explained it better: sometimes, you just need to be sad. **Good.**

Mac's emoji wipes sweat off its brow. **Thank God. Wasn't sure how that one would land.**

The music is amazing.

Jeanine Tesori and Lisa Kron. They're badass. It's based on a true story.

Oh. Tears well in my eyes again. **I didn't know that.**

Does that make it better or worse?

I consider this and remember what Jay said to me: if you can embrace your pain and turn it into something useful, it loses some of its power. This woman—the real Alison—used her pain to create something beautiful and moving.

Better.

"SWEET DREAMS (ARE MADE OF THIS)"

Number three on my kindness list: bring candy to rehearsal. I hand around a bag of gummy bears while we wait for Jay.

Joss picks out a pink one. "You all should come to my house tomorrow night. We can order pizza and watch BroadwayHD or something."

"In." Mac takes a handful.

Casey agrees, Rory and Arlo nod, but I bite the head off a green bear and chew the sticky candy to give myself time to think. *How do I convince Mom to let me drive home late?*

With a little research in hand, I broach the topic at dinner, pointing out that Joss's house is less than five miles from ours.

Geography doesn't win Mom over. "I'm still uncomfortable with you driving in the dark, and on a Friday night...I'm sorry."

"What if I promise to be home by—" I do quick mental acrobatics to balance having enough time at Joss's with getting Mom to agree to let me go at all. "—ten?"

She wrings her hands, her fork set to the side and her dinner abandoned, another culinary casualty of our mother-daughter conversations. "That's still a lot later than you usually get home."

"Mom. You do realize I'm a teenager? Who should be spending Friday night with her friends? I'm not even going *out* out."

Her face softens, and I think for a second I might have won.

"I don't know, Rae. You know why the driving thing is harder for me than for other parents."

Maybe I'll earn points for being sympathetic. "I get it. But it's got to happen sometime, right?"

Several seconds pass, then Mom rubs her forehead. "What if I take you and pick you up?"

"Ugh. Pass."

"Why?"

"Because it's embarrassing."

"So, lie. Say your car is being worked on."

So, lie. Easy for her to say. Easy for her to do. My stomach clenches at the memory of her lying to me about Dad. "You know what? Forget it." I turn my back on her surprised expression and run to my room.

The night the police came, I waited for Mom to come tell me. And waited. And waited. She didn't knock on my door until 5:30 the next morning.

With red eyes, she sat next to me on the bed and took my hands in hers. "Your dad...was in a car accident." Struggling to speak, she shook her head. "He...didn't make it."

Despite the fact that this was not news, hearing it a second time was every bit as horrible as the first.

"A deer ran in front of him.... He hit it...and the car rolled."

"Couldn't he have swerved?" My mind was foggy by that point, but I was pretty sure I remembered the police officer saying he swerved.

"The deer ran right in front of him.... I guess there wasn't...." She couldn't—or chose not to—finish the sentence, and that was the first moment I suspected she wasn't going to tell me the whole story.

"There wasn't *any* time to swerve, or slow down, or...?" *Or do something to avoid hitting a massive animal? No, because he was speeding. Because of me.*

"I don't think so."

"What did the police say, exactly?"

She looked down. "They said it was too close for him to avoid it."

Too close because he came upon it too fast.

"Why didn't he slam on his brakes?"

"He probably did."

"Then, how fast was he going?"

Mom turned to face me, the tears momentarily suspended in her eyes. "What?"

"I know he was hurrying to get to my concert...."

Her eyes burned with intensity as she held my gaze. "He finished earlier than he thought he would. There was plenty of time."

I could have left it at that. Maybe he was only speeding a little, like he did sometimes, and not racing against the clock to get to school. But I had to know. If his death was my fault, I didn't know how I would ever forgive myself, but it would be better than always wondering.

"So...he wasn't speeding?"

Before she answered, Mom paused for a long moment. Finally, she raised her eyes to meet mine and said firmly, "No."

She lied.

She lied because she couldn't face the fact that his death was my fault, so now I have to face it alone.

BEFORE SCHOOL STARTS, I find Joss. "Hey, I'm really sorry, but I can't make it tonight."

"Oh no! Why?"

"Um...I haven't had my license long, and my mom won't let me drive late at night." My face burns at the lameness of my semi-truthful explanation.

She grabs my forearm, eyes wide. "You should spend the night."

"Really?"

"Oh my gosh, it will be so much fun. After we kick the boys out, we'll stay up late and talk and—you'll stay, won't you? Your mom will be okay with that?"

"Yeah, probably."

"Yay!"

Joss bounces away, her blonde ponytail swinging. I text Mom and, thankfully, she agrees without argument.

After rehearsal, we all head to Joss's. Her basement is nice—professionally finished, unlike mine, which has mismatched furniture on a concrete floor.

Arlo goes straight for the air hockey table, and Casey follows.

Mac walks behind a bar backdropped by a wine bottle–shaped piece of art made from corks. "Ladies? Gentleman?" He tosses a towel over his shoulder as Joss, Rory, and I sit on the stools.

"What do you have?" Rory asks.

"Nothing too exciting," Joss says. "Mom and Adam lock up the good stuff."

Mac turns and opens the mini fridge behind him. "We have a number of choices of the soda pop variety, an assortment of sparkling water flavors, and a plethora of juices."

"Pepsi, please." Joss holds out her hand, and Mac places a can into it.

"And for you, sir?"

Rory strokes his chin, dons Clarence's accent, and says his line from the play. "'I was just thinking of mulled wine. Heavy on the cinnamon and light on the cloves. Off with you my lad, and lively now!'"

"Ha!" Mac slaps the table with his towel, and we all laugh.

"But for real, I'll take a KeyLime LaCroix. Thanks, Mac."

"And for the lady?" he asks as he hands Rory his can.

"Snapple Apple."

"You picked that just because it's fun to say." Mac twists off the cap and hands me the bottle.

Out of the corner of my eye, I see a puck go flying across the room and hit the wall. "My bad!" Arlo calls. The three of us spin around to watch the game.

They're playing to seven, and it's tied at five. Arlo hits a shot straight down the middle, which Casey blocks, but then his paddle slips and the puck slides into the goal.

"Gah!" Casey raises his hands in the air.

The next time the puck flips off the table, Joss runs to get it, then stands at the side of the table to watch. The rest of us join her.

"Too much pressure!" Casey cries, but the next shot he takes slides into Arlo's goal.

"Damn." Arlo pulls it out and serves it back. *Thuk-thuk-thuk.* The puck whizzes back and forth for a solid two minutes.

"My arm hurts," Casey complains, just as Arlo makes the shot.

The guys set down their paddles, and Arlo gives Casey a fist bump before they both collapse on the couch.

"Our turn," Mac says. "Boys versus girls?"

"Do you really want to play against me?" Joss leans forward over the table. "I have three stepbrothers, and I can beat them all. I will own you, Reddington."

"Bring it, Cohen."

Joss hands me a paddle. "We cannot let them win."

I nod as I take my place. Joss serves first and sends the puck straight toward the goal. Mac is quick, though, and blocks it. "How's that ownership thing work again?"

Eyes narrowed, Joss hits it toward the wall so hard it bounces back to us without Mac or Rory touching it. She executes several moves like this in quick succession, and the puck zooms back and forth so fast I can barely keep my eyes on it. While the guys swing their paddles wildly, Joss keeps zinging it until she gets it lined up, and then wham! Goal!

She gives me a high five and smirks at Mac. He nods. "You know what you're doing, there's no denying it. But now we know your style, and two can play at that game."

Mac performs his own rapid-fire back-and-forth, but Joss follows the puck. When he takes his shot, she's ready for it and sends it straight back, into the goal.

"Do you realize how many hours I've spent doing this?"

The fact that Mac doesn't have a retort makes me think Joss is getting to him, and I wonder if he's a sore loser. My gut says I'm about to find out.

When the puck winds up in my corner, I do the best I can, but my best ends up giving them a goal when I accidentally knock the puck into our pocket. "Sorry."

"No worries. That's the only point they'll get."

Our next two points come quick; the puck flies in untouched. "What was it you wanted to know about ownership?" Joss taunts.

Mac slaps the puck down and hits it as fast as he can, but Joss isn't caught off guard. They go back and forth a few times before she sends it in again.

The score is six-one. Mac and Joss stare each other down. Joss gets it zigzagging around the table and lines up the shot for the win.

"Ha!" She raises her paddle, and I clink it with mine.

Lifting an imaginary cap, Mac says, "I am humbled by your air hockey prowess."

The basement door opens, and Joss's mom appears. "Pizza's here." She sets a stack of boxes on the bar.

Arlo and Casey open the lids, and Joss pulls paper plates and napkins from a drawer. I grab a couple slices of pepperoni, then settle in the lounge area of the basement. Under a giant quote about kindness and laughter that stretches across the wall is a sectional couch and a chair that face a big-screen TV.

Mac wipes his mouth with a napkin and points at Rory. "Favorite performer: go."

"Do they have to be living?"

"Doesn't matter."

"Gene Kelly." A dancer, of course. Rory turns to his left. "Casey?"

"Uh...I don't know a ton. Maybe Hugh Jackman?"

"Not a bad choice." Mac takes another bite, then says, "Rae?"

"Julie Andrews."

"Old school. I like it."

"Joss?" I ask.

"Mm...this is hard. But if I have to pick, I'd say Audra McDonald."

"Who?" Arlo asks.

"This amazing singer and actress. She's won six Tony Awards. I fell in love with her in *Ragtime*. Is there anyone you like?"

Arlo looks at the floor. "I don't know this stuff like y'all do."

"That's okay," Joss says. "It means there's so much for you to discover."

"Ahem." Mac looks pointedly at her.

"And who, pray tell, is your favorite performer, Mr. Reddington?" She pinches a string of cheese with her fingers.

"Thank you for asking. For performance, I have to give it to Christian Borle, but as far as talent across the board, you can't not say Lin-Manuel."

Joss shakes her head. "None of us got to pick two. If you're going to make us play these silly games, you have to stick to your own rules."

"Fine, Christian it is." The guy *is* hilarious as a rock star version of William Shakespeare in *Something Rotten*, one of the soundtracks on Mac's feel-good musicals list that I've started listening to.

Now that Mac is pacified, Joss grabs the remote. "What do you guys want to watch?" She navigates until musicals fill the screen. "Call out if you see something you like."

"What's *The Toxic Avenger*?" Arlo asks, and Joss pulls up the description.

"They made a musical about a toxic waste dump?" Rory says incredulously.

Mac grins. "I'm sold."

People shift so everyone can see the TV. Casey sits on the floor with his back against the couch in front of me; I scoot toward the side of the cushion, so I don't bump his head with my knee.

Not long after it starts, Mac pops up to get food, bringing the smell of sausage back with him. Arlo steps over Casey to get a drink. Joss adjusts the pillow behind her several times, and Rory repositions himself so his legs are hanging off one side of the chair, then the other. All the fidgeting is distracting, but by the time Toxie's heart is broken and his lady love, Sarah, is crying, we're all settled, quiet.

Casey doesn't seem to mind my feet in the least; in fact, he's leaning so far into my legs that he's practically sliding them out from under me. Mac is wedged against the arm of the couch on my other side, leaving plenty of space on his cushion. But will it be weird if I move toward him? Will he think I'm trying to get closer, rather than merely claiming my fair share of lounge space? And what if I *do* want to get closer—would he mind?

When Casey pushes my legs even further, the situation becomes untenable. Trying to be as subtle as possible, I extricate myself and put my left leg on the edge of Mac's cushion. He looks at me, and my cheeks burn. *Busted.* Then he leans forward, sizing up the Casey situation, before putting his arm across the back of the couch. With a jerk of his head, he invites me over.

Okay. My hands start sweating, but I swing my other leg onto the lounge. *How close am I supposed to sit?* My right leg is barely on the cushion—I actually have to clench my muscles to keep it from slipping off.

Mac whispers, "I won't bite," so I scooch ever closer, barely leaning against him. Tense, I let our bodies touch, but not *too* much. And my head—*what do I do with my head?*

Turtle-slow, I relax one muscle at a time, gradually letting more of my weight shift onto him. Mac drops his hand so it's touching my shoulder (*ohmigod*), so I rest my head on his shirt, the material soft on my cheek.

I pretty much stop paying attention to the movie, riveted instead by the delirious mix of shampoo, soap, and cologne coming from Mac's neck.

Too soon, the credits roll. I let my head linger until Joss climbs over Arlo to turn on the lights, then I take one more whiff of Mac's scent and sit up. Since no one else moves, I stay near him, getting chills when he lowers his arm, and the back of his hand touches mine. Our skin stays in contact for the rest of the night.

We watch clips from Broadway performances, concerts, and *Saturday Night Live* theatre skits until it's time for the guys to leave. When Mac stands, the left side of my body (*and my heart*) mourns the absence of his warmth.

Upstairs, Joss leaves me in her room to change into my pajamas. Once I'm finished, I sit on the end of her bed and look around. Her bulletin board is full of theatre memorabilia—pictures from *Little Shop* and other past shows, Playbills, ticket stubs from *School of Rock* and *Cinderella*, and a *Wicked* key chain. A bookshelf holds titles by Jenny Han and Rainbow Rowell. The closet door is slid open, showing shoe boxes piled so high they collide with the clothes, which are crammed so tightly together I don't know how she ever finds anything.

Being here, this moment, is achingly familiar, and I realize it's been a minute since I hung out with a girlfriend. *Don't get emotional and weird about it*, I caution myself.

Joss comes in and plops on the bed. "So, let's talk about you and Mac."

"What about us?" I can't help but smile.

She tosses a heart-shaped pillow at me. "The sparks—hello?!"

Hugging the pillow to my chest, I grin.

"You like him, right?"

I nod, then she says, "He's totally into you too."

My heart flits around my chest. "You think?"

"Come on—it's obvious."

The words sound like what Mac would say, and I'm struck by how similar they are. "Were you and Mac ever...?"

"A couple? God, no. He's like my brother—some days I love him and some days I hate him. But I think you two would be really cute together."

"What kind of guys do you like?"

"Mmm...." She leans against the headboard. "Someone humble —which, no offense, Mac is not." We share a laugh because I don't disagree. "And I always appreciate a guy who's willing to be vulnerable."

Maybe that's something everyone appreciates. I probably wouldn't have told Mac about my dad if he hadn't first told me about Finn.

"I'll never forget my first boyfriend," Joss continues. "We were each other's first kiss, and even though neither of us knew what we were doing, maybe *because* neither of us knew, it was scary and special and huge, and there was something perfect about that."

My pulse accelerates before I ask the next question. "Has Mac had many girlfriends?"

"Eh. I've tried to set him up before, but he was always resistant. But he's never acted around another girl the way he acts around you."

Her words echo in my mind as I slide into my sleeping bag. The memory of my head on Mac's chest fills the darkness, and my body thrums as I remember the warmth from his skin, the little puff of air I felt on my forehead when he laughed. *What would his mouth feel like on mine?* I wonder. *Is he asking himself the same question?* My lips curl up as I drift off to sleep.

"PHOTOGRAPH"

I wake up Sunday morning to two texts—one from Mom saying she had to go into work because her IT team is having a production issue and the other from Grandpa inviting me over for breakfast. He's the best chef in the family, so whatever he'll make will far surpass the cereal I'll have if I fend for myself.

"What are you in the mood for?" he asks when I come in. "Sweet or savory?"

"Mm...sweet."

He nods and pulls out a pan. I sit at the table and watch him work. We both know it's better this way—he tried to teach me when I was younger, but I burnt bread, scorched a pan by heating milk too long, and made a notorious French toast that tasted like raw egg.

"Would you wash these?" He hands me a container of blueberries.

The berries should be safe from my ineptitude, so I grab a colander and turn on the water. "You don't have a baseball glove from the '40s, do you?"

Grandpa tilts his head. "You know, I just might. I've got a box of things from my childhood. I'll look after we eat."

I set the table and wait until he brings plates over.

"Does this fit the bill?"

Crepes stuffed with a cream cheese filling and smothered in blueberry sauce. "Definitely."

We dig in, eating in happy silence, blueberries popping satisfyingly in my mouth, the hint of lemon in the filling brightening the dish and the morning.

My phone buzzes as I'm clearing the dishes.

Mac: **Wanna come over and drop stuff in a tub?**

Grandpa notices my smile. "Something amusing?"

"A friend wants to work on sound effects for the show. Do you mind if I go?" I was going to ask Grandpa to run lines with me, but I don't have to know my lines that well. Since it's a radio play, we get to have scripts onstage.

"Sure, eat and run." He winks. "But tell this friend—?"

"Mac," I say. Grandpa raises his eyebrows, and I blush.

"Tell Mac he owes me. Let me check on the glove."

♪

"Hey—where did you get that?" Mac takes the worn glove from my hand as soon as he opens the door.

"It was my grandpa's."

"Killer." He motions me in, and I'm immediately struck by how neat his house is—way neater than mine.

"Keep your coat on. We have to do this in the garage. Sorry." He leads me down a hallway, the walls of which are crowded with pictures, all in matching gold frames. A family portrait, little boy Mac and his baby sister, Mac with his face resting against a dog I assume is the illustrious Finnegan Reddington Fuzzypaws the Third. Older Mac's sister in a basketball uniform—many such pictures, in fact—and a surprisingly large number of Mac in the boy version of said uniform.

"Hi there." Mac's mom turns from the kitchen sink, wiping her hands on a towel. "You must be Rae. It's nice to meet you."

"Nice to meet you too, Mrs. Reddington."

"Okay, Mom, you met her. We're going outside now."

"I'm sorry it's so cold," she calls after us. "The garage is the only place you can splash water around."

At least the garage door is down, but my breath still makes visible puffs in front of my face. I stuff my hands in my pockets as Mac kneels by the tub of water and picks up a rock, which he holds out to me. "Do the honors?"

I hold my arm over the tub. "Time to save George, Clarence," I tell the rock, then let go.

It makes a *splash*; water sloshes over the sides of the tub, but Mac shakes his head. "You hear it hit the bottom. Do you think we need a deeper tub?"

"A rock is heavy enough it won't matter. We should try something lighter."

Mac has assembled a variety of items. Picking up a plastic bowl, he extends his arm and releases it. The fact that it floats solves the *thunk*ing problem, but its contact with the water is more *slap* than *splash*.

I crouch before his pile and examine the options. "What if we use something heavy but put a towel at the bottom of the tub?"

"Genius. I'll see if my mom has a towel she'll let us use."

While he dashes inside, I blow into the space between my hands. A couple minutes later, he rushes back out waving a ratty old towel. He drops it into the tub and uses a broom handle to push it down, so he doesn't have to submerge his arms.

Take two: good *splash*, less *thunk*, but there's still no mistaking the sound of it hitting the bottom.

"Damn." Mac wraps his arms around himself and stares at the water. And I stare at his face. There's a little wrinkle in the space between his eyebrows and the bridge of his nose. His look of concentration is endearing, and I like that this matters so much to him.

With his head tilted to the side, he says, "Maybe the bowl *could* work," and picks it up.

"It's too light."

"Yeah, to drop. But maybe we're going about it wrong."

"What do you suggest?"

He hesitates for a moment, thinking, then kneels in front of the tub; I do the same. After pushing up his sleeves, he slowly dunks the bowl under the water until it fills up, then he turns it upside down, keeping it under the water. He looks at me, and I nod. With a quick intake of breath, he pulls the bowl out of the tub.

The effect is perfect—when the bowl breaks contact with the water, I hear George and Clarence jumping in the river. The water rushing out of the bowl sounds like waves splashing around them. Even the aftereffect of the water sloshing a bit as it settles reminds me of gentle waves surrounding our heroes once Clarence rescues George.

Mac and I look at each other, and he breaks into a huge grin. He tosses the bowl aside and wraps his wet arms around me. I squeeze him back. *Damn the layers of puffy winter coats between us.*

When he speaks, his mouth is so close to my ear, his breath warms my skin, sending a shiver down the rest of my body. "Let's go in. I'm freezing."

I don't disagree but am still disappointed when he pulls away.

The blast of warm air that greets me makes my cheeks sting, little pins pricking the surface as my face thaws. I follow Mac to the kitchen table, keeping my coat on because the heat from the house hasn't seeped into my bones yet.

Mac's mom approaches. "I'm making soup. Will you stay for lunch, Rae?"

I glance at Mac to see if the invitation extends from him too.

"She makes a mean potato leek."

"That would be nice, thanks," I say to Mrs. Reddington.

As she returns to the stove, Mac's dad and sister appear. She's wearing a basketball uniform, and given Mac's height, I'm surprised she's so tall. Good for her game, I'm sure, but maybe not so good for Mac's ego as the big brother.

"How'd your little experiment go?" his dad asks.

I smile at Mac, but his eyes are focused on the table. "We found something that works."

His dad walks over to his mom and places a hand on the small of her back. "You sure you don't want to come to the game?"

She glances at me and Mac. "No, I've got some things to take care of here."

Is that true, or is she not going because she doesn't want to leave us unsupervised? What is she afraid might happen? *What* would *happen if the two of us were alone in the house?* I hope no one notices the pink that's probably creeping into my cheeks at the first thought that pops into my head. I try to read Mac's expression, but he's scrutinizing his fingernail like it's the most fascinating thing in the world.

After his dad and sister leave, his mom brings us steaming bowls of soup. She takes hers into another room, calling, "There's plenty more if you want it."

The refrigerator hums, reminding me of the hushed meals at home.

"Your sister plays basketball, huh?" I blow on my spoon. "I saw your pictures. I didn't know you played."

Mac nods without looking at me. "All through elementary and middle school. Only stopped last year."

"Why?"

"Too hard to do that and theatre. And I never got any playing time anyway."

Part of me wants to ask why he started playing in the first place, but the topic doesn't seem like one he's eager to discuss. Trying to be nice, I say, "If you played for that many years, you must have been decent."

"Not as good as my dad wanted me to be."

I don't know what to say, how to steer the conversation toward our normal easy, jokey style. Is it something about me being at his house? Maybe Mac is wishing I didn't stay, so once I finish, I take my bowl to the sink and reach into my coat pocket for my keys.

"You're leaving?"

I'm surprised he's surprised. "Um...."

"Want to watch a movie or something?" His tone shifts and he sounds like himself again.

Relieved, I put my keys back in my pocket. "Sure."

I take off my coat as Mac clears his place, then follow him down the single step into the family room. More pictures on the walls—all black frames here—and a blanket that looks too perfectly draped over a chair to have actually been thrown haphazardly.

Now comes the decision of where to sit. I'd be afraid to disrupt the staging of the blanket chair, but it doesn't face the TV anyway. A couch is along the back wall and a second chair is cornered with the couch, an end table in between.

Mac grabs the remote and sits in the chair, and I hate myself for feeling disappointed. I curl up in the corner of the couch.

"Do you like *Guys and Dolls*?" he asks.

Please—obviously. "I think it's nicely-nicely."

He smiles at my reference to the film's character of gambler Nicely-Nicely Johnson and points the remote at the TV. Although there are many Sinatra gems, this has always been my favorite. *Take Me Out to the Ball Game* is delightful, and one not everyone knows about. *On the Town* is a classic. But the music in *Guys and Dolls* is so fun, the lyrics so clever.

When it starts, though, I turn abruptly to Mac. "What is this?"

"It's a documentary about making the cast album for the '92 revival."

"That's not *Guys and Dolls*."

"No, not the show. But it includes glimpses of the performances."

"I thought you meant the movie."

Because I'm talking too much, Mac presses pause. "Yeah, I mean, that's great, but anybody can see that. This captures a moment in history."

A concern has surfaced in my mind that I truly hope is unfounded. "You have seen it, right?"

"I wasn't alive in '92."

"Not the show—the movie."

He looks down, trying to hide that sheepish grin, and *oh my God*, I can't even. "How do you call yourself a fan of the theatre?"

"To be fair, movie musicals aren't technically theatre."

"But it's a classic. It's Sinatra!"

"This is Nathan Lane!" he counters.

I roll my eyes. "No one tops Sinatra."

"No? Have you heard Nathan?" He knows I haven't, so he doesn't give me a chance to answer. "For crying out loud, the man chose his stage name because of Nathan Detroit—*this* character. How can that not make him the best actor for the part?"

"This is blatantly unfair, you know. You're judging something you haven't seen."

"So are you. I have a solution—we watch both and then decide."

A wave of heat rides up my body at the thought of spending the next several hours with Mac. "Deal."

He wants to watch the movie first, and it's like spaghetti and meatballs for my heart. It's been a few years since I watched it, but it's just as wonderful as I remember.

At the end, Mac turns to me. "I grant you Sinatra is a charming rake, but I think you'll agree Nathan beats him on vocal chops." He sets the remote on the table and stands. "Popcorn?"

"Yes, please. I seriously doubt Nathan Lane is a comparable crooner."

Mac opens the door to the pantry as he says, "Sinatra is a great crooner, but he doesn't have a theatre voice. Nathan Lane is indisputably *Broadway*. After you hear him, you'll have to admit at least that."

A moment later, kernels pop and the smell of fake butter wafts into the family room. Mac brings in a big bowl and sits next to me—right next to me. Apparently, he didn't suffer from an agonizing internal debate about how much of his body he should let touch mine. Thigh, torso, arm—they're all dizzyingly close, only a couple layers of fabric separating our skin.

I try to pay attention to the documentary, I do. But I'm also paying very great attention to Mac's hand—when it goes in the bowl and whether my hand should or should not go in at the same time.

This behind-the-scenes view of recording an album makes me think of Mrs. Whaley, my old choir director. She knew how to make all our different voices blend to produce something transcendent.

The song "Sue Me" is one of my favorites. Nathan and his gal Adelaide fight through their overlapping words and melodies as he proclaims his love despite his lousy way of showing it. After the last note, Mac hits pause and stares at me. "Come on, that was pure gold."

Reluctantly, I concede. "Okay, fine, that song is more theatrical in this version."

"And by *theatrical*, you mean...?"

"Dramatic, I guess?"

"And by *dramatic*, you mean...?"

I'm not sure what he wants me to say. He leans closer, so close I can smell his heady mix of shampoo, soap, and maybe cologne, and whispers, "The word you're looking for is *better*."

Mock-glaring, I push him away. *Stupid.* But after he resumes the documentary, he settles back against my side and stays there until it's over.

As if that isn't enough to put some extra heartbeats in my pulse, he caps it off by leaning over me to set the bowl on the table, pressing a good quarter of his surface area against me. I steel myself for the tragic moment when he will get up, but he slouches down and rests his head against the back of the couch, so I scooch to mirror his position. *Our faces have never been this close.*

"So, how'd you fall for movie musicals?" he asks.

"My grandpa."

"You watched them together?"

I nod. "That's our thing. How about you? Why musicals?"

"It started with Mrs. Faatz. Bad name, but badass teacher. First grade. She was big into using the arts in education. Did a whole unit around the Frog and Toad musical. We planted seeds in little plastic cups and then listened to Toad sing about how hard it is to wait for them to grow. Learned math after listening to Frog and Toad eat countless cookies. That show is full of life lessons for six-year-olds—patience, friendship, kindness. She was brilliant to use it."

"You should tell her that."

"Yeah, I should." A moment passes. "How about stage shows? Have you seen anything live?"

"Some, not many." I pause. "A few years ago, my parents and I saw *Rock of Ages*." A musical about '80s rock—how could Dad and I not see that together?

Mac seems to choose his next words carefully. "Did he ever see you perform?"

I shake my head.

"That's hard."

"Everything's hard." We stare at each other. "I thought after a year, it would be easier, you know? No more firsts of all the things I used to do with him. But it's not. His birthday is Tuesday, and that day is going to suck just as much this year as it did last year."

Mac nods. "It's been two years since Finn died, and I still hate going to bed because seeing it empty feels like someone is pushing on my bruised heart with their thumb."

"Stupid sadness."

"You're profound, Raina-Rae."

I don't know if it's the way the corners of his lips curl up slightly or because I know if I don't laugh, I'll cry, but I start to giggle, then Mac joins in. And then it's a cycle that feeds on itself, and we're laughing because of how hard we're laughing at something that wasn't even funny. By the end, we both take shuddery breaths and wipe our eyes, and I have to remind my lungs how to work.

Neither of us says anything as we compose ourselves; we just stare at each other with our faces inches apart. My heart whaps my rib cage, distracting me from Mac's eyes, which, up close I realize, are a mix of brown, gray, and green.

Is this the moment? I wait to see if Mac will lean forward and close the gap between us. He shifts almost imperceptibly toward me. Maybe that's a sign? I inch closer but am interrupted by a noise in the kitchen.

I sit up quickly and look over my shoulder—Mac's mom pulls a casserole dish from the fridge. When I turn back to Mac, his expression is inscrutable.

"HAVE A NICE DAY"

Given what happened during my first concert, choir wasn't something I had any intention of continuing. But after enough no-showing at practice, Mrs. Whaley found me at my locker one day. Before I had a chance to apologize, she wrapped her arms around me. "Raina, I'm so, so sorry."

That was all it took—damn tears. She discreetly guided me to the teachers' lounge, led me to a couple chairs in a corner, and lightly placed her hand on my knee. "I know you need time to grieve. But please know you'll always be welcome in the choir if and when you're ready to come back."

She checked in periodically last year, and again a few months ago when school started. Every time I said I still wasn't up to rejoining, she gave me a nod and a frowny smile, sympathetic but disappointed.

It's nice that she keeps trying.

On my way to school, I stop at Kroger and buy a "crazy daisy" bouquet of unnaturally neon flowers. At the end of the day, I'm swimming in their floral scent on my way to the choir room when Mac steps into the hall from the back of the theatre.

"For me? And I didn't get you anything."

He reaches out, but I pull my hand away. "Why would I give you flowers?"

"The better question is: to whom *are* you giving flowers?"

I hesitate. "Do you know Mrs. Whaley?"

Mac taps his chin with his finger. "Can't say I do. Do we have a botany program I don't know about?"

"She's the choir director." I walk past him, but he keeps pace at my side.

"And you've wronged her egregiously and are making amends?"

"Watching the documentary yesterday made me think of her, and I feel bad I'm not doing choir anymore."

"Mm hm." Mac nods. "I think I understand. You're denying her your lilting voice to lend your talents to our show. She's jealous the theatre department has stolen another singer, so this is a peace offering."

One door away, I stop walking and face him. "We had a concert the night my dad.... After that, I couldn't do choir anymore, but Mrs. Whaley was really nice about it. She wanted me to do it again this year...but I'm not ready yet."

Mac purses his lips, done with the jokes. "She'll love them."

Before I go in, I peek through the door, afraid of running into Shelby, Maya, or Carolyn. But from what I can see, the few kids congregating in the room aren't among my former BFFs.

Mrs. Whaley is looking at some sheet music. When I approach, she smiles and opens her arms for a hug.

"Thanks for being so understanding. I'm sorry I keep saying no."

She waves away my apology and takes the flowers. "These are beautiful, Raina. Thank you. You'll come back to us when you're ready."

I take a deep breath as I step into the hall, where Mac is waiting. "You okay?"

Nodding, I start walking, and Mac jogs to catch up. We enter the stage from the back and see Joss in the wings, examining props. "Where did you two come from?" she asks.

"Rae was delivering kindness."

She smiles at me. "What does that mean?"

"I owe someone for a favor and I'm trying to pay it forward."

Mac picks up an ice cream scoop and tosses it from one hand to the other. "Operation: Good Deeds."

Joss's eyes twinkle. "Ooh, fun. I want in. Do you have, like, a plan? Or do you just do nice things when you think of them?"

"I'm still figuring that out."

"Do you want to talk about it after rehearsal? I mean, if you want help. It's fine if it's just your thing."

"No, two Good Samaritans are better than one."

"Great, let's brainstorm at Starbucks." Joss leads me downstage, and Mac hurries after us. "Hey, I want to go too!"

After Mac gets his cappuccino, he stakes out a table in the corner. Cinnamon dolce steamer in hand, I sit across from him and unzip my backpack. Joss flounces over with a strawberry Frappuccino, sits next to Mac, and props her elbows on the table. "So, whatcha got?"

I place my hands on the notebook before opening it. "These are just some ideas that popped into my head. I haven't given it a whole lot of thought."

They stare at me, waiting expectantly. I gently flip back the cover, pause, then turn the notebook around so they can read the list.

1. *Buy Starbucks for the car behind me*
2. *Compliment someone*
3. ~~*Bring candy to rehearsal*~~

4. Call Gramma and Pops more often
5. Leave money in vending machines
6. Donate stuff I don't need anymore
~~*7. Do something nice for Mrs. Whaley*~~

"These are great." Joss shakes her plastic cup, swishing the slushy ice inside. "We should do some at school." She pulls the notebook toward her, takes a pen from her purse, and starts writing.

8. Pick up trash after lunch
9. Pass notes saying how great our teachers are
10. Leave positive notes on bathroom mirrors

"Or stall doors," I interject.

Joss amends: *10. Leave positive notes on bathroom mirrors and stall doors*

We're quiet as we contemplate. After a moment, Joss says, "I love these, but should we think bigger?"

"Poster board, not Post-its?" Mac offers.

Joss rolls her eyes. "No, I mean should we try to make a bigger difference?"

I've been trying to figure out how ever since the day at the Rock and Roll Hall of Fame—suddenly, the memory of my visit sparks inspiration. "What if we organized a fundraiser?"

"Yes," Joss says. "For what?"

"Well, Jon Bon Jovi has this charitable foundation...he raises money to fight hunger and homelessness."

"Bon Jovi?" Mac says. "Seems kind of random."

"My dad loved Bon Jovi."

His eyes jump up to mine. "Oh. Then we should definitely do that."

Looking from him to me, Joss says, "Because...?"

Deep breath. "My dad died last year."

Dropping the pen, Joss reaches for my hand. "Rae...."

I swallow the lump in my throat and manage to hold back the tears. "I'm sorry I didn't tell you sooner."

"I actually already knew. I heard about it right after it happened."

"Why didn't you say anything?"

She shrugs. "I figured you would tell me when you were ready."

No one says anything until Joss lets go of me. "We should absolutely do a fundraiser for Bon Jovi's charity," she says. "And while we plan it, we'll do the other things on the list." When we leave, she pulls her wallet from her purse, takes out a ten, and drops it in the tip jar.

"JUMP"

November 12. No chance of forgetting my dad's birth date. I know the tears will come eventually, but I can't bear a whole day of misery, so I play *Something Rotten* as I get ready, tapping my foot to the lively music. When I walk into the kitchen, Mom points to her ear, and I reluctantly pull out an earbud.

"What do you say we have dinner at Luigi's?"

Dad's favorite pizza place, a carryover from his and Mom's college days when they would go there late because it's open around the clock. We haven't been since...we haven't been just the two of us.

"The cast is grabbing dinner after rehearsal." May or may not be true, but I'll go through McDonald's and eat in my car before I'll go to Luigi's with Mom on Dad's birthday.

Her face falls. "Oh, okay. Maybe after we could go to Buckeye Donuts." She's clearly craving campus nostalgia, but these spots don't hold any memories for me, so why should I have to go?

"Sorry," I say brusquely. "We'll be out for the night."

"Dinner is one thing, but I don't want you driving past nine."

"I know, I won't." Backpack in hand, I leave before she can say anything else.

At the end of rehearsal, Mac jumps off the stage and hurries up to me, standing so close it seems he no longer feels we need to maintain personal space. *No complaints here.*

"I rallied the troops," he says. "An hour at Rockin' Jump, then Romano's."

"What—"

A word into my reply, he cuts me off. "I know the day still sucks, but maybe we can make it a little better than last year."

He remembered. I'm in serious danger of getting weepy, but he playfully bumps my shoulder with his, making me laugh as I swipe at my eyes.

Madness reigns at the trampoline park, a hotbed of sensory overload. Music blasts from the speakers, the bass vibrating in my chest; kids crisscross from one activity to another and make me dizzy with their nonstop zigzagging; and the smell of pepperoni hangs thick in the air. It's fantastic—because it's impossible to concentrate on anything other than what's right in front of me.

Once we're all standing on a giant grid of trampolines, Arlo and Casey race from one side to the other, sliding down the bouncy walls on their stomachs. The rest of us claim four nearby pads, forming a square as we bounce higher and higher. Joss flips in the air and turns a perfect somersault; Rory mirrors her.

"How do you know how to do that?" I ask.

"Cheerleading," Joss says.

"I did gymnastics for a few years before I committed to dance," Rory adds.

The best I can manage is bouncing on my butt and popping onto my feet again.

"Who's game for the foam pit?" Without waiting for an answer, Mac runs off. Joss and I follow, while Arlo and Casey get in line to battle each other with ginormous foam mallets, and Rory heads for the obstacle course.

The three of us take off and fall into the foam abyss below. I clamber my way out, and Mac offers me a hand—my fingers tingle at his touch.

After several more leaps, I start to sweat and brush off the hair that's stuck to my forehead. We jump until we're exhausted from our efforts to escape the foam, like trudging through four feet of snow. Then the boys hop onto the dodgeball court while Joss veers toward the bathroom.

I don't mean to look at the clock. Being here has been an excellent diversion. But at 6:41, with only two minutes to go, I can't not watch.

Most people probably don't make a big deal about the exact moment they were born. (A lot don't even know the time of their birth.) But my dad did. It helped that all of us were born during waking hours. He might not have made such a fuss if one of us had been born at three in the morning. But at 10:27 a.m. on July 17, he would text Mom at work or wrap his arms around her and give her an embarrassingly long kiss. At 8:19 p.m. on April 24, he would cup my face in his hands and tell me the world became a better place when I entered it. And so, at 6:43 p.m. on November 12, Mom and I would play his silly little game and smother him in a group hug that lasted way longer than I ever would have admitted to anyone but that I was secretly in no hurry to leave.

My breath catches in my throat, and I try to slow my pulse. *Watch the game.* I attempt to focus on the ball whizzing back and forth, but my eyes glance repeatedly at the clock.

6:42.

I count the seconds in my head. *One-one-thousand, two-one-thousand, three-one-thousand....*

A line on the bright red 2 shifts to make it a 3.

With a sharp inhale, I close my eyes until a hand on my shoulder makes me jump. "Are you okay?"

Joss's concern distracts me enough that I manage to fight the tears. "Yeah, thanks."

Like I can outrun the heartache, I dash back to the trampolines, then bounce as high as I can, pushing my body until my heart beats so hard that my physical pain is the only kind I can think about.

"Five minutes!" Mac calls from the air. When we return to the earth, he takes my hand and pulls me toward the foam pit.

I'm about to jump when a new song starts, and my smile falters. I stand frozen listening to the opening melody, but when the vocals cut in, I lose all control of my limbs and sink to the bouncy ground.

Mac kneels by my side, bending his head close to mine. "What's wrong?"

I wave my hand around, as if that will tell him it's the song that's wrong, because seriously—"Sweet Child O' Mine"? Today? *Thanks, universe.*

Understanding well enough, Mac gently guides me to my feet and wraps his arms around me. As I sob against his shoulder, he strokes my hair, which is so perfect it only makes me cry harder.

Soon more bodies approach; more arms encircle me. The song ends, but the five of them continue to hold on.

The buzzer buzzes—our hour is up. Still, they don't break the huddle. Instead, ten arms squeeze tighter, and then our whole mass slowly starts to tilt. I lose my footing, lean precariously far to the left, grab onto some part of someone, and lose contact with the ground. All six of us tumble into the foam pit amid squeals and shouts and elbows and tears and laughter.

Once we're seated at Romano's, Joss puts her arm around my shoulders and leans her head against mine.

The mood is somber. Even Mac is quiet. Finally, Rory looks at me. "What was it about that song?"

Only the fact that we listened to it together a million times. I take a deep breath. "My dad loved '80s rock, and 'Sweet Child O'

Mine' has the best guitar solo ever. When I heard that lyric...." I trace my finger along the red squares on the vinyl tablecloth.

"Did he ever see Guns N' Roses in concert?" Arlo asks.

"I don't know. He saw Bon Jovi a bunch." *I saw them in concert 23 times*, he says in my head. "They were his favorite."

"I'm glad we're doing something for his charity," Joss says.

Casey looks at her. "What are you talking about?"

"We want to organize a fundraiser for Jon Bon Jovi's Soul Foundation. It fights hunger and homelessness."

I smile at Joss, touched that she looked up the foundation.

She continues, "That's the big thing, but we're doing small acts of kindness too."

Rory takes the paper ring off his napkin. "Like what?"

"We've got a list." Joss nods at me, and I pull out my notebook and pass it around.

"Cool," Rory says. "My dance studio likes this kind of thing. Maybe I could do something there."

While the others talk, I look around the table, wishing Marlene from the Rock and Roll Hall of Fame could hear us. Maybe I'll pay it forward with interest.

"WHEN I SEE YOU SMILE"

J oss and I only have one class together, fifth-period English, so that's when we pass our note. I write, *I love Mrs. Nicolosi. She's the best teacher I've ever had.* Because I sit in the third row and Joss sits in the front, my mission is to initiate the note's journey; Joss's is to be conspicuous enough that Mrs. Nicolosi confiscates it.

Ferrying the note across the room will require the assistance of four people to my right and one behind Joss. I run into a hiccup right away, because sitting next to me is Paul Chen, the most awkward human I've ever encountered.

Although I don't make a point of talking to him, on the rare occasion he engages me in conversation, it always starts with, "Did you know...?" The kid knows more than a *Jeopardy* champion.

When Mrs. Nicolosi turns toward the whiteboard, I finger the note in my palm, then quickly dart my hand out. The air swirls around my fingers for far too long. I shake my hand, watching Paul out of the corner of my eye.

He knows what I'm doing; he's looking at my hand, at the note. But he doesn't take it. I'm just about to tap the shoulder of Xavier

Ruhl when Paul whispers, "Did you know the Hawaiian alphabet has only twelve letters?" He moves a pencil horizontal so it makes a *T* with two others he's lined up on his desk. "Every word ends in a vowel."

With a sigh, I poke my knuckle into Xavier's back, then let the note rest on his shoulder. Without turning around, he reaches back and takes it. *Was that so hard?*

The note encounters far fewer obstacles on the rest of its trek. It's a challenge not to laugh at Joss and how obvious she's being about it. Mrs. Nicolosi doesn't catch on, though. She frowns at Joss as she holds out her hand.

Joss looks over her shoulder and grins at me. I smile back, then return my gaze to our teacher, feeling a surge of pride when she reads the note and blushes.

♪

AFTER REHEARSAL, Mac bumps his fist against my arm. "Hey. I brought all the prop stuff I had at home. Want to help me bring it in?"

I grab my coat and follow him to his car. He pops the trunk and lifts out the tub, which is filled to the brim with a cuckoo clock, the baseball glove, high heels, and plenty more I can't see. I'm tasked with carrying a doll-sized door with a bell over the frame that tinkles as I walk. Together, we hurry back to the warmth and set everything onstage.

A couple trips later, Mac kills the lights and drags the ghost light to the middle of the stage. Like a moth to a flame, I scurry over, not wanting a repeat of his Halloween prank. "I'm not letting you out of my sight."

It's quiet as we stare at each other over the glowing bulb, less than six inches separating our faces. Because he isn't looking away or saying anything, maybe he feels the same connection I do.

My heart does somersaults, and my armpits start sweating, because—confession—I haven't kissed a boy before.

Sure, I've had crushes, starting with Wyatt Gardner in kindergarten. At the end of the first day, my head was so full of things the teacher had said—where to store my lunch box and which side of my folder my papers were supposed to go in and where the bathroom was—that my conversation with my mother that morning was long forgotten, as was the number of the bus I was supposed to get on. I stood on the sidewalk, tears welling in my eyes. Wyatt turned me around so he could read the tag attached to my backpack, took my hand, and led me to my bus.

Then there was Max Abner, who picked me first for red rover during field day at the end of second grade. A couple years later, it was Micah Jaffe—let me say, sharing your magic pens and exchanging invisible messages is a surefire way to a nine-year-old girl's heart. The feeling was mutual, and we were one of the first "couples" in our class. The idea of kissing was gross then, but that didn't stop a group of girls from planning our wedding at recess.

In middle school, I liked my lab partner, Zander Eisley. He was the closest I ever came to a kiss. At a party in eighth grade, we played spin the bottle. Zander spun it, and it landed between me and Emilee Masters, arguably—*clearly, one might say*—slightly more on my half, but stupid Emilee said, "Spin it again," and he did.

Last year, from the first day of school until October 21, I hoped Keegan Macek from choir would ask me to homecoming. As of October 22, crushes were meaningless, along with pretty much everything else in my life. Not being kissed was ranked last among my concerns in the black hole that was freshman year.

But now butterflies flit around my stomach. *Is he leaning forward? Should I lean toward him? Is it weird if we don't kiss now that we've been staring at each other for so long?* Time has slowed to allow an infinite number of thoughts to fill the few seconds that actually pass.

Mac blinks, the clock resumes its normal functioning, and he says, "I won't try anything funny this time."

♪

Joss and I are armed with pens and stacks of rainbow Post-its, ready to kick off our next note campaign. We start with the girls' bathroom closest to the auditorium. I write *You are beautiful* on a pink square and stick it to the mirror as Joss says from within a stall, "Should we put one on every door?"

"Are we doing every bathroom? That's a lot of notes."

"How 'bout every other."

At the other end of the mirrors, I stick *Let your light shine.* "Sounds good."

On our way to the next bathroom, I say, "I feel bad not doing anything for the guys."

"Don't you think they'd make fun of the notes?"

"Probably. But it might make them feel good inside. We could make them funnier."

Joss looks over her shoulder, grabs my hand, and pulls me into the boys' room. "Okay, show me what you've got."

I scrawl a note and stick it to the mirror: *Hey, stud.*

Inspired, Joss starts writing, then presses a blue sticky next to mine—*Lookin' hot*—before going into a stall.

Besides the urinals and fewer stalls, the boys' bathroom is pretty similar to ours, although the colors are different—their stalls are forest green, whereas ours are cream.

We hit all the bathrooms on the main floor, then head upstairs, where I write for the boys, *Smiles are sexy* and *You're a rock star.* After we finish, Joss links her arm through mine and says, "So, how are things with Mac?"

Heat infuses my ears and I shrug. "A couple times I thought he was going to kiss me...but nothing happened."

She rolls her eyes. "Sometimes boys are chickens."

"Maybe he's not sure if I like him."

"How can he not know? The rest of us know." She pokes me playfully in the arm.

"Maybe he doesn't like me."

"Oh, come on. He lights up when he's with you."

Picturing his face warms my insides. That grin—he does always look happy to see me, like a kid in a candy store. "Then why hasn't he kissed me?"

"He just needs a little nudge. And I am not afraid to give him a push."

I stop. "What do you mean?"

"Just trust me."

"NO ONE LIKE YOU"

F riday morning, Joss finds me at my locker. "I'm having a party."

"Cool."

"No. I'm having a party for you and Mac."

"What?"

She leans closer. "This is the nudge."

I open my mouth to ask more questions, but she straightens up and backs away. "Tomorrow, party starts at eight. You can come earlier if you want to get ready together. And spend the night!"

What just happened?

BEFORE MRS. NICOLOSI starts her English lecture, Paul Chen leans over. "Did you know fermented drinks have been around since 10,000 B.C.?"

I never know what to say to his trivia. "Huh."

He settles back in his chair and nods in Joss's direction. "I heard your friend is having a party."

How does he know about it? Granted, I don't know who runs in Joss's social circles besides our little group, but I can't imagine any of the circles include Paul.

"Did you know bourbon is the official spirit of the United States?"

Because I'm excited and nervous and ready to throw caution to the wind, I say, "Yeah, I did," just to mix things up.

Paul tilts his head all the way to the right, almost resting it on his shoulder, stares at me for a minute, then gives a little snort.

♪

WHILE I PACK up after rehearsal, Mac hovers. "What are you doing tonight?"

Holing up in my room or the basement to hide from my mother. "Nothing. You?"

"That is to be determined, Raina-Rae." His eyes dart around to see if anyone was within earshot of his slipup, if I now have the right to share his full moniker with the group. He got lucky. "I'm too jazzed for a mundane Friday night at home. Let's do something."

"You want to grab the gang and go to dinner?"

Mac taps his foot and the lion head on his toe bounces up and down. "As much as I revel in the company of our motley crew, I was thinking tonight could be just you and me."

Ohmigod. Is he asking me out? My heart beats so hard it could propel me forward without my feet taking any of the initiative. All that energy finds its release in my face, spreading my lips into a giant grin. "Yeah, that sounds fun."

Ohhhkay. I have a date with Mac—I mean, I could have a date with Mac. What if Mom says no? And if she says yes, is what I'm wearing okay? Do I have breath mints in my purse? Do I actually have to worry about whether I'll need a breath mint?

Before I can get too far ahead of myself (*a little late for that*), I pull out my phone. "Give me a second."

Can I go out to dinner? I type, careful to avoid a direct lie that might trip me up if Mom asks questions.

I smile awkwardly at Mac while I wait for a response.

Home before 9.

A quick thumbs-up emoji and I drop my phone into my purse. "Let's go."

Mac and I follow Joss and Arlo to the parking lot, and I sneak glances at him, like we're doing something illicit. Every time our eyes meet, I have to look away or I'll laugh.

"Oh," he says, "Rae, I got the old box of Corn Flakes. Want to see it before you go?" His tone practically winks, and he gives me a mischievous smile.

I'm sure Mac's ruse is as obvious to Joss and Arlo as it is to me, but they're talking and don't even acknowledge us as we stop and they continue to their cars. I go with Mac to his Fusion—Dinah— and wait while he unlocks the doors.

"Romano's?" I ask.

"Nah, we always go there. Do you like sushi?"

"I've never had it."

He raises his eyebrows, tilts his head, and gives me his "you did not just say that" look. I know he won't rest until he has remedied this situation, so obviously, we're getting sushi.

And now I have something new to be nervous about. "It's raw fish?"

"Not all of it. Shrimp tempura is cooked. One of my favorites."

Okay, fried fish I can get on board with.

The restaurant Mac parks in front of is in a strip mall, but the inside is far more elegant than the outside would suggest. Plush carpet and soft lighting welcome us in. It's quiet except for the babble of a water fountain and the murmuring of other diners.

As we peruse the menu, Mac says, "If you like cucumber or avocado, try one of those rolls with eel."

I scrunch my nose.

"It's sweet; trust me, you'll like it."

By the time a waitress comes to take our orders, I haven't decided whether to heed Mac's advice, but after I order a shrimp tempura roll, he watches me with a slight smile.

"And an eel avocado roll, please."

Our server leaves, and Mac reaches into a beautiful blue and white porcelain tray on the table and takes two pieces of paper, sliding one to me. I take the short pencil he offers me next and ask, "What are these for?"

"Haikus. Kind of what this place is known for."

Huh. More unique than drawing on the tablecloth.

We learned about these poems in middle school, seventh grade, I think, but I don't remember the structure. "What are the rules?"

"Three lines—five syllables, seven, five."

Mac bows his head and writes, and I agonize over whether to be funny or serious...or romantic? He finishes before I've started and raises his hands to question my lack of action.

Can't go wrong with humor, I decide and get to work.

It's a good call—he laughs when he reads my composition:

> No raw fish for me.
> Tempura might be okay.
> Jury is still out.

"You'll have to write another one after you taste the awesomeness that is deep fried shrimp," he says.

His poetic masterpiece reads:

> Pets prolong your life.
> Loving, loyal companions.
> Dogs are the best pet.

"Solid effort, but I object to the last line," I say.

"Care to refute it via haiku?" He hands me another piece of paper, and I craft my counterargument:

Cats aren't demanding.
Independent but loving.
Superior pet.

It doesn't win over Mac, who says, "An animal demanding to *snuggle* isn't a negative."

At the conclusion of our mental exercises, I'm faced with a physical challenge—aka chopsticks. Mac smirks as I flounder, watching until he can no longer bear my ineptitude, then he slides into my side of the booth. He places the chopsticks in my hand and curls my fingers around them appropriately, sending my body temperature up several degrees. His skin is warm, and I struggle to focus on the utensil lesson and not on how good his touch feels.

Once I retain enough to successfully pick up a piece of the tempura roll, I give it a try. "Not bad."

"High praise."

"I'm a tough critic." The roll is delicious, the spicy mayo adding a creaminess and some tang to the crispy shrimp, but I'm not giving Mac the satisfaction of thinking he's right until I've tried the eel.

He points to my other roll with his chopsticks. "And?"

The eel is covered in a brownish sticky sauce, which I'm hoping will mask the fishy flavor. I tentatively put a piece in my mouth.

Damn, he *was* right.

The sauce is delectable, and I wouldn't even know I'm eating a serpentine-like fish. "It's okay," I say, but he sees through me.

"You love it. Admit it."

I take my time chewing and swallowing. "It may be better than I thought it would be."

"And by *better*, you mean...?"

Rather than set him up to tease me, I take another bite.

Still, he continues, "The phrase you're looking for is *the best thing I've ever tasted and thank you for insisting I order it.*"

"No, I don't think that's what I meant." I wipe my mouth to hide my smile under the napkin.

"You're right, I misunderstood. What you were actually trying to say was, *You're wise beyond your years, Mac, and I will never doubt you again.*"

"I'm definitely sure that wasn't it." I'm outright laughing now.

He shrugs. "Fine. Then I'll keep my future recommendations of awesome things you should experience to myself."

We stare at each other. "No, you won't," I say.

"You're right, I won't." He smiles around a bite of sushi.

ON OUR WAY to the car, Mac says, "Can I tempt you with a hot beverage?"

It's only 7:40, so I nod.

The instant I open the door to Starbucks, I'm hit by the smell of coffee beans, a gentle reminder of Dad. We sit at the same table where we brainstormed kindness ideas. Maybe that's what causes Mac to say, "Oh, I keep forgetting to tell you—I had a thought about Bon Jovi's charity."

"Yeah?"

"I was thinking we could volunteer at a homeless shelter first. Might be good to check out the place, see what they do for people, where they need help. We could get some ideas for how to help the Soul Foundation."

"Sounds great."

"I checked online, and they need volunteers on Thanksgiving. Do you think you could go, or would that mess up your family plans?"

Last year's Thanksgiving consisted of Mom crying, me crying,

Grandpa making dinner and watching us cry, and nobody eating. I'd be thrilled to skip this year's encore. "No plans to mess up."

Starbucks is clearing out, and by 8:15, we're the only ones left. A barista says to us, "We close in 15 minutes, if you want anything else," and my heart sinks. I don't want to go home.

Neither, apparently, does Mac. "It's early. We can find something else to do. Bookstore? Arcade? Bowling?"

Picturing Mac in bowling shoes puts a smile on my face; remembering my curfew erases it. "I have to be home by nine."

I frown at him, but he says, "Any chance your mom would make an exception? It *is* Friday—you can sleep in tomorrow."

If only she were worried about me not getting enough sleep. But maybe if she thinks I'm not *driving* after nine....

"Let me see." I text Mom, **Can I stay at Joss's tonight?**

The more minutes that pass without a response, the more I'm sure she's going to say no. But I'm not willing to have Mac take me back to school until she answers.

Since we can't stay at Starbucks, we walk through the darkness of the parking lot toward Dinah, the cold tickling my nose hairs. It's a clear night; as I wait for Mac to unlock the doors, I look up at the stars sprinkled throughout the sky.

Inside the car, Mac cranks up the heat and plays the hilarious soundtrack to the musical *Avenue Q*.

Mom finally writes, **Aren't you spending tomorrow night there?**

Too bad I only have one friend I could conceivably be overnighting with. **Yes, but we'll hardly get any time together after the party. Please?**

Did she suggest it? You didn't ask to sleep over, did you?

Wow. Nothing like realizing how desperate your own mother thinks you are. I roll my eyes. **No, I didn't. She invited me.**

Mac is watching, so I unclench my jaw.

Her next text reads, **Okay. Have fun.**

I exhale with relief, and Mac asks, "Does that mean yes?"

"Yes."

He grins like I just handed him a puppy, which dissolves (or at least buries) any guilt over deceiving my mother.

"What did you say to convince her?"

Well, I can't use the same line with Mac. "Um...." More important, I don't want to lie to him. "I told her I was spending the night at Joss's."

His next words shoot fatal holes in my cover. "Won't she have questions when you come home later?"

Ah, shit. I blame hormones for sabotaging my ability to think clearly.

I sigh, then tell him the whole truth. "I'm not allowed to drive after nine. If she had her way, I wouldn't drive unless it was broad daylight."

"Because of your dad?" he says softly.

The way he asks, Mom's unreasonableness sounds less... unreasonable. "Yeah."

"I can give you a ride. Anytime."

"Thanks. But I don't think she'd agree to me being in a car with anyone under forty this late at night either." My brow furrows.

"She's a little overprotective?"

"About that, for sure. In the pie chart of things we fight about, driving and curfew are the biggest slices—and it's a giant pie."

"Things are rocky between you, huh?"

"You could say that."

"Has it always been that way, even before your dad?"

"No, we used to be close." Mother-daughter pedicures. Friday nights binge-watching the hottest new show on Netflix. Capping off a rough day by downing a pint of ice cream each. "It's not just that my dad died and we're both grieving or whatever," I tell Mac. "She lied about how he died. The police officers said he was speeding, which I know is because he wanted to get to my choir concert in time for my solo, and she flat-out said he wasn't. We both know he died because of me, but she won't talk about it." My voice catches, and I swallow the lump in my throat.

Mac's eyes seem to get bigger when they're full of sympathy. *No wonder people can't resist puppy eyes.*

"I'm really sorry, Rae." He takes my hand, quelling any doubts about whether I should have shared so much. "I would tell you that his death wasn't your fault, but if I were you, I would feel the same, and I wouldn't believe me. You shouldn't feel responsible, because it was an accident, and I shouldn't feel like Finn died because of me, but I do."

Both glassy-eyed, we stare at each other. Mac leans against the headrest, and I do the same.

After a moment, he lifts his head and says, "I'm going to suggest something crazy."

I sit up.

"Let's say you don't go home till tomorrow morning. I'll tell my parents I'm sleeping over somewhere, and we'll live it up."

"You mean, stay out all night?" The thought of so many hours yet to unfold both thrills and terrifies me.

"It'll be an adventure, Raina-Rae." He gives me a mischievous grin, and his knee bounces under the steering wheel.

My insides click-clack up the hill of a roller coaster, then plummet down the other side, my stomach dropping to my toes as I say, "Okay!"

Not wanting to go somewhere else that will close 45 minutes after we get there, we head to Waffle House. We park under the yellow sign with the Scrabble tile letters and enter to the smell of sugary fried batter because, here, waffles are appropriate anytime—literally, they're open 24/7.

We opt for salt and fat and quickly have a plate of hashbrowns between us. I poke my fork into the mound and pick the crispy ones off the top.

Because Mac got me talking about Mom, I wade into his familial waters. "What's your relationship with your parents like?"

"There's a question." He gives me a tight smile.

"Give me one word for each."

His eyebrows do a little jump. "I don't know if it's that simple. But with my mom...let's go with *patient*. And my dad...." He shovels a forkful of hashbrowns into his mouth, then says, "*Disappointing*."

I don't know if I should pry further, but Mac has done his share of sticking his nose in my business, and now, I'm kind of glad. "The relationship is disappointing, or your dad disappoints you, or you think you disappoint your dad?"

"D—all of the above." He sets his fork down and picks up his straw wrapper, which he twists around his finger, the paper crinkling as it bends. "I'm pretty sure I'm not what my dad pictured when he found out he was having a boy."

"What do you think he imagined?"

"He's a sports guy, so not a son who's five-one, hates basketball, and thinks musicals are the reason for living."

"Does he give you a hard time about theatre?"

"During the whole basketball-theatre showdown, things got ugly, but now at least he accepts it." Mac stares at the white paper ring around his thumb, then unwinds it and starts over. "Did I tell you Jay took me to my first show?"

I shake my head.

"*The Lion King*; I was eight. Hands down the best theatricality of any musical that's ever been produced. Jay and Rob, his partner, now husband, have lived next door forever. They were always friendly, and my parents seemed to like them, my mom especially. So, when *Lion King* came to town, they asked her if I might like to see it with them."

His straw wrapper has been wound and unwound so many times, it's disintegrating, so he drops what's left and picks up mine.

"She told me about it at dinner and was so excited. I was

thrilled—it was my favorite Disney movie, and I knew every song by heart. My dad didn't say anything at first. Then, like it was an innocent question, like he genuinely wanted to know and wasn't being judgmental, he asked, 'Is that normal?'

"The smart thing would have been for my mom to ignore it, to have a conversation with him when my sister and I weren't around. But he set her up, and she fell for it. She said, 'What do you mean?'"

Mac pauses, and I don't know if it's because he's trying to remember or because he remembers all too well.

"He said, 'I don't know, I just think two grown men taking an interest in a young boy is a little unusual, is all. I want to make sure everything is on the up-and-up.'" Mac looks at me, and I frown at him.

"My mom, thankfully, told him, 'They love the theatre, and they know Mac loves *The Lion King*. I think it's nice they're taking him.'

"We didn't talk about it anymore, and when the night of the performance came, my dad wasn't around to ruin it, so I went, and it was amazing, and I'll never forget it. That night changed my life, Rae."

His eyes take on the happy twinkle I'm used to seeing, and my heart unclenches, relieved to see the pain leave his expression.

"You knew then, huh? That theatre was your passion?" I ask.

"From the moment those giraffes walked down the aisle. It was majestic. I was hooked."

Reluctant to take Mac back where he doesn't want to be, I nevertheless say, "I'm sorry things with your dad aren't better."

He shrugs. "They could be worse. I still love the guy, you know?"

Yeah.

"Okay, I need something sweet," he says. "Waffle? Or, I know a donut place that's open all night."

My vote is for donuts, so we take Dinah for another spin. I grab his phone and pull up Spotify. "My turn."

"What auditory treasure are you treating me to?"

Something '80s—Bon Jovi. But which album? I choose *Crush* and tap "It's My Life." Mac bobs his head and taps his thumbs on the steering wheel.

"Thank You for Loving Me" starts just as we pull into the parking lot of Bob's Donuts, a dive if I've ever seen one. It's a lone shack in the middle of another strip mall parking lot that's nearly deserted at this time of night. But I can smell the donuts from here, and my mouth waters.

I move to open the door, but Mac leans back and closes his eyes, apparently having a moment. I don't judge; I've certainly had my fair share with Jon and his gang.

When the song ends, we exit the car and walk into the brightly lit shack in silence. Once we've chosen our sugary confections and are seated at one of three tables, Mac says, "People take being loved for granted."

"I think many classic love songs would beg to differ." I bite into a chocolate donut hole, then lick the gooey glaze off my fingers.

"Not romantic love. Family, friends—how often do you think about who you're loved by?"

Unbidden, Shelby's face pops into my head. To Mac's point, I never thought much about the "Luv u" texts we exchanged or our kissy smiley faces, but now that what we had is missing, I know how significant it was.

I swear Mac can read my mind because he asks, "Who are you thinking about?"

Nosy.

"I had a best friend before my dad died. We were there for each other through everything—breakups, family drama, all of it. Even the shitty memes people made of me. But eventually, even she couldn't deal with my moping."

Mac narrows his eyes at me. "Don't say *moping*," he scolds.

"That sounds like you were obsessing over some guy who didn't like you. You were *grieving*. And she wasn't there for you?"

"She was...." I don't know why I'm defending her. "For a while. But sympathy has its limits, right?"

"No." He crosses his arms on the tiny table and leans forward. "If she was your best friend, she should have been there for you forever, no matter what."

A weight lifts off my heart, like maybe I'm not crazy for thinking Shelby failed me and not the other way around.

"And what memes?" Mac asks.

Crap. That slipped out. "It's not a big deal. After my dad's accident, I kind of had this moment when I cried so hard I passed out, and someone took a picture, and, well, you can fill in the rest. Or you can look them up, but I'd really love it if you didn't."

His donut remains untouched. "That's bullshit. Those people are assholes." He stares at me intently, with such fire behind his eyes that I truly hope it's never me he's mad at. "You didn't deserve that. I'm sorry, Rae."

Maybe it's because I'm tired or maybe because it's been a long time since I've opened up like this, but I cry. Not *Of Mice and Men* hysterics, but tears, nonetheless.

Mac comes around the table to sit next to me in a seat barely big enough for one, but I'm grateful it forces us to be close. He puts his arm around my shoulders, and I lean my head against his chest. There will be a wet spot on his shirt, but I don't stress about it, because I know he won't care.

"I wish I'd been there for you last year," he says over my head.

"Me too," I whisper.

I CAN'T STOP YAWNING. This night has been so perfect, I don't want to give up a minute of the time we have left, but I'm afraid I might fall asleep mid-sentence, so when Mac suggests we try to get some rest, I agree.

We stay in the strip mall parking lot and recline Dinah's front seats. Mac keeps her running so we have heat, and *Crush* plays quietly in the background. We give each other small, sleepy smiles before closing our eyes.

The sky is faintly grayish blue when I wake up a couple hours later. I'm massaging the stiffness out of my neck when Mac opens his eyes and sits up. "Did you sleep?" he asks.

"A little."

He nods. "Do you think Joss will be offended—" For a second, I'm afraid he's going to bail on tonight's party, but he finishes by saying, "—if I'm carrying a Red Bull all night?"

To prove the necessity, he yawns, then rubs his eyes and raises his seat. "Shall we greet the day in style?"

Although I don't know what he has in mind, I'm game for anything he might propose. "I think we should."

Mac drives to a park I've never been to. It's so quiet I can hear the frost on the grass crunch beneath my sneakers as I follow him onto the trail. It's darker under the canopy of branches, and I can barely see my breath in the early morning light. The puffs of air come quicker as he leads us uphill, the incline getting steeper as we climb.

As we near the top, he turns back and offers me his hand. I take it, some welcome warmth in the cold, and he pulls me the last few steps forward. Then we look out over a wide expanse of forest, the brightening sky clearly visible above the trees.

He doesn't let go of my hand.

A breeze swirls around us, and we inch closer together. Clouds catch the light, turning their undersides pink, while the tops still have a purplish hue. It's wonderfully peaceful. I glance at Mac, and his face is relaxed, serene. Seems we're both happy to bask in the moment as the dawn gradually chases away the night.

We stand in silence, palms clasped, and watch the sun rise.

♪

Back at school, my car is the only one in the parking lot. Before I get out of Dinah, Mac says, "You, Raina-Rae, are something special."

"And you, sir, are a charmer."

I open the door, but Mac grabs my wrist. "I mean it, Rae. This was one of the best nights I've had in a long time."

"Me too." I stare into his eyes. "I'm...since my dad, I haven't...I needed this." I didn't know just how much until tonight.

He squeezes my arm, then lets his fingers trail down my hand as I step into the chilly morning air, a smile playing on my lips and a long-absent joy dancing in my heart.

"KNOCKIN' ON HEAVEN'S DOOR"

Still on a high from the night, I take advantage of the serotonin and ask Mom about volunteering with Mac on Thanksgiving.

"We've never not spent Thanksgiving together," she says.

"I know. But it's hard without Dad." I look at the floor. "I can't do what we did last year again." Lifting my eyes, I add, "Plus, it would be nice to help other people who are having a hard time."

She can't disagree with that.

I ARRIVE at Joss's carrying five outfits because I have no idea what I'm supposed to wear. She surveys them, then picks up a simple black dress with three-quarter sleeves and a button-down shirt and skirt and hands them to me. "Not sexy enough."

That leaves a tight long-sleeve dress with leggings, which Joss shakes her head at, as well as a miniskirt with a peasant blouse, to which she says, "Maybe with boots."

My last choice consists of jeans and a jacket over my *Hamilton* shirt—the one I bought because it makes me think of my dad, with the definition of "legacy" based on the song "The World Was Wide Enough."

"This could work," Joss says. "Try it on."

When I reappear, Joss hands me one of her hats, a burgundy, velvet military cap, and I study my reflection in the mirror. I like it; will Mac?

Downstairs, Joss plants herself by the front door. "You can run things in the basement."

I descend another level and ready the space—dim the lights, tell Alexa to play some music, open chip and candy bags and plastic cookie containers. Then I pop a nacho cheese Dorito in my mouth, slide onto a bar stool, and wipe my clammy palms on my thighs. Tonight will be the most social interaction I've had since the infamous party where Sadie Haddix grilled me about my dad, and I'm praying this gathering is far less dramatic.

Footsteps sound above me, and a moment later, I'm greeted by a familiar face. "Hey, Rae." Casey grabs a handful of M&M's and sits next to me.

"Hi, Casey." Before I can say anything else, more people arrive —two guys from the football team. My pulse quickens a bit, but I meet their eyes and smile.

One guy nods at my chest, and I'm momentarily offended, until he says, "Cool shirt."

"Oh, thanks."

They go to the mini fridge and grab drinks. Rory and Arlo show up in quick succession, and then I can't help but wonder why Mac isn't here yet.

My heart drops to my knees when I see Shelby on the stairs. I shouldn't be surprised she's friends with Joss; there's overlap between choir and theatre kids. But now all I can think about is whether Maya and Carolyn are here too and what will happen if any of them notice me.

Fight or flight—*yes, please*—kicks in, but Mac's appearance quells my desire to escape. He nods when he catches sight of me and makes his way over. "You look great."

Picking the right outfit: check. "Thanks."

From behind the bar, he asks, "What are you drinking?" and I realize I haven't gotten anything yet.

I need a Mac smile fix and get it by saying, "Snapple Apple."

After he hands it to me, brushing my fingers with his, he points at my shirt. "I approve. Most girls go for the Schuyler sisters."

Some guy who's rooting around in the fridge behind Mac grabs a can, then joins us. "Are you talking about *Hamilton*? I love that show. It was my gateway musical."

Mac smirks as the guy thrusts his hand in the air, shouts, "Yo, Devon!" and hurries away.

"I wonder if Lin-Manuel Miranda knows he led someone to a life of addiction," I say.

"Among the common folk who don't understand that *intermission* is not called *halftime, Hamilton* is everyone's gateway musical." Mac shakes his head.

"Have you seen it? I've only heard the cast album."

He nods. "In Chicago. It would have been epic to see the original Broadway cast, but no one was getting within a mile of those tickets."

I fiddle with the Snapple cap. "Have you ever been to New York?"

"Once. My mom and I went last summer while my dad and sister were at a basketball camp."

"What shows did you see?"

"*Beautiful*, which my mom picked since she likes Carole King, and *Dear Evan Hansen*."

"I haven't listened to that one yet."

Mac slaps his hands on the bar and leans so far forward our noses almost touch. "Tell me you did not just say that."

Chastised, I press my lips together.

"Raina. Do you remember me saying there are certain theatrical imperatives you must understand?"

I start to justify my lack of familiarity with the soundtrack, but Mac cuts me off. "*Dear Evan Hansen* is one of the best musicals to come along in our generation. You *will* listen to it this weekend." He raises his eyebrows until I nod.

Someone calls Mac's name. He holds up a finger and says, "Be right back."

Left alone at the bar, I scan the room for friendly faces and accidentally catch Shelby's eye. She chokes on her cookie, and I quickly look away, my heart thumping again.

I drafted so many texts to her after Maya's intervention, but I never sent any. What would have been the point? She chose to cut me out of her life.

To put more distance between us, I move to the other end of the room and watch air hockey. When the game ends, Rory picks up a paddle and nods at me. "Want to play?"

Without Joss crowding me, I make the mistake of resting my hand on the side of the table. The puck slams into my thumb, and pain shoots up my arm.

"Rae, I'm so sorry!" Rory drops his paddle and rushes over.

Tears like little needles prick the corners of my eyes. "It was my fault. Let's keep going."

Rory raises his eyebrows as he walks slowly back to his side. "Are you sure?"

I nod and pick up my paddle. Concentrating on getting the puck in the goal is the only way I might manage not to cry. *Thuk-thuk-thuk.*

The longer we go, the more people gather to watch. I wish I'd taken off my jacket. We alternate scoring until we're tied six-six. The crowd around us cheers. Focusing, I line up the puck and send it flying straight at Rory's goal. He blocks it, then zigzags it back to my side. In an attempt to mimic Joss's trick, I hit it again and again as fast as I can until I send it into the open slot.

Rory holds up his paddle, and I high-five it with mine. Bodies push against me as other people scramble to take our places. Like I'm bursting through a wall, I finally reach open air—and nearly bump into Shelby.

"Rae—hi."

"Hey."

The party is loud, but the space between us is empty. She doesn't move away, though, so I stand, mute, until she fills the void with, "I didn't know you knew Joss."

"We're doing *It's a Wonderful Life* together."

"You are? That's great." She looks genuinely surprised, and I don't know if it's over the fact that I was cast or the idea of me doing anything other than being sad. After another moment, she says, "I can't wait to see the show."

"Thanks."

Awkward. I wait to see if she wants to exchange more pleasantries or if I'm free to hightail it to the bathroom, the snacks—anywhere else would be fine—then the music stops.

Joss stands on the end of the sectional and waves her arms to get the group's attention. "Let's play 7 Minutes in Heaven." She looks meaningfully at me, and my cheeks flush.

Murmurs ripple through the room as Joss hops down and writes everyone's name on a scrap of paper. After she writes mine, she folds down a corner, then does the same for Mac. The girl has no shame.

I slide my palms down my jeans as Joss drops the names into two red Solo cups. "Once you're paired up, go in there." She points to the pocket doors at the back of the room. "You get seven minutes—make 'em count."

With her hand over the top, she shakes the cup, then holds it above her head and picks out a piece of paper. "Chloe!"

The girl joins Joss and waits for the next name to be drawn.

"Bryce!" Joss ushers them both into "Heaven," sets a timer on her phone, and resumes the music. I stare after them, but the white paneled doors offer no clues as to what's happening on the other side.

Casey is nearby, so I slide unobtrusively into his group. Another guy nods at him. "So, uh...you're doing the play, right?"

"Yeah.... We open in a few weeks."

The guy nods and glances at the doors, and I do the same. Still closed. Still mysterious.

"When's your first swim meet?" someone asks the guy who asked Casey about the show.

He doesn't answer right away, like maybe he didn't hear him. Then he blinks and says, "What? Oh, December 10." *Guess I'm not the only one preoccupied with that closet.*

In the seven minutes of waiting, caterpillars build cocoons in my stomach, metamorphose, then incessantly beat their wings against my insides. When the timer goes off, Joss knocks, and Chloe and Bryce come out immediately, suggesting they were poised by the door, and I wonder if they kissed at all. *Is that an option? Will all this be for nothing?*

Joss draws the next name—"Devon!"—then picks up the other cup. "Jenna!" And two new people disappear behind the doors.

I'm not sure where Mac got off to, and imagining that Joss will call our names and he won't be here makes those butterflies clamor to get out of my body through my mouth. I swallow and scan the room, feeling a palpable sense of relief when he appears among a group of guys who could probably bench-press him. The butterflies resettle in my abdomen.

During the turns of various people who are not me, I down a second Snapple Apple because drinking it gives me something to do, but now I need to pee. I don't want to miss the next selection, but if I wait and Joss picks me, then I'll have to pee during my seven minutes. I'm debating what to do when I hear, "Cierra," and rush gratefully to the bathroom.

A line has formed, so by the time I'm done, Joss is holding a cup again.

"Mac!" she shouts, and my heart hammers in my chest.

It takes her longer to draw a girl's name since she has to fish around to find the paper with the folded corner.

"Rae!"

My face feels frozen—I'm not sure if I smile or not. Mac appears beside me, and I have only a second to meet his eyes before Joss pushes us behind the doors and slides them shut, dampening the noise from the party.

The space is crowded, full of shelves and bins and a washer and dryer. And a bench. I sit, then the bench creaks as Mac sits next to me.

Now what? I force my eyes to be brave.

He's looking at me, but like all the other times, I can't read his mind. Should I say something or wait for him to take the initiative? If he wants this to be a make-out session, shouldn't he be kissing me already? Does the fact that he isn't—that he hasn't—mean he doesn't want to kiss me? Or is he trying to force his lips to be brave?

It's probably only been ten seconds, but when you're dealing with a mere total of 420, even ten seconds assume mythic proportions.

I can't take it. "So...." *Clearly, it's my wit that Mac finds charming.*

"Yeah."

"I think Joss wanted us in here together."

He rolls his eyes. "No shit."

Did he see her cheat too, or does he simply know her well enough to guess she did? And is the eye roll an indictment of Joss's meddling or a reflection of his feelings about me as a Heavenly partner? Despite Joss's confidence that Mac only needs to be urged into leveling up our relationship, I'm suddenly self-conscious of all the times we've been in kiss-conducive situations, and he hasn't made a move.

"I'm sorry if you don't want to be here," I say and feel the familiar rise of tears to the rims of my eyes.

"No, it's not that. I just hate when she plays matchmaker."

I nod and take a breath as I stare at my lap. Maybe his frustration with Joss explains our rocky start, and if I can steer things back to where we're *us*, everything will be okay....

Nudging my leg with his, Mac says, "Hey," and leans forward to make me look at him. When I do, his gaze is so deep, I know there's *something* special between us, even if I can't say exactly what.

"You know I always have a great time with you, right?" he asks.

Who wouldn't—I'm delightful. I don't say that, even though it's the kind of response that could get us back on track, because I'm afraid a "But..." lingers in the air. I say carefully, "I always have fun with you too."

Mac jerks up, nearly bouncing on the bench. "Yes! See, why doesn't Joss get that? We're amazing friends. Why do we have to be something more?"

Don't cry...don't cry....

"Do you...want us to be something more?" he asks quietly.

"I don't know." *Yes, you do.* "I just...know I like you."

He picks up my hand. "I like you too, Rae."

Our heads are bent together, and I can feel his breath, warm on my face.

Then he does it—darts forward and puts his lips on mine. .... He's not moving his lips. I'm not moving my lips. I feel like we should be moving our lips. In movies, there's a lot of tongues, but our lips are pressed too firmly together for either of ours to get any action. *Get out of your head,* I admonish myself. I don't want to be thinking about my first kiss, I want to be enjoying my first kiss, and—

Mac pulls away and looks at me for a split second. "I'm sorry, I can't do this." Then he opens the door and rushes out.

What the hell?

Faces peer in at me, making my ears burn. I don't know how much time we had left, but no one knocked, and this is *not* how this was supposed to go.

I hate that every step I'll have to take to get as far away from this bench as possible will take me closer to people's staring eyes. But the longer I wait, the more the fire spreads over my face, and tears rush in to extinguish the flames.

Willing them not to spill out yet, I bolt and hurry up the stairs. As I run up to Joss's room, my vision blurs and wetness cascades down my cheeks.

THERE'S a gentle knock on the door.

"Come in," I say, feeling awkward inviting someone into a room I'm crashing.

Joss gives me a small smile as she sits across from me. "I'm sorry."

"I thought he liked me," I whisper.

"I thought he did too."

In the silence that follows, I pick at my chipped nail polish.

"Come back to the party," Joss encourages.

I give her a 'you-can't-be-serious' look.

"He's gone, if that's what you're worried about."

That, and everyone else who witnessed my humiliation. "I can't."

"C'mon. The party will be a better distraction than staying here by yourself." She grabs my hand and tries to pull me off the bed, but I resist and shake my head. "You go, though. Have fun."

Although she lets go of me, she doesn't move, and I brace for her attempt to convince me to join her. My expression must say it's pointless, though, because she eventually walks away.

By the door, she turns back. "If you change your mind...."

I nod, knowing I won't.

♪

Before we change into our pajamas, I check my phone and see a text from Mac: **I'm so, so sorry. Forgive me?**

I don't respond.

"SHOT THROUGH THE HEART"

When I get home, I lug my clothes upstairs but don't bother putting anything away, just dump it all on my bed, sink to the floor, and close my eyes.

My brain is exhausted from two nights of almost no sleep and from spending the past twelve hours trying to answer impossible questions.

Am I that bad at kissing? Maybe I am, I have no way of knowing. I mean, I sat there doing nothing. If you kiss someone who wants to be kissed, they kiss you back. If the girl responds like a pillow, surely that prompts you to take your lips off hers, stat.

But every time I curse myself, I hear Mac's voice: *I can't do this.*

What couldn't he do? Be peer-pressured into making things physical? Let our first kiss be dictated by a teenage party game? Or keep pretending to have feelings for someone he's not romantically interested in?

Tears pool at the corners of my eyes and spill out at the thought of what it looked like from the other side of the door—on top of being the girl whose dad died, the girl who lost her shit in English, am I now also the girl too repugnant to kiss?

I need to drown out the noise in my head. Possibly against my better judgment, I type "Broadway cast" in Spotify and choose *Dear Evan Hansen* from the search results.

The song "For Forever" gets me, and I play it a second time, then a third, and let my heart break open. Before the party, this moving ode to friendship could have been our anthem. Now it's a reminder that Mac ruined what we had.

It's while I'm wiping snot off my cheek that the text from him pops up: **You okay?**

A cry of anguish bursts forth. Afraid Mom will hear me, I smother my face in my comforter until I can breathe without sobbing.

The next text comes a couple hours later, but I resist the urge to look. I've had my fill of show tunes and moved onto algebra equations, and I don't want to reopen the floodgates....

Curiosity eventually wins.

Don't forget your homework. *Dear Evan Hansen*!!

Heat rises within me. Is he seriously going to act like nothing happened last night? Like what he did didn't change everything? I turn my phone to silent.

My head is down as I walk through the halls on Monday, but the brightly colored squares in my periphery are too intriguing to ignore. Cautiously, I raise my eyes, making sure the *entire* student body isn't staring at me, then look at the notes on the lockers.

I'm not the only one whose attention they've caught. Other kids are stopping in front of them, looking around for the perpetrator, talking in groups while pointing them out. Smiling.

In my bay, I slow down and read:

Seize the day.

You'll never walk alone.

Put on a happy face.

No one is alone.
Climb every mountain.
Make them hear you.
Breathe.

Even if I didn't recognize the handwriting, I would know Mac wrote them. They're titles of songs from musicals. My pulse quickens as I approach the purple square on locker 223 and read the song he picked for me:

You will be found.

From *Dear Evan Hansen.* A beautifully melodic promise that we're not alone, that *I'm* not alone.

At the bottom of the paper, in letters almost too tiny to read, he wrote, *I'm very sorry.*

I look at the ceiling and swallow hard. *I will not cry, dammit!* Then I open my locker, shove my backpack inside, and grab my algebra book. Only after I've taken my seat and pulled out a notebook does my heart resume normal functioning.

Before class starts, a girl behind me asks the person next to her, "Did you have a note on your locker this morning?"

"No, did you?"

"Yeah. It said, 'Always look on the bright side of life.'"

"Aw, that's cool. I wish I got one."

CASEY and I share a lunch period, and after we eat, he suggests we clear the trash people have left on the tables. Throwing away empty chip bags and water bottles isn't a big deal, but I'm horrified by some of the messes people do not feel compelled to clean up—half-eaten French fries, congealing ketchup, sticky pop remnants, and a few unidentifiable substances I choose not to think about.

On one of my trips to the trash can, I swear I hear, "That's the girl...."

I spin around, but the rest of the words get swallowed by the other conversations happening in the cafeteria.

My ears go several degrees warmer as I imagine people talking about me behind my back, just like they did with the memes, and finish the sentence in my head. *That's the girl whose dad died last year.* Or maybe, *That's the girl who cried so hard she passed out in class.* Or, *That's the girl who got rejected in 7 Minutes in Heaven.*

I don't want to be any of those girls.

With my head down, I hurry from table to table. When I do a final scan of the room, I notice the lack of chatter and feel certain everyone is staring at me.

But it's not quiet because people are struck speechless by my pitifulness; it's quiet because Paul Chen, at the table next to me, is sitting alone.

Everyone around him is engaged in a flurry of activity—talking, gesturing, eating, laughing. In the eye of this social hurricane, Paul is still, hunched over, his only movements the repetitive arc of his hand lifting his sandwich from the table to his mouth and the subsequent slow chewing.

My heart thumps in empathy as I recall my banishment from Maya's table and having nowhere else to go.

AT THE FINAL BELL, my stomach ties itself in knots, and not because today's health lesson was on communicable diseases. I consider feigning sickness and skipping rehearsal, but this is not a long-term solution; I'll have to see Mac at some point.

Still, I avoid making eye contact and hover by Joss until Jay claps and we begin.

I go three hours without exchanging any words with Mac. When we wrap for the day, I'm the first off the stage. But I don't grab my coat quick enough.

A touch on my shoulder so light I barely feel it at all. "Hey." He removes his hand immediately.

I'm debating my next move—Turn around? Walk out?—when Joss rushes to my side. "We have to go." She puts an arm around me and heads for the doors. But as I'm swept forward, I glance back, and there's no mistaking the pain in his expression.

Once we're in the hallway, I turn to Joss. "I feel bad."

She stops. "No. You don't feel bad. He's the one who should feel bad."

"I think he does."

"Good."

"Shouldn't I talk to him? Let him explain?"

"What is there to explain?" She puts a hand on her hip. "He ran out on you in the middle of a kiss and said he can't do the whole boyfriend thing—he doesn't get to go back to flirting and pretend everything is fine when you want something more and he won't give it to you."

I don't know if I agree, but Joss is staring me down, so I nod. As I drive home, though, I'm not sure which is worse: the idea that Mac and I will never be more than friends or the idea that we might not even be that.

"EVERY ROSE HAS ITS THORN"

We're each meeting with Janice this week to try on our costumes. I'm up after rehearsal on Tuesday, so I slip out the door at the back of the stage and avoid an awkward encounter with Mac.

On Wednesday, Joss invites me to her house. On the floor in her bedroom, leaning against her bed, I scroll through pictures of Mac and try to decide whether to delete them.

Joss nudges my foot with hers, and I realize she's peering over my shoulder.

"I don't want to sound mean, but Mac Reddington is not worth being miserable over."

With a sigh, I set down my phone. "I don't know what I did wrong."

"Who says you did something wrong?"

"If I didn't, why did he stop kissing me?"

"Look," Joss says. "I've been friends with the guy for years, but Mac is going to do what's best for Mac."

I think of her story about the prank he pulled on her during *Little Shop of Horrors* last year and wonder if she's right.

She continues, "As long as you're okay with that, he can be a lot of fun, but if you want more from him, you're going to be disappointed."

Maybe Mac is more of a flirt than I realized and was just playing me. But it's not like it was all fun and games—the times I opened up to him, he was so comforting it definitely felt like he was doing what was best for me, not himself.

Unless getting me to be vulnerable was somehow best for him? I was pretty damn vulnerable on that bench, though, so why did he bail?

"There has to be a reason he ran out," I say.

"Yeah, the reason is he's a coward."

"If I let him explain—"

"No. Mac needs to learn there are consequences for his actions." Joss grabs a notebook from her desk, crosses her legs, and rests the book on her thigh. "Let's think of more kind things."

If I learned anything from Maya's intervention, it's that people don't want to be pulled into my downward spiral. "Okay. Do you have any ideas?"

Joss looks pensive. "What about a reverse burn book?"

"A what?"

"Have you seen *Mean Girls*?"

I shake my head.

"It's a fun movie they turned into a great musical. You should listen to the soundtrack. But anyway, this girl has a book where she and her friends write awful things about their classmates—embarrassing stories, secrets, vicious rumors. But what if we had one—" She waves the notebook in front of me, "—where we wrote nice things?" Apparently too energized for her current position, she shifts so she's kneeling and practically bounces as she talks. "Things we like about someone or a story of when they did something kind!"

Swept up by her enthusiasm, I add, "We could leave it where

other people will find it and put a note in the front encouraging them to write in it."

"Perfect!" Joss dangles her notebook by the spiral binding. "But we can't use this. We need something special. Let's go shopping."

We end up buying a black leather number with a gold ribbon and thick, creamy pages. Once we're back in Joss's room, she opens the cover and looks at me. After a moment, she clicks her pen and starts writing. She finishes the first entry, flips several pages ahead, and writes a second. Then she hands the book to me. "Your turn."

I leaf through it. "Can I read what you wrote?"

"Sure. That's the idea, right?"

The first comment says, *Abby Meyers has an amazing sense of style. Her outfits always look so put-together and chic.*

I nod and go in search of the second: *When I moved here in sixth grade, Deepa Bakshi invited me to sit with her and her friends at lunch.*

Following Joss's lead, I go to a blank page toward the back and write, *I'm jealous of Cami McCallister's hair—it's so beautiful and effortless.*

Joss reads over my shoulder. "Nice."

For my next entry, I stick with the hair theme: *Jasmine Valdes donated her hair to Locks of Love.*

"I didn't know that," Joss says.

"Yeah, in seventh grade."

"That's so cool."

After trading the book back and forth for half an hour, Joss examines our efforts. "I think this is good. We should leave plenty of room for other people too."

Joss BLOCKS me protectively when Mac approaches after rehearsal. I hunch over my bag, zipping it as slowly as humanly possible. But I turn my head slightly and watch him from around Joss's legs.

"Do you mind?" He leans to Joss's side to make eye contact with me, and I quickly look away.

"As a matter of fact, I do."

"Jesus, Joss. I just want to talk to her."

My ears burn. As Joss says, "Well, she doesn't want to talk to you," she grabs my arm and pulls me up. "If you hadn't humiliated her, things might be different."

He growls, "If *you* hadn't meddled—"

We move swiftly through the doorway, but Mac hurries after us and stops Joss with a hand on her shoulder. "Wait. Just tell her... that I miss her."

♪

RATHER THAN GO HOME, I stop at Grandpa's.

"To what do I owe the pleasure?" he asks when he opens the door.

"I have a new movie musical to watch."

He leads me in, toward a *whirring* noise coming from the kitchen. "I'm making bread, and soup. Stay for dinner?"

I nod as I drop my bag on a chair, then plop down on the couch to relax, hoping that will release some of the tension in my body after the scene with Mac.

One of the soundtracks I listened to on Sunday was *Into the Woods*. I pull up the movie on Netflix and try to forget it's one of Mac's favorites.

Grandpa puts up his feet and leans back, then offers me half of the blanket that spans the length of the couch. I stuff a pillow under my elbow and curl my legs under me.

We're halfway through the movie when a *beeping* sounds in the kitchen, and Grandpa gets up to check on dinner. "Soup's on."

Steam rises from the piece of bread he sets in front of me. I lean forward and inhale. "Smells great."

"Herb and Parmesan."

It's almost too hot to pick up, so I hold it by the edges to spread butter over one side and watch it melt instantly. Taking a bite, I burn my tongue, but it tastes so good I don't care. "You should open a restaurant."

"I'm glad you like it. I'll send some home for your mom." Grandpa digs in himself, then asks, "How'd you discover the movie?"

I remembered the Playbill from Mac's shoes. "My friend Mac likes it a lot," I say without thinking.

"Mac? Same friend from last weekend?"

Crap. I nod, wishing desperately to change the subject.

"Should I commit his name to memory?" Grandpa smiles, but when I don't smile back, he stops. "Something tells me there's a story here," he says softly.

"He's...we...it's complicated."

We're quiet as we dip our spoons into our bowls of creamy potato soup. Once my insides are toasty, I look at Grandpa until he returns my gaze. "Why do guys act like they feel a certain way if they don't?" It comes out more accusatory than I mean for it to, like my grandfather is a proxy for the entire male species.

He sets down his spoon and wipes his mouth with his napkin. "Feelings are a tricky business. They don't always act in isolation. And they can change from one minute to the next."

"That doesn't answer my question," I criticize.

"Maybe not. But perhaps this Mac fellow does feel a certain way sometimes, or he might be feeling lots of ways, all at the same time."

I shake my head. "This isn't like that. It's an either/or scenario."

"In my experience, things aren't always that simple."

I must be giving him a *look,* because he reaches for my hand.

"Here's what I'll leave you with: I've been a teenage boy. Granted, it's been quite a few years, but some things never change. And I'd bet dollars to donuts he thinks it's complicated too. Give him some time to figure it out."

"ANOTHER ONE BITES THE DUST"

Jay looks especially excited when he claps his hands together on Friday. "Okay, magic-makers. We've got three days, then some time off to stuff our faces full of turkey, potatoes, and pie, and then it's tech week. We're in the homestretch."

We make it to the scene right before Uncle Billy loses the company's big stash of cash. Jay puts up his hand. "Let's stop there. We'll wait until next week to see George get desperate."

I think about Jay's turkey and pie comment. "Should we do something kind for Thanksgiving?" I ask Joss as we're getting ready to leave.

She picks up her backpack, letting her arm hang at her side. "What do you have in mind?"

"Well, I know we've done a lot of notes." My stomach churns as I remember Mac's musical-inspired Post-its. "But what if we write something we're thankful for on people's lockers?"

Casey stops as he walks past. "Are you talking about what you're thankful for? My mom always makes us go around the table on Thanksgiving."

"Rae's thinking we put notes on people's lockers."

"Sounds nice."

"What does?" Rory joins us.

"Writing something we're thankful for on people's lockers."

Rory purses his lips.

"What?" I ask. "Not a good idea?"

"No, I really like it. It's just that the last time there were notes on people's lockers, not everyone got one, and from what I heard, some people were disappointed."

We're all quiet. Arlo has come up behind Joss, and a couple feet away, clearly listening, stands Mac.

"Do you think we could do the whole school?" I say hesitantly.

"That's, like, a thousand people." Mac raises his eyebrows as our eyes lock; I quickly look away.

"But wouldn't it be great for everyone to know something someone values about them?" I counter.

"How would we know whose locker is whose?" Joss asks.

"Maybe we could get a list from the office," Casey says.

"I bet Jay would help." Mac rushes off. A minute later, he waves to us from the window of the sound booth, where he's now standing with Jay and Dave.

The rest of us cram inside, and I put myself at the back, with several bodies between me and Mac.

Once we've laid out the plan, Jay says, "I admire the idea, but are you aware this school has twelve hundred students?"

"Maybe we need some help." Arlo shifts so he can see Jay from behind Rory. "What if we get a bunch of people to write the notes?"

"We could spend the weekend recruiting," Joss offers.

I add, "People could stay after school on Monday, and then everyone would see them on Tuesday before the break."

"Let me see what I can do." Jay smiles. "But there is one condition: I get to write notes on your lockers."

We leave with our assignments for the weekend: Joss and Mac are covering anyone with ties to theatre, plus Mac will reach out to some guys he played basketball with, and Joss will talk to all the people she knows just because she's Joss. Rory will enlist kids from his dance studio; Arlo has played a variety of sports over the years; and Casey has connections with the chess club, the debate team, and student government. I reluctantly agree to ask the non-thespian choir kids.

In my room that evening, I stare at my phone for ten minutes before sending a single text. It's been so long since I talked to these people I feel like I need to introduce myself before soliciting. I type:

Hi, this is Raina, I was in choir last year. I know we haven't talked in a while. I sort of fell off the face of the planet after my dad died, but I'm trying to rejoin humanity, and I have a group of friends who are not only kind to me but also really supportive of this pay-it-forward mission I'm on. We're going to put Post-it notes on every student's locker to say something about them we're thankful for, and we could use help. If you're interested, hang out in the lobby after school on Monday.

Hard pass.

I delete everything and pause again because I'm also hung up on the fact that I don't know if these kids still have my number or if it will seem like a stranger asking them to participate in some random paper project.

In the end, I text, **Looking for volunteers to write thankful notes on RHS lockers Monday afternoon. If you're interested in spreading some kindness, meet in the lobby after school.**

Part of me expects a lot of **Who is this?** replies, but I only get one. Besides that, I get no responses at all.

On Saturday, Mom pounces on me as I come into the kitchen, popping out from behind the fridge door like she was lying in wait. "I could use some help. Please?"

"With what?"

"Dinner. I want to do something fancy for Grandpa's birthday, but I might be in over my head."

Utterly faithless in my ability to provide culinary assistance, I'm about to decline, but Mom's face is so full of nerves and hope that I sigh and say, "What do you need?"

"Thank you." She pulls out ingredients. "I'm making baked cod with béarnaise sauce, but I haven't done it before." The tablet is propped up on the island, and she points to the recipe. "Can you prep the butter while I chop the shallots?"

"Okay." I've never attempted butter foam, although it kind of does that in the microwave when I melt it for cookies because I'm too impatient to let it come to room temperature. Maybe that's why my cookies are always so chewy.... More proof I'm a disaster in the kitchen.

I turn on the stove as Mom pulls a knife from the block. "Hey, I wanted to ask you something."

Oh, lord.

"I was reading on one of the parent message boards about some kindness campaign going on at school. Do you know about it?"

My cheeks flush. "Kindness campaign?"

"I guess some kids are leaving uplifting notes in bathrooms and on lockers. Have you seen them?"

"Yeah...."

"That's nice. Do you know who's writing them?"

Me, for one. I couldn't ask for a better opportunity to tell her about the whole pay-it-forward thing, but she might ask what inspired me, and I'm not coming clean about ditching class to go to the Rock and Roll Hall of Fame. "They're all anonymous."

"Well, I guess that adds to the fun."

I stare at the butter and try to determine if the white layer forming on top qualifies as foam.

"You know who I could see doing something like that?" Mom has pushed the shallots to one side of the cutting board and is now chopping a green herb. I don't answer, but she continues anyway. "Shelby."

It takes supreme willpower to not snort. *Like she's one to lead a kindness campaign.* "Hmm," I say through gritted teeth.

Mom puts a saucepan on the burner next to mine and looks into my pot. "Did you turn off the heat? It has to settle off the heat."

"Yeah, I did."

I lean against the counter as Mom starts adding things to her pan, but apparently waiting for butter to cool isn't useful enough because she points to the egg carton. "Separate the eggs. We need eight yolks."

Goopy liquid runs over my fingers as I liberate the yellow orbs.

"Shit, I forgot the peppercorns. Can you crush them?"

I hold up my eggy hands.

"Right." Mom darts back and forth between the stove and the spice rack, where she picks out two peppercorns, then alternates between hitting them with a meat mallet and stirring her sauce.

Once the eggs are done, I wash my hands and return to the butter, which I'm supposed to scoop out without getting any of the white stuff at the bottom. As I'm spooning the butter into a bowl, Mom holds up her saucepan. "Does this look like it's reduced by half?"

"I don't know how much was there to start with."

Mom stares at it a moment longer, then reaches around me to pull a strainer from a drawer. "Will you finish the sauce, and I'll work on the fish?"

I mix the egg yolks with the sauce, add some white wine, and start stirring, my job for the next 8 to 10 minutes. Halfway through, I'm thinking about what kinds of things I might write on people's lockers, my arm going steadily counterclockwise, when Mom interrupts my thoughts.

"The week after Thanksgiving is tech week, right?"

"Yeah, why?"

"Do you know what time rehearsals will end?"

"I don't know. Late, I guess; they're bringing in dinner."

"Can you ask to be home by nine?"

I stop stirring and turn to face her. "Mom. Seriously?"

"That's what we agreed to."

"Yeah, and that to and from school is okay."

"I just don't like—"

"Me driving at night. I know."

She doesn't say anything, just stares at me. "Fine. But I want you to come straight home after." Because I don't respond, she prompts, "Okay?"

"*Okay*." I roll my eyes and resume stirring. *Shit.* "Uh, is this bad?"

Mom peers over my shoulder. "Raina! The heat was too high— you cooked the eggs!"

"Well, I didn't know how high the temperature was supposed to be."

"Were you watching it?"

"No, because I was trying to convince you to let me be a normal teenager!"

Mom stalks to the refrigerator. "We can't use this now. We'll have to start over." Flinging open the door, she mutters, "I don't know if there are enough eggs...."

I look down at the scrambled mess, then pull the pot off the stove and drop it in the sink. Mom glances over her shoulder at the clatter. "Wash that so we can use it again."

A "please" would be nice. But if she's not concerned with civility, then neither am I.

"Do it yourself." I bump her with my shoulder in my hurry to get the hell out of the kitchen.

♪

During Grandpa's birthday dinner of a Costco casserole Mom pulled from the freezer, I try to make it a happy night for him without acknowledging her any more than I have to. As soon as he leaves, I descend to the basement and watch *Sweeney Todd*. Tonight seems just as fitting as Halloween, given that my attempt at dinner was a horror show.

Multiple times, I wish I could text Mac—to vent about the night's catastrophe, to tell him I'm watching the movie, to ask what kind of responses he's gotten about the notes, to forget things are weird between us.

But I resist the urge.

"A KIND OF MAGIC"

Casey and I clean up after lunch, and Paul Chen is alone again. His head is bowed, causing his glasses to slip down the bridge of his nose. The hair above his forehead is messy in a way that looks more disheveled than stylish.

On an impulse, I grab a bag of chips from the vending machine and walk to his table. "Mind if I join you?"

He glances up from his sandwich, shakes his head, and adjusts his glasses. "Did you know it would take approximately 506,880,000 Post-it notes to encircle the world?"

Even in light of the other random trivia the guy has shared with me, this is unexpected. Does he know about our plan? "That's a lot of Post-its."

"You're one of the kindness gurus, are you not?" He spits out a little bit of apple when he speaks, and I look away.

"One of the what?"

"Over the past eleven days, kind notes have appeared on bathroom mirrors, stall doors, and lockers. Three different sets of handwriting. One of them is yours."

"I'll neither confirm nor deny it." I suppress the smile that wants to curl the corners of my lips.

"I've seen you put money in the vending machines and not buy anything. And now you're sitting with me."

Is what I'm doing an act of charity? "I just...I've spent my fair share of lunches alone, and I thought you might want some company. But if I'm wrong, I can leave."

"You're not wrong." He takes another bite. Before he finishes chewing, he says, "Did you know the winner of a hot dog eating contest in New York ate 66 hot dogs in 12 minutes?"

"No. Did you know Jon Bon Jovi's favorite movie is *The Godfather*?"

"Did you know Francis Ford Coppola made the cast of that movie eat dinner in character?"

So much for steering the conversation toward a topic I know something about. Time to get to the point. "Did you know a group of us—the kindness gurus, as you say—are staying after school today to put up notes saying what we're thankful for about everyone?"

Paul stares at his lunch. "That's nice."

"Thanks.... Do you want to be a part of it?"

He shakes his head. "People around here don't care what I think."

"The notes will be anonymous. We've got twelve hundred to write, so we need all the help we can get." I pick up my Doritos bag and stand. "If you change your mind, meet us here this afternoon."

I walk toward Mrs. Nicolosi's class, calling, "See ya," and Paul replies, "Did you know the phrase 'goodbye' was popularized by Shakespeare?"

AFTER THE MASSES exit the building, it takes me a minute to realize that all the people left standing in the lunchroom aren't loitering. They're here for us. My chest tightens—in a good way.

Joss stands on one of the tables. "Hey! Hi, everyone! Hey.

Thanks for coming. Here's the deal: we're going to put a note on every single locker saying something we're thankful for about that person. Casey—do you all know Casey? Casey Sammons is your guy for Post-its." Casey holds up a stack of notes.

"And Mac Reddington has the list of locker owners." Mac waves sheets of paper in the air.

"Get a list and a pad of Post-its, and find lockers for people you know. If a locker already has a note, move on. We'll keep going until we hit every locker." As people start to disperse, Joss yells, "Thank you!"

I help Casey distribute the Post-its as kids crisscross the cafeteria. Once no more hands reach out to us, I take off running, snatching a list from Mac without further interaction.

Starting with last names beginning with *A*, I write to Olivia Abbott, *I'm thankful you shared your sparkly stickers with me in first grade.* To Summer Ackroyd, whose mom used to pack the best lunches, I write, *I'm thankful you traded your snacks in elementary school.* Next, I find Sofie Alejandro, who tutored me in math two years ago. *I'm thankful you're so patient.*

On my way to Rylee Applebaum's locker on the second floor, one of the choir girls I texted races past me down the stairs. She grins and hollers, "Hi, Rae! This is fun!"

I double back toward her locker. *I'm thankful you're so positive.*

Making my way upstairs for the second time, I pass two guys I remember from Joss's party.

"Hey, Rae," one says.

"Hi," I say over my shoulder, surprised he knows my name.

At Rylee's locker, I scrawl, *I'm thankful we bunked together during the class trip in middle school,* then stick the pink square onto the door. Danielle Bache's locker is up here too, so I write, *I'm thankful you learn music fast and took time to help me,* before swinging around the end of my row and hurrying down the next.

When I leave that row, I nearly bump into Paul. "Hey! You came."

"Yeah."

I smile. "Well, I'm thankful you're here."

"Did you know 46 million turkeys get eaten on Thanksgiving?"

"Do you eat one?"

"Of course."

He stares at me for a moment before brushing past and heading toward the stairs. I continue down the row he came from and attempt to figure out which note is his.

Thanks for letting me borrow your jacket that one time. Nope.

I hope you know how pretty you are. Doubtful.

I appreciate how you always let people go in front of you in the lunch line if you get there at the same time. Don't think so.

Only one remains: *I am thankful you look sorry when your friends act like assholes.* It's his. Does Paul get bullied? So, he's eccentric; maybe he's uncomfortable in social situations. Why do people have to make things harder when someone is already struggling?

I shake my head.

Toward the other end of the second floor, I find Erika Beasley's locker and write, *I'm thankful you sent me postcards when you went on vacation the summer between fourth and fifth grades.*

As I step from the locker bay into the walkway, I almost run into someone again. "Sorry," I say as I look up—and see Shelby.

"No prob—oh. Hey.... This is a cool idea Joss had."

I simultaneously want to roll my eyes, run away, and scream, "It was my idea!" But instead, I force my face muscles into a smile and say, "Yeah."

"We've got a lot done already." She looks around at all the colored paper.

"A lot of people are helping." I shift my weight to my other foot.

Shelby's eyes are like elusive hummingbirds, darting away every time they meet mine. "Okay, well, I guess we should keep going."

I nod and wait until she disappears into another bay of lockers, then exhale.

Further down the list, I hit a stretch of lockers in close proximity. In the span of ten minutes, I knock out seven notes:

I'm thankful you gave me the other half of your friendship necklace in second grade.

I'm thankful you were my partner in freshman science.

I'm thankful you taught me how to French braid my hair.

I'm thankful you sat with me in the nurse's office when I broke my arm in third grade.

I'm thankful you make me laugh in class.

I'm thankful you shared your makeup with me in middle school.

I'm thankful you thought my book club idea in fifth grade was cool.

After the last one, I shake my hand to soothe its cramping.

So many lockers are covered. I slowly spin around—bright squares of pink, purple, teal, green, yellow, and orange wave from the metal doors—and pride swells within me.

But we're not done yet.

Joss goes up and down rows, consulting her list and crossing off names. When I approach, she grabs my shoulder. "This is phenomenal." She shakes her list in my face. "We only have, like, a hundred to go."

Adrenaline surges through me as I circle some of the remaining names. "I'll take these."

She nods, then bounds toward Casey to assign him some of those that are left.

We go back and forth for the next fifteen minutes, writing notes, checking with Joss. Other kids start to leave, presumably having run out of names they know. I wave at Paul when I see him heading for the door.

In our last huddle, Joss holds the list out to the five of us. We take turns pointing at names, then disperse one final time. I finish first and run back to the middle of the cafeteria, sweaty and out of breath. Arlo races Casey down the stairs as Rory and Mac jog toward me. Joss sprints toward us, squeals, "We did it!" and throws the list in the air.

♪

TUESDAY MORNING, I'm out the door so early, I have to wait until they let students into the school. The walk down the hall is magical, thousands of rainbow notes making RHS look the happiest and most welcoming I've ever seen it.

I take my time getting to my locker. Jay's sticky is waiting for me: *I'm thankful you decided to take a chance and audition.*

But his isn't the only one.

From Joss: *Thank you for being my partner in kindness. I'm glad we're friends.*

And Casey: *Thanks for being the best scene partner George could have.*

Arlo: *You're brave.*

And Rory, with his perfect printing: *I'm thankful you give me a fighting chance at air hockey.*

Mac's is separate from the rest; I squat to read it: *No matter what, I'm glad I got to know you. Truly.*

I touch my fingers to the paper and close my eyes. When I open them, I become aware of the voices building around me, of snippets of conversation as I walk through the lobby.

"How long did it take someone to do this? There's a note on every locker."

"I know, right? How cool."

"This is the nicest thing anyone ever wrote to me."

"I'm keeping this note forever."

"These are from people who actually know us. That's amazing."

As I head to first period, I soak in all the smiles, note waving, and laughter, and my heart expands inside my chest.

I think I've done Marlene proud.

"FREE FALLIN'"

Because we're amped up from our kindness coup and it's the last day before a five-day weekend, our focus is scattered at best. Jay lets us off easy, working the commercials and tolerating an excess of shenanigans. We struggle to get through the song about "Dux Toilet Cake, the Soap of 100 Uses" on a good day, but today, we dissolve into giggles at every chorus. I'll never hear "Santa Claus Is Coming to Town" the same again.

Jay finally gives up on us, raising his hand for quiet. "Things are coming together nicely. On Saturday, we'll take it cue by cue and perfect the sound effects. Monday, we'll run it all the way through. But take a break these next few days. Enjoy your families. Eat your weight in pie. Think about the things you're grateful for."

Rory comes up to me as we walk offstage. "Do you have a second?"

"Sure."

"It's killing Mac that you won't talk to him. He's been giving me a ride to school, and your name comes up *a lot*."

My heart skips a beat. "Comes up how?"

"He wants you to know he feels terrible about 7 Minutes in Heaven and how it played out."

How it played out. Does that mean he feels terrible because he humiliated me or because he wishes he hadn't left?

I shake my head, tired of feeling confused. "Tell him to forget it."

Rory looks hopeful. "Like, you forgive him?"

"Like, we're working on the school play together, same as you and me."

Before Rory can say anything else, I grab my stuff and hurry out of the auditorium.

♪

THE NEXT MORNING, I get a text from Mac: **Can we talk? Please? I need to tell you something. Kind of a big deal.**

I warn myself this could be an attempt to intrigue me into saying yes. But dammit, I am curious. And we're still supposed to volunteer at the homeless shelter tomorrow, which will be harder if we're not speaking. **Fine.**

Really? Okay, great. Meet at Starbucks in 10?
Yes.

My hands are clammy as I grip the steering wheel; I wipe them on my pants several times along the way. After I pull into a parking space, I sit for a second to calm my body.

When my phone buzzes, I grab it, thinking it might be Mac. It's a text from Rory with a picture of a forest green square that looks like...a bathroom stall door? He wrote, **Mac didn't want you to see this.**

There's more to the text, but I immediately zoom in on the image, sliding it around to read the messages scribbled on the door until I find it: *For a good time, don't call Raina Ballester!*

My nerve endings shoot pinpricks through my hands, and my heart pounds.

He scratched them out after I took the picture, Rory's text says.

Them? How many are there?? My breaths are shallow and coming fast. I grab at the door handle, desperate for air. But Mac is inside—I can't see him now.

As I start the car, I glance at my phone and see the end of Rory's message:

You gotta forgive the guy—he defaced school property for you.

I put a hand on my chest as I back out. Mom would have a fit if she knew I was driving in this condition, but I have to get away from here.

It's a short drive and I make it home in, arguably, one piece. Mom's car is gone, so I don't proceed past the garage, just turn off the engine, close my eyes, and lean my head back.

A chill seeps into the Jetta, but I don't go inside; this way, I can pretend the temperature is the reason for the numbness in my hands.

I can't believe this is happening. It's the memes all over again.

The last thing I need is a text from Mac, but that's what the universe decides to give me.

Will you be here soon?

The contents of my stomach churn. I told Mac about the memes. He *knew* what those assholes did to me, and because of him, they're doing it again.

Another text comes through: **Are you okay, Rae? Please answer.**

The heaviness in my chest twists into something different—anger tempered by enough guilt that I send a quick reply:

I changed my mind.

Three dots flash while he types.

Like, you're not coming?

I don't know what to write that won't lead to more questions—until the perfect response pops into my head.

I'm sorry. I can't do this.

Let's see how he likes those words.

…

Are you serious? I thought you were going to let me explain.

My heart thuds. **Nothing you could say would make it better.**

…

Oh my God, Rae. I know you've been through a bunch of shit, but not everything is about you.

Now I want to write "Are you serious?" But before I get the chance, Mac digitally cuts me off with a tirade that makes my phone buzz so fast and furious I can barely read each text before the next one comes through.

And also? When you didn't show, I was worried about you.

Like, maybe you were in an accident. You know how scary that is, right?

You of all people should have known what a shitty thing you were doing.

So you shouldn't have done it.

And if you can't see that, maybe you're not the one to lead this whole kindness crusade.

The pause that comes before Mac's next text gives me a chance to breathe, if my lungs remembered how to take in oxygen. Instead, I hold my breath, like if I keep that in, I can stop the tears from bursting forth from my body.

Mac ends with, **You're on your own tomorrow. *I changed my mind.***

Nope, there's no holding it in after that. I fling my phone on the passenger seat and cover my face with my hands, sobbing and hiccupping so hard I barely sound human.

Mom's Camry rolls into the space next to me in the garage—too suddenly for me to get even a tiny bit of my shit together. After she gets out, she spots me, then leans down and cocks her head. When I don't immediately do anything, she opens my door.

"What's wrong? Are you okay?" Between those two sentences, her voice escalates dramatically on the panic meter.

"I'm fine," I say. Obviously not true, but it assuages her fear that I've suffered bodily harm in connection with the vehicle I'm sitting in.

"Come inside." Mom pulls gently on my elbow, and I slowly get out of the car. "What's going on?" she asks once we're in the kitchen.

"I got in a fight with Mac. He doesn't want to volunteer tomorrow, so I'm not going either."

Her expression goes from pity to pissed in one-point-two seconds. "Whoa, hold on. I'm sorry you're fighting, but what do you mean you're not going?"

"We were supposed to do it together. I don't want to do it by myself."

Ah, the you're-wrong-and-I'm-about-to-tell-you-why look. "You may not want to do it, but you made a commitment."

"So did he," I interject.

She puts up a hand. "I agree, but I can't make *him* go…. Raina, come on. You know better than to back out of something like this. It's Thanksgiving. At a *homeless shelter.*"

A new wave of tears clamors to get out, so I say, "Fine," and rush upstairs. Then I let them come, hot on my cheeks, because she's right—I can't bail on people in need—but I'm so tired of doing hard things alone.

"SOMETHING TO BELIEVE IN"

I snooze my alarm twice and spend the bare minimum amount of time getting ready. Hair in a ponytail, no makeup. I don't say anything to Mom before I leave for the homeless shelter.

When I arrive a short, quick woman named Tonya greets me. "Welcome, welcome." With a hand on my back, she leads me to the kitchen, where she says, "You're going to be refilling plates with Nancy," before disappearing.

"Hello." Nancy rolls a cloth napkin and adds it to a stack in front of her. "Normally, people plate at the counter, but for the holidays, we like to serve them." Two more napkins make their way onto the pile. "After people have got their plates, you will walk around with a tray of turkey or potatoes or such and ask if they want more. Yes?"

I nod.

She uses five napkins to form the base of another pyramid. "You wear an apron and gloves. Find what fits you closest."

Once I've found an apron and grabbed a pair of gloves, Nancy pauses in her rolling and directs me to extra ladles and serving forks. "You can talk to the residents if they seem to want it, but remember, this is a hard day for a lot of them."

I take my place among other volunteers waiting by a table filled with trays sitting over Sterno cans. Juicy turkey is piled high in one tray, creamy mashed potatoes fill another. Green bean casserole with crunchy fried onions on top; gooey marshmallows so thick I can only assume sweet potatoes are hiding underneath; and glistening buttered corn complete the spread, all the smells mingling in the air.

After a different group takes plates to the diners, Nancy gives us our marching orders. "What's your name, hon?" she asks me.

"Raina."

"Raina, you take the sweet potatoes. If you empty your pan, there will be another waiting for you."

I pick up the steaming pan and am surprised by the heft. My hand cramps from holding the ladle and the edge of the pan, but the bottom is too hot to rest it on my forearm.

It's hard to tell if people are out of sweet potatoes specifically, so I check for plates that are nearly empty. The first man I approach sits alone, staring at his food.

"Would you like more sweet potatoes?" I ask.

He doesn't look up but nods.

The next table is more lively; three women and two men are talking and laughing when I walk up.

"How are you this fine day, miss?" One of the men stands and offers me his hand. I set down the tray in order to shake it. I'm glad he has a strong grip because my arm feels like jelly.

"I'm fine, thank you. How are you?"

"Very thankful, very thankful. It's a good place here. They do us right."

I smile and offer, "More sweet potatoes?"

"You know it."

After I've served them all, I say, "Happy Thanksgiving," as I head for the next table.

"God bless," the man calls after me.

Soon I need a new tray. The benefit of doling out food is that the tray is more manageable when there's not much in it, so my muscles scream at me when I pick up another full one.

Once I'm sure I've got a good grip, I turn around and am startled by a girl at the nearest table. She looks younger than me, and she's thin—too thin, which is obvious in spite of the oversize jacket she's wearing—and shaking.

Quietly, I say, "Can I get you more sweet potatoes?"

She doesn't respond. I'm debating whether to ask again or move on when she whispers, "Thanks."

I lean forward to spoon the potatoes onto her plate—and realize she's pregnant.

She bows her head and places her hands in her lap, presumably waiting for me to leave. I pick up the pan and move swiftly to the next table.

But my thoughts stay with her. Did her parents kick her out because she's pregnant? What will she do after the baby comes?

With the second pan, I'm looking more than scooping, but I eventually come upon a table with plates so clean they barely look used, and I feel guilty I didn't notice them sooner.

"Would you all like more sweet potatoes?"

Each of the women shakes her head. One says softly, "No, thank you, honey."

I hesitate. "Is there anything else I can get for you?"

"Not from the kitchen."

Feeling fifty shades of inadequate, I stand there a moment longer. "Well, I hope...I hope tomorrow is a better day."

The woman looks into my eyes. "That's always the hope. Maybe one day it'll be true."

People begin to leave, but some men in the corner appear to be in no hurry to go. Although their plates are empty, they're laughing, slapping the table periodically. When I approach, one of them throws his arms out and yells, "Ask, and ye shall receive!"

Smiling, I hold up the ladle, and the guy waves me on. I scoop a generous portion of potatoes onto his plate, but he keeps motioning for more. I continue scooping, giggling, until he finally tells me to stop.

"Now, this is a feast!"

By the time I finish, my arms feel like lead. Even after I return the tray to the kitchen, my forearms keep burning.

Nancy appears as I pull off my gloves. "Everything go well?"

I nod and untie my apron.

On my way out, I say goodbye to Tonya, who says, "I hope you're going home to give thanks with your loved ones."

That girl. I can't stop thinking about her. How long has she been homeless? Months? It looked like she was pretty far along. Thank goodness she has the shelter, assuming she's been staying there and not out on the streets.

Has she seen a doctor? I don't know if it's possible to have a baby by yourself, to literally birth a human with no one to help you. She could go to the emergency room—surely they would take care of her, even if she couldn't pay for anything. But then what?

A picture in one of our photo albums flashes in my mind. I haven't looked through the albums in at least a year, but this image is crystal clear because it's my favorite. I'm a baby, sleeping in Dad's arms. He's looking down at me, and if love could be captured in an expression, that picture would do it.

My eyes burn as tears spring up. I blink so I can see the road.

Did the girl feel loved before she got pregnant? Is it better or worse if she did?

I should have talked to her. About more than stupid root vegetables. Found out if there was some way I could help her.

A pit forms in my stomach. How on earth could I help her? I've failed everyone I care about.

The tears fall harder now, and I repeatedly take my hand off the wheel to wipe them away. Holding my breath makes my eyes go squinty, which threatens my visibility even more. And focusing on breathing more than staying the proper distance behind the SUV in front of me makes me wonder if anyone has ever crashed a car because they were weeping. That thought causes snot to run out of my nose, because if *I* died in a car accident after Dad, I honestly don't know if Mom would have the will to go on living.

I pull over and give my sorrow unfettered release, sobbing until all that's left is a hollow shell of a person.

"UNDER PRESSURE"

The day after Thanksgiving, I don't leave the basement except to go to the bathroom or get food. I eat a bowl of Honey Nut Cheerios in Dad's recliner while watching *Holiday Inn*, my legs crisscrossed under his old nubby blanket. Lunch is a PB&J with *White Christmas* playing. Microwavable ramen accompanies the falling darkness outside and *The Nightmare Before Christmas* on the screen. I spend so long in Dad's chair that my butt hurts, but all that prompts me to do is change positions.

Inside the fridge I find three-quarters of a pumpkin pie, and Mom isn't around, so I take the whole thing downstairs. I cue up *The Polar Express* for the gazillionth time, stab my fork into the creamy orange filling, and wallow in cinnamon and nutmeg.

By the time only a quarter of the pie is left, my stomach is on the verge of exploding, but I keep shoveling forkfuls into my mouth. Only after it feels like the only place left for food to go is up do I set the pie on the floor and pick up my phone.

I've already read everything on the Soul Foundation website, but I pull it up again. If only we lived close enough to volunteer at the Soul Kitchen, the Foundation's nonprofit community restaurant that serves paying and in-need customers. Beyond that, there's a Donate button, but it's not like I have fifty thousand dollars lying around, and fifty bucks feels pointless. How is that going to help someone like the girl I saw?

It's past midnight when I climb into bed, but I'm still so full I toss and turn for hours. At 4:00, I wake up sweating and abandon any further attempt to sleep.

♪

Rehearsal on Saturday is long—five hours of constant starting and stopping. Arlo practices making "ice crack" by crushing cornflakes with a rolling pin. It takes several tries to figure out how many cornflakes to put on the baking sheet. Too many and they clatter off the side. Too few and it's too quiet. We get it eventually, but you can't reuse crushed flakes, so we're down half a box before we've gone ten minutes.

When Gower the druggist slaps George, Rory bends a belt and snaps it while Arlo says his lines, but Jay holds up his hand.

"Let's work on the slap." He runs up onstage and confers with Rory, who practices snapping until it actually sounds painful.

The next one to trip us up is the rock breaking glass in a window of the old Granville house. Rory is supposed to break ribbon candy with a hammer, but doing it on a baking sheet doesn't give the right *tinkle*.

"What about on one of the dinner plates?" Casey suggests. We try it. Better, but not enough better.

"Someone could hold it so the broken pieces fall." Mac reaches out his hand for a piece of candy and holds it by both ends over the plate. Rory hits the confectionery ribbon, but he's afraid of accidentally hammering Mac's fingers, so he doesn't hit it with enough force to break it.

"Harder. But accurate," Mac warns.

Rory breaks it this time, and the shower of sugar shards on the china makes a delightful shattering sound.

"Excellent. Moving on." Jay returns to his seat in the auditorium, and we continue.

It goes like that until we wrap for the night.

On my way out of the bathroom, something on top of a locker catches my eye. I move closer and recognize the corner of one black leather notebook. *Our reverse burn book.*

I stand on tiptoe, pull it down, and leaf through the pages. Ample messages in a rainbow of colors pepper the paper—from top to bottom, in corners, sideways along edges, and in cramped letters butted up against the binding.

Before bed that night, I read everything:

Isabella Valdez volunteers with Big Brothers Big Sisters.

No matter what, Mia Newsome never breaks her word.

Brooklyn Kahn doesn't think she's pretty, but she's gorgeous.

When I came out, Bianca Rowley didn't treat me any different.

Sasha Dyas is nice to my brother with Down's.

I pause and rest my hand on the page, touched by the beautiful words these girls have written and by the kind acts that inspired them.

Eden Ulrich came with me to mosque.

Carmen Jiminez spends her summers working at a camp for kids with cancer.

When my parents are fighting, Paola Cafarelli lets me sleep at her house.

Lily Devlin used her own money to pay for my prom ticket.

Rae Ballester is stronger than some people made her believe, stronger than me, and I hope she knows I never wanted to stop being friends with her.

I stare at the words—Shelby's—written in loose cursive in purple ink. I read them again, then a third time, and dab at my eyes.

"CAN'T FIGHT THIS FEELING"

Hope. It feels like floating to the surface instead of being pushed underwater, like being weightless on the moon rather than pulled down by gravity, like maybe I didn't drive all my old friends away.

Like I might be able to fix things with Mac.

I should have told him about seeing the stall door, explained why I bailed. Just like he should have told me why he walked out during our kiss—and I should have given him the chance.

My heart pounds as I text, **I'm sorry. I've got more to say (I know you do too)—can we talk? Starbucks, on me?**

Come on, flashing dots.

A minute goes by.

Two minutes...three.... I shouldn't stare at my phone, tapping the screen every time it goes dark—a watched pot and all that. But as Paul Chen would say, Did you know water boils at 212 degrees Fahrenheit no matter how many eyes are on it?

He'll respond.

He has to.

Ten minutes....

Ugh. I set my phone aside and flop face-first onto my bed.

It buzzes—my phone buzzes!—and I scramble to grab it so spastically that I knock it to the floor. I slide sideways on my stomach and thrust my arm down.

Just woke up. Meet you there in 20 minutes?

Yes, okay. Twenty minutes. I take a breath and gather the papers I printed earlier, my brilliant idea for winning Mac over.

I don't see Dinah in the Starbucks parking lot, but it's only been thirteen minutes. Inside, I order a raspberry steamer and a cappuccino.

Drinks in hand, I sit at a corner table facing the door. After four non-Mac people come in, I try to distract myself by watching the floor and predicting each time the door opens whether or not the feet that step through will be wearing the only pair of shoes I want to see.

Given how insistently my heart has been beating all morning, I wouldn't have thought it could beat any harder, but seeing those Playbill collages proves emphatically that I was wrong.

I'm too chicken to make eye contact as Mac takes a seat, so I hand him the "program" I created and watch his face as he reads.

RAINA-RAE'S APOLOGY
Starbucks

CAST
The Girl Who's Sorry and Regrets What She Did...Raina Ballester

WHO'S WHO IN THE CAST

RAINA BALLESTER (*The Girl Who's Sorry*): Raina was hurt and humiliated by 7 Minutes in Heaven, but she missed her best friend. Just when she was ready to hear his explanation, she received a text with a picture of a certain graffiti-covered bathroom stall, and her worst fear about that party came true. She was reliving a school nightmare, and her friend was the reason why. But she should have talked to him instead of running away. She believes he didn't mean to hurt her, hopes he will forgive her, and say what he wanted to say the day she stood him up. Life hasn't been the same without him.

MUSICAL NUMBERS
"This Nearly Was Mine"
"Not a Day Goes By"
"What Would I Do"
"Time Heals Everything"
"Maybe This Time"
"Take Me or Leave Me"

First, he sighs. Then he glances at me. Then his eyebrows knit together, and at the end, he runs his hand through his hair.

Finally, *finally*, he looks up. "I'm so, so sorry, Rae. I one hundred percent never meant to hurt you."

The release valve in my body opens, letting out some of the tension. "I should have told you Rory showed me the picture. Bailing on you wasn't fair. I'm sorry I was selfish."

He shakes his head. "You had every right to be upset."

"But you were right—it's not all about me." After a moment, I ask quietly, "What happened at Joss's party?"

Nodding, he stares at the table. Takes a sip of his drink. Cracks his knuckles, then makes eye contact. "Okay...." His leg bounces up and down. "You need to know it's not you, it's me."

What kind of line is that? I narrow my eyes.

"Sorry. What I mean is, I'm kind of going through something." His leg is bouncing as fast as my heart is beating.

He swallows. "I miss you, Raina. You're the best friend I've ever had, and I hate that I screwed things up between us, but it's not bullshit when I say it's not you, it's me, because you're perfect, and if I don't want to make out with you...I don't think I want to make out with any girl."

It takes a second for his words to sink in. He stares at me, waiting for me to respond.

Is he telling me I turned him gay?

"How long have you known?" I ask.

He hesitates. "It wasn't like I was leading you on, if that's what you're thinking."

"But did you know before or after?"

"I don't know. I wasn't sure."

"But you are now?"

Slowly, he nods. So, kissing me cemented his desire to never kiss another female. *Swell.*

"It's not you, Rae. I mean, it is you in the sense that if there was any chance I were—" He leans forward before lowering his voice, "—straight, I would absolutely want to kiss you because you're amazing. You're sweet and funny and brave, and I love—"

His eyes widen and he looks away. "I love hanging out—"

A hint of a smile graces my lips, but I don't say anything.

He stops bouncing his leg and takes a deep breath. "I love you."

I lean back in my chair, like the force of his words physically overpower me. My heart is such a jumbled mess I don't know where one feeling ends and another begins.

"Say something, Rae, I beg you."

We lock eyes, and this time, it's easy to read his expression. It's full of need—for understanding, for acceptance, for compassion. For me to be the kind of friend who's there for him when it matters most.

I reach across the table and take his hand. "I love you too, Mac. I'm really glad you told me."

"Yeah?"

"Yes. I'm sure it wasn't easy."

"You're the only one," he says and squeezes my hand.

"Are you going to tell your parents?"

"Ever? Sure."

I roll my eyes.

"Soon?" He shrugs. "How do you think that will go over with my dad?"

We both stare at our entwined hands. "He loves you. It'll be okay." *I hope.*

"I'm just not ready yet, you know?" He looks up, and I nod. "I was nervous as hell about telling you, and I was pretty sure you would be cool with it."

"You were that nervous?"

"Are you kidding me? I barely slept at all Tuesday night. But I was afraid you would never forgive me if you didn't know why I walked out, and the thought of that was worse than the thought of telling you this."

"I'm sorry. Again. I knew I was being a bitch, but I didn't know *how* bad a friend I was being."

"You couldn't have known. I should have told you right after it happened. And I'm sorry I got so mad when you didn't show. I wish I'd known you'd seen the picture, but really, I was just stressed that I'd gotten all worked up for nothing."

"Can we agree—no more secrets?"

He squeezes my hand again. "It's a deal, Raina-Rae."

We linger over our drinks and catch each other up on everything that's happened since the party, including Mac deciding to volunteer at an animal shelter.

"My first session is this afternoon—want to come with? I suppose we can even see the cats."

"You will be *privileged* to spend time with the cats. What time?"

"I'll pick you up at 2:45."

Pick me up. That would involve introducing him to my mother. "I could meet you there; otherwise, my mom will insist on talking to you."

"Great."

When I raise my eyebrows, he says, "Now that we've professed our love for each other, I think it's only fitting I meet the fam."

If I weren't so happy Mac and I are *us* again, I might resist. Instead, I trust he'll somehow make it okay.

In the time we've spent reconnecting, it started to snow—giant flakes that leave my hair wet within minutes of stepping outside. Still, Mac seems reluctant to leave. He walks me to my car, and when I go to open the door, he throws his arms around me and holds on tight. I squeeze back just as hard.

"ANIMAL"

At 2:40, I stand guard by the front door while Mom hovers in the living room. Dinah pulls into the driveway, and Mac walks up.

I close the door behind him but don't move from the foyer. "Mom, Mac. Mac, my mom."

Mom raises her hand. "Hi, Mac."

"Hi, Mrs. Ballester. Nice to meet you."

When I told Mom that Mac would be coming over, I set some ground rules: no embarrassing stories, no personal questions, and no lengthy conversations.

"I can't wait to see the show," she says. "Rae mentioned you're the student director?"

Mac nods.

"What does that involve?"

I stop Mac before he can answer because he would talk about theatre all day. "I'm sorry, but we don't have time for that." I open the door to a blast of cold air. "We're going now."

"Okay, have fun." Mom smiles as I push Mac toward his car.

Once we arrive at the animal shelter, Mac fills out some

paperwork, then a guy not much older than we are takes us to the dog area. We step inside, and I fight the urge to cover my ears.

Cages line both sides of a corridor, and as we walk the length of it, dogs put their paws on the bars or run around their tight quarters, yapping, barking, and howling nonstop.

"After you walk 'em, flip over this tag." The guy, Jerry, shows us an "I've been walked" card hanging on the cage doors. "Try to keep 'em out for at least 15 minutes. Any questions?"

"Seems simple enough." Mac takes a leash from Jerry, who nods before leaving.

Mac turns to me. "Which one first?"

"You pick," I shout over the noise.

He settles on a reddish-brown dog with skinny legs and long ears—named Rusty, according to another card on the cage.

"Hey, buddy." Mac holds out his hand as he opens the door, then hooks the leash onto Rusty's collar. "Are you ready for a walk?"

I don't know what I thought we'd be doing here, but I somehow neglected to consider we'd be doing it outside. Having left my gloves, scarf, and earmuffs at home, I zip my coat as high as it will go and shove my hands in my pockets.

Mac came prepared. He pulls out a pair of gloves and hands me the leash. I fight Rusty's eager straining while I wait for Mac to resume his dog duties.

We follow the circular path that foot and paw prints have made in the snow. Rusty licks the air to catch the flakes as they fall, nearly tripping us as he twists his body left and right. Mac laughs. "See? You don't get this with cats."

"You also don't have to be outside in twenty-degree weather."

"It's brisk, refreshing."

"It's dangerous for the extremities."

We dash around the loop until Rusty calms to a comfortable pace. I perk up when Mac says, "Should we go in?" But I realize he means only to swap out the dog.

Next, he chooses a poodle mix named Gracie, whom I quickly determine will suit me fine. She walks by Mac's side, never pulling ahead.

"So...how was Thanksgiving?" Mac purses his lips, like I've forgotten I was there alone and asking will remind me that he bailed.

"Kind of overwhelming."

He nods. "It's good you went. I'm sure it meant a lot to people."

"I hope so. There was a girl...." I haven't stopped thinking about her.

"A girl?"

"Our age. Maybe younger. And pregnant."

"Damn." Mac stares ahead. "We take so much for granted."

It's easy to forget how fortunate we are without a reminder of how hard others have it. If more people knew about her—and those like her; I'm sure she's not the only one—maybe we could do something...but how do I make them aware? I can't very well bring the whole student body to the homeless shelter—but maybe I can bring a little bit of the shelter to them.

I stop and put my hand on Mac's arm. "What if we did a sleep out?"

"What?"

My pulse quickens as everything swirls together in my head. The girl. The shelter. The Soul Foundation. "For Jon Bon Jovi's foundation."

"Okay...."

"We could organize a sleep out to raise money to fight hunger and homelessness. If people see what it's like to spend a night without a roof over their heads, they'll be compelled to help the actual homeless, right?"

"Assuming they have a heart, I would say yes."

"Anyone who wants to participate can get sponsors or something, and we'll raise money leading up to the sleep out." I hold my breath and wait to hear what Mac thinks, but before he responds, I hurriedly add, "And we should do it soon—people are more charitable around the holidays."

"Just so I'm clear: you're suggesting we spend the night outside in December?"

"I know it'll be pretty miserable—"

He holds up a hand. "We need to work on your marketing skills."

"—but even if it's miserable," I continue, "we get to go home in the morning to a hot shower, a warm bed, and a family that loves us.... Not everyone does."

Done joking, Mac frowns. "You're right." His expression brightens as he says, "A sleep out is a great idea."

My cheeks tingle, and I'm not sure if it's because they're gradually turning to ice or because I'm smiling so hard.

When Mac's shift is up, he hands in the leash. "Can we see the cats?" he asks Jerry, who directs us to a door at the end of the hallway.

Another thing cats have going for them is their decibel level. The door closes behind us, and it's quiet except for toys being batted or paws landing on the ground. I crouch beside a tortoiseshell cat and let her rub her whiskers against me.

Mac dangles a feather over a sleek black cat until it gets bored, then he sets off in search of someone else to play with.

My cat can't get enough attention, so I sit on the floor and stretch out my legs. She steps onto my lap and settles into position. Her eyes close, and she purrs.

By the time Mac comes over, my legs are asleep. He sits next to me. "You look happy. Both of you."

"I've missed this."

"You had a cat?"

I shake my head. "My grandpa had two when I was little. Mickey and Rooney."

"Ha, nice."

I'm glad Mac appreciates the nod to Mickey Rooney, an actor

who was in some of Grandpa's favorite movie musicals. "They were both tigers, super friendly." I haven't thought about them in a long time. *Wonder why Grandpa never adopted others.*

Eventually, the cat hops off my lap and saunters away, and I reluctantly agree to leave. On our way out, we pass the front desk, and Jerry offers me a piece of paper. "You looked pretty comfortable in there. Interested in volunteering?"

I grab a pen.

"TRUE LOVE TRUE CONFESSION"

On Monday, everyone looks at me and Mac when we walk into the auditorium arm in arm. Joss pulls me by the elbow and demands, "What happened between the two of you?"

"We talked. Mac has a thing about first kisses—he thinks they should be special—and he didn't like being forced into it." His secret isn't mine to share.

"So, that's it? That's enough for you to forgive him?" She puts her hand on her hip.

"I can't argue with wanting a kiss to mean something or wanting it to be spontaneous."

"But he humiliated you."

"And feeling like he *had* to kiss me humiliated him."

Joss eyes me critically. "Then where do you guys stand?"

"Where we've always stood." I smile before running up onstage.

For dinner, the theatre parents' group brings us these Thanksgiving burritos I lament not knowing existed before today. Giant flour tortillas filled with mashed potatoes, stuffing, turkey, and corn. Just like the Pilgrims ate.

Around a mouthful, Mac says, "You know I have to do it—what is everyone most thankful for? I, for one, am grateful for friends who won't judge me if I get another one of these tasty monstrosities."

"I'm thankful we all decided to do this show and are here together now." Joss takes a bite and looks at me.

"For the five of you." I swallow. "After my dad...I kind of closed myself off. I...didn't really have friends."

The eyes that stare at me are full of warmth. Joss nudges my shoulder with hers. It's nice to feel understood.

Arlo takes his turn. "Uh...I know I'm not a theatre person, but y'all took me in anyway, and that's cool."

We look at Rory, and he gives a quick smile. "Um...I asked out a guy from my dance studio, and he said yes."

Silence follows until Rory, seeing our gaping mouths, says, "I don't keep it a secret that I'm gay, but I wasn't sure if you knew or not, and, well, I thought you should."

"That's great, man." Mac raises his hand and Rory high-fives it, then Mac meets my gaze for a second before looking away.

"Yeah, we're happy for you," Casey says.

Arlo leans forward and offers Rory his fist to bump. "Good for you, dude."

I'm touched by all the support, and a lump rises in my throat. "When are you going out?" I ask.

"He's coming to the Saturday show, and we're going out after."

"Ooh, can we meet him?" Joss squeals.

Rory blushes. "I guess?"

She claps her hands. "Yay!"

Grinning at us, Rory looks relieved.

Mac clears his throat. "Uh...." He looks at me again, and my heart tumbles over itself in anticipation of what I think he's going to say. I smile and subtly nod. "So," he continues, "I guess if we're confessing...." He takes a deep breath. "I, too, am of the homosexual persuasion.... You're the first ones I've told."

Everyone is still for a moment, then Rory squeezes Mac's shoulder, which seems to shake the nerves out of Mac's face. Joss launches herself off the floor and smothers him in a hug. Arms around his neck, she doesn't let go for several seconds, and he grasps her just as tight.

Once she's back on our side of the circle, she looks from Mac to me. "I am so sorry about 7 Minutes in Heaven." She looks like she might cry.

"It's okay," I say.

As if she doesn't believe me, she stares at Mac, who says, "Really. Forgiven, I promise."

Apparently, she needs physical confirmation because she hugs me and then Mac again. And then she hugs Rory for good measure.

With the few remaining minutes of our break, I tell the group my idea for a sleep out.

Joss gushes, "You're brilliant," and my cheeks flush. She continues, "We should do it soon, before it gets too close to the holidays. I bet we could do it at school." Popping up, she beelines for Jay, and the rest of us follow.

He wipes his hands with a napkin as he listens. "I love it. Can I make a suggestion? Find someone tech-savvy to build a website. You can use it to promote the event and collect donations."

"I know someone who might be able to help," I say. It's a hunch, but something tells me Paul Chen is our guy.

Before I go to bed, I text Mac, **Did you know Rory was gay?**

He responds, **I suspected.**

Clearly, I need to get better at detecting these things. **Were you into him? Are you disappointed he's with someone else?**

Raina, just because two people are gay doesn't mean they're automatically attracted to each other.

As soon as the text comes through, three dots flash. Of course, he's got more to say—several texts' worth, it turns out.

Are you attracted to every straight boy who comes your way?

...

Oh my God—are you? Were you attracted to me just because I was *there*?

...

I feel so used.

My fingers fly over the keyboard. **Shut up. I actually liked you. But sometimes I forget why.**

Please. You luuuuv me.

"THE FINAL COUNTDOWN"

The next day at lunch, I find Paul in his usual spot, sit opposite him, and slide my open bag of Cheetos across the table. *A little bribe can't hurt.* "Hi. Random question, but do you know how to build a website?"

"Yes." He puts an orange puff into his mouth.

"Great. Would you maybe be willing to build one for me?"

"Okay." He pinches his napkin, leaving a streak of orange dust. "Did you know Google is a play on the word *googol*, which is the numeral one followed by a hundred zeros?"

Since I'm asking for a favor, I resist rolling my eyes. "We're organizing a sleep out to raise money for the Jon Bon Jovi Soul Foundation. It fights hunger and homelessness."

"That's good."

I pull out my phone. "We'll do more planning at rehearsal. If you give me your number, I'll send you the details tonight."

After I add him to my contacts, he says, "Did you know Alexander Graham Bell's mother and wife were deaf?"

♪

During that evening's dinner break, I'm all business. "We've got our website guy, but he needs the details. When are we thinking?"

Mac inhales his food like he hasn't eaten in days. "How about the Saturday after the show?"

I text Paul, **Hi, it's Raina. The sleep out will be a week from Saturday, here at school.**

Holding a wrap in one hand and her phone in the other, Joss scrolls and says, "Other sleep outs go for twelve hours. We could do seven to seven."

"What do we want the site to look like?" Rory stretches his legs out in front of him and leans back on his hands. "Should there be a theme or something?"

"Since it's Jon Bon Jovi's foundation, we could make it about music," I offer.

"Or the '80s." Mac grabs the lapels of his imaginary blazer.

"Ooh, people could come in costume!" Joss exclaims.

I smile as I type another text to Paul, but pause and look up. "Is it okay to have fun when we're talking about homelessness?" The last thing I want is to make light of the situation.

Everyone looks down.

"Do you think we shouldn't have a theme?" Rory asks.

"I like the idea," I say, "but does it trivialize what we're doing?"

"We want people to come, though, right?" Arlo asks. "The more people who come, the more money we'll raise."

"And we'll make sure people know what the Soul Foundation is all about," Joss offers.

My guilt assuaged, I tap send.

Casey suggests playing '80s songs during the sleep out, then my phone buzzes. I read the incoming message, and my heart dances.

"For the URL, Paul proposed, 'SleepOutForSoul.' What do you think?"

"That's perfect," Joss says to a chorus of enthusiastic nods.

♪

A COUPLE DAYS LATER, Paul finds me at lunch and opens his laptop. "Here's the preliminary site."

No question Paul was the right person to ask—it looks professional. "Sleep Out for Soul" arcs across the top, followed by "A night on the streets to benefit the Jon Bon Jovi Soul Foundation and its efforts to fight hunger and homelessness."

The paragraph beneath that reads:

"On Saturday, December 14, join your fellow students outside Rickenbacker High School for an '80s-themed sleep out. Wear your oversize blazers, your leg warmers, your jean jackets and slap bracelets. Bring your New Kids on the Block sleeping bag and your Alf pillow. Let's see how much money we can raise to put more people, more youth, in warm beds and warm homes."

And then there's a DONATE button.

The page design is bright and colorful, very '80s. Vivid shapes —triangles, zigzags, spirals, and waves—surround the text like confetti.

I stare at Paul for a minute before he looks back. "This is incredible," I say. "You did this in two days?"

He shrugs. "Did you know that in the human brain, information transmits as fast as 120 meters per second in certain types of neurons?"

His eyes return to the computer. But I keep staring at him. "Is there anything you don't know?"

Sometimes I wonder if he understands rhetorical questions. He seems to think for a moment, then turns to me. "Probably."

I shake my head.

♪

As we gather for rehearsal—our final, dress rehearsal—Paul enters the auditorium. When our eyes meet, he hesitates, then takes a tentative step forward. I walk down the stairs to meet him in the aisle.

He reaches into his backpack, pulls out a box, and hands it to me. Inside are what look like business cards. Our URL with a QR code plus a blurb about the sleep out are on the front, and info about the Soul Foundation is on the back.

"You can give those to people to drive traffic to the website." Paul turns abruptly to leave.

"These are awesome, thank you—" I reach out my hand to stop him from walking away. "Hey, do you want to stay and watch? We could use more people in the audience."

After a moment, he nods and takes the nearest seat.

I make my way into the wings and wait to start, shaking my hands to make the tingliness go away.

"Nervous?" Mac appears by my side.

"Yes. I didn't know I would be tonight."

"You're a natural. You'll be great." He bumps me playfully before heading out to watch with Jay.

The first act is largely uneventful, the only mishap being the ribbon candy. Rory doesn't break it the first time, but Arlo, who's holding it, nods at Rory to hit it again. It shatters successfully, and we keep going.

At intermission, we stay backstage like we will tomorrow. Mac and Jay appear from the back entrance, and Jay motions for us to gather around.

"Nice work, everybody. It's looking great. Arlo, make sure you keep your script down so it doesn't block your face. All of you, try to look at your scripts with your eyes while keeping your heads up. Joss, I like what you're doing with the props in the background but be a little more subtle with your movements so you don't upstage whoever is speaking." She nods. "Casey, Rae, when we come back for act two, don't be afraid to engage a little more. People want to see that the actors are friends."

Casey puts his arm around me. "Got it."

"That's it for me. Mac, do you have anything else?"

He looks at his notes. "During the commercials, you guys need to stand closer together. I could only hear Casey on the mic."

A few minutes later, Mac gives us our cue for places. Arlo goes out first and mills about, checking props, reviewing his script. Casey and I go out together, laughing at a pretend joke our radio actors have exchanged. After Rory and Joss come onstage, Mac slips out the back and resumes his seat next to Jay.

Even though we've practiced dozens of times, I still hold my breath when Joss lifts the bucket out of the tub. But it sounds perfect. I slide the tub back and forth to make waves.

At the end, Arlo as the announcer signs off, and we all sing "Auld Lang Syne." The lights go down, and applause bursts forth, louder than I anticipate. Dave brings up the house lights, and I'm surprised to see twenty-ish people in the audience—a handful of teachers and staff, Joss's mom and others from the parent booster group, Janice, and Mrs. Whaley, plus Jay, Mac, and Paul.

Mrs. Whaley reaches me first and opens her arms for a hug. "You were wonderful."

I sink into her embrace. "Thank you."

Holding onto my shoulders, she looks me in the eyes. "I'm so glad you're doing this." Before I can respond, she pulls me in again.

Paul walks around onstage and checks out the props. I climb the stairs and join him.

"Did you know John Harvey Kellogg was a doctor, and he invented Corn Flakes for a patient with bad teeth?"

I take the box from him and set it back on the table. "So, what did you think?"

"It was good. You're a good actress."

"Thanks. Are you going to come to one of the real shows?"

"Okay." He picks up the belt and examines it. "Did you know there are multiple theories as to the origin of the phrase 'break a leg'?" Some people think it's based on how women curtsy when they bow, but others say it carried over from when men would bend to pick up coins the crowd threw at them when they performed well."

I listen with a bemused smile on my face.

Paul flicks the bell over the doll-sized door. "There's also the possibility that it's a superstition, saying the opposite of what you mean so you don't tempt the gods. One theory even maintains it has to do with John Wilkes Booth, but that one's far-fetched."

Once he finishes enlightening me, he looks up to find me staring at him. In the silence that follows, my smile widens. I've never heard Paul so talkative.

"Well, whatever the origin, break a leg tomorrow," he says and walks swiftly out of the auditorium.

"DON'T STOP BELIEVIN'"

The time from when school lets out at 2:05 until our call at 6:00 is interminable. Mac and I camp out on my bed and look on my phone for a Playbill quiz to take.

"How about this one?" I flop onto my stomach. "*Which Broadway writing team are you and your BFF?*"

"Color me intrigued—go." Mirroring my position, Mac scoots close so he can read over my shoulder.

The first question is, *How often do you and your BFF hang out?*

"Easy." Mac taps, *Every day.* "But unfair."

"Why?"

"We're in high school together. Not all fabulous friends who take this quiz are. The fact that we see each other daily is a foregone conclusion."

"So, you don't think we would see each other every day if it weren't educationally mandated?"

"I'm not saying we wouldn't. I'm just saying the fact that we do doesn't necessarily accurately reflect our relationship as it pertains to whichever songwriting duo we're destined to be compared to."

I roll my eyes. "Next question: *Someone just broke your BFF's heart. What do you do?"* I flip my phone over so I can hear his answer sans the multiple-choice options. I want to know what he would have done if some other guy had broken my heart.

"Such an act of betrayal would not go unpunished. As to the specifics, it would depend on the gentleman-turned-snake. The sporty type would deserve an embarrassing prank designed to humiliate him in front of his jock friends. For the artist, flat-out destruction of one of his creations. A theatre geek would never be such a cad."

The mock-innocent grin Mac gives me makes me laugh. "I'm going with, *Throw on a funny movie and make popcorn,"* I say. "Next: *What kind of music do you and your BFF like to listen to?"*

"Show tunes," we say simultaneously.

"Which Sondheim musical do you and your BFF like best?" I ask.

"Alas, I must confess to not having seen any but *Into the Woods* onstage, so I will strike my memories of said show from the record and choose based solely on soundtracks."

We agree on *Sweeney Todd*.

"Question 5: Which lyric best describes your friendship?"

I expect Mac to choose the first one: *When other friendships have been forgot, ours will still be hot.*

He stares at me for a moment, then says, "The second one." *It may seem there's nothin' to it, but I simply cannot do it alone.* As I tap it, he nudges my shoulder with his.

The next question gives us pause: *Are you and your BFF more like fire or ice?*

"I'm fire, and you're ice." Mac looks at me. "How do we answer?"

"I don't think I'm ice." I tap, *Fire.* "*Are you and your BFF more east coast or west coast?"*

"We're both too uptight to be west coast."

"Are you and your BFF more into In the Heights *or* Hamilton?" I read.

"Again, the question is unfair. *Hamilton* is newer, which enhances its repeatability."

I tap, *Hamilton.* "You think too much. Two more. *How similar are you and your BFF?*"

Mac reaches over me and taps, *We've got lots in common.*

"Okay, last one: *What's your favorite way to spend a day with your BFF?*"

"I'm torn," he says. "*On the couch watching TV* or *At the bar gossiping over cocktails.*"

"We can't drink," I argue.

"Imagine."

"You're the one quibbling about legitimacy."

"Fine. I was leaning toward the couch anyway."

After I tap his choice, I pull my phone in close so only I can read the result. Mac practically shoves his head under my chin to try to see the screen.

I roll over and hop off the bed. "We, my friend, are Jeanine Tesori and Lisa Kron."

As Mac ponders, I read the description: "You and your BFF might be newer friends, but that doesn't mean you aren't a history-making match made in heaven. You're composer Jeanine Tesori and lyricist Lisa Kron, the team behind *Fun Home*! Though you both have an excellent sense of humor and a bit of a wild side, your defining feature is your shared ability to traverse complex situations, offering valuable insights and reflections."

He nods. "I approve." A moment later, he says, "I wonder who the other pairs are."

I sigh, resume my position on the bed, and tap *Play again.*

BEFORE WE LEAVE for the theatre, Mom meets us at the door. She gives me a hug, which I allow for a couple seconds before pulling away. Then she hugs Mac too. "I can't wait to see the show. Break a leg!"

On the ride over, the butterflies in my stomach beat wings of steel. Mac parks, and I exhale loudly.

"It's okay to be nervous," he says. "Hell, I'm nervous and no one will see me. But you've got this. Mary is a part of you now, and you're going to be great up there."

With a deep breath, I nod, and we open our doors.

Inside, Mac heads for the stage while I make my way to the girls' dressing room. As Joss and I change into our costumes, she talks a mile a minute.

"I know so many people who are coming tonight. I think the Friday show is the best because it's the first. But Saturday is good because people aren't coming from school or work. Sunday's usually a little quiet since it's an afternoon show, but it's the last one, so that makes it special for us. Who do you have coming tonight?"

She pauses to let me answer. "My mom and grandpa."

"Nice. My mom and stepdad and stepbrothers are coming. They usually come to all the shows. Well, my mom and stepdad, anyway. They only make my stepbrothers come once. Let me fix your tag."

I turn around so Joss can tuck in the tag of my blouse. Then I fasten a pearl necklace around my neck and fix the toe of my tights before slipping on my shoes. Once we're done, we look each other up and down.

"You look swell, Lana Sherwood," I say.

"You're a fine-looking dame yourself, Sally Applewhite." Joss holds her elbow out to me, and I crook my arm around hers.

The guys are already backstage. Joss straightens Arlo's tie. Casey studies his script, even though I know he doesn't need to. Rory smiles, looking the least nervous of any of us.

A few minutes later, Jay and Mac appear. Jay claps his hands together silently, then waves us closer. "I want you all to know how proud I am of what you've created. This isn't a traditional play, and it makes you stretch in different ways. I've seen each of you grow, as performers and as people, over the past six weeks, and I am honored to have been a part of it. Enjoy your moment. You're gonna knock their socks off.

"I have a little something for you." He walks into the wings and returns holding a box, then hands us each a package wrapped in tissue paper. I tear it open and find a silver bell inscribed with the words Clarence writes to George at the end of the play: "No man is a failure who has friends."

♪

My body buzzes like a current of electricity courses through it, from the moment I walk onstage till after the lights go down at the close of tonight's performance. That extra energy must sharpen my focus because this opening night show goes even better than last night's dress rehearsal.

When the five of us walk backstage, Mac and Jay have rushed there to meet us. Jay opens his arms, and we all pile in for a group hug.

"Bravo, magic-makers. Bravo."

We make our way to the front hall, where people are waiting. After a minute, I spot Grandpa waving his arm as he and Mom walk toward me.

He puts his hand on my back as Mom wraps me in a hug, then pulls me close for a hug of his own. "You knocked it out of the park."

At first, Mom doesn't say anything, just smiles and wipes her eyes. With a shake of her head, she envelops me again and whispers, "You were wonderful."

She releases me but takes my hand, and I don't pull it away. A magical bond forms between performers and the audience, and I'm not ready to let that feeling of connection go.

Mac appears by my side. "Hey. Hi, Mrs. Ballester." He nods at Grandpa, who offers his hand and introduces himself.

"Congratulations," Mom says as she sweeps him into an embrace. "The show was phenomenal."

"Thanks. I knew Raina was a star from the moment I met her." He raps his knuckles lightly on my arm and says, "My mom wants to see you, whenever you're done."

"Go," Mom says. "Visit with your friends. We'll stay for a bit."

Before I leave, I hold her gaze. I almost don't recognize her expression, it's been so long since I've seen it: she looks genuinely happy.

It's how I feel too. Following Mac to his family, I'm tempted to leap in the air.

His mom hands me a bouquet of flowers. "You were fabulous, Rae."

I don't know what to say. "You didn't have to do this. They're beautiful. Thank you." With my nose buried in the bunch of pink roses, I breathe in their sweet scent.

"We've seen Mac do quite a few shows, but he seemed to have the most fun with this one, and something tells me you're the reason why."

Does his mom think we're a couple? What has Mac told her?

"Well, he's the reason I decided to audition, so I'm grateful."

Someone throws their arms around me from behind, almost knocking me off balance. Joss's face appears over my shoulder as she squishes me into a hug. I turn to find her and her mom, who says, "You were great, Rae."

"Thank you."

Joss's mom starts talking to Mac's parents, so I look around and see Casey and his family. His younger brother and sister are running in circles around him, but when they see me, they stop and stare with their mouths open.

"This is my friend Rae," Casey says. "Do you recognize her?"

"You were in the show," his sister says.

"You love Casey." His brother seems awed by this. Casey and I laugh.

"You did a fantastic job." His mom puts a hand on his little brother's head.

His dad, an older, grayer version of Casey, grabs hold of his sister before she darts off. "Indeed."

"Thanks. Casey was the best to work with."

As they attempt to wrangle his siblings, I spot Rory talking to a guy I don't recognize. *Ah—the dance studio date.*

I head in his direction, and he waves. "Hey, Rae. This is Logan."

Logan is tall and trim, not unlike Rory, but Logan's hair is white-blonde, in contrast to Rory's dark brown. They look cute together.

"Hi, Logan." I smile.

"The show was great. You were incredible."

"Thanks."

Rory takes Logan's hand and leads him away. "Let's say hi to Mac before we go."

Someone taps me on the back—Arlo, with an elderly woman. "Rae, my grandma wanted to meet you."

The woman takes my hand in hers. Her skin is dry and warm. "You were divine." Arlo is supporting her by the elbow, stooping since she's so much shorter than he is. It's sweet.

"Thank you very much. I'm so glad Arlo decided to do the show. He's amazing."

She squeezes my hand before letting go. Arlo loops his arm around hers and leads her away, calling over his shoulder, "See you tomorrow, Rae."

I make my way through the crowd toward Mom, who is talking to Jay. As I approach, she says, "A sleep out?"

Uh oh.

"She's the one organizing it," Jay says, "pulling everything together. It's quite impressive—on top of all the kind things she's done around the school."

Before Mom notices me, I attempt to read her expression. Mostly, she looks confused. But there's more underneath. Pleasant surprise? Pride? ...Hurt?

As I debate whether to interrupt the conversation, Paul plants himself in front of me and says, "Did you know a French businessman in the 1820s hired people to clap at theatrical performances?"

I peer behind him and strain to hear what Mom and Jay are saying, nodding distractedly. "Hi, Paul. Thanks for coming."

"The show was good. You were good."

"That's nice of you to say," I add, not meeting his eyes.

Jay extends his hand to Grandpa, leans toward him, and says something I can't make out. Then Jay shakes Mom's hand before walking away, raising his palm to me as he passes.

Paul takes a step back and turns. I place my hand on his arm and refocus my attention. "I'm glad you came."

His head drops as he looks at my hand. "Okay. Well, have a good show tomorrow. And Sunday."

He disappears into the crowd, and Mom and Grandpa capitalize on my moment of solitude. "Here's our star." Grandpa gives me a squeeze.

I glance at Mom, waiting for her to say something about what she heard from Jay, but all she says is, "Are you heading home?"

No one mentioned doing anything tonight, so I nod.

"Mind giving me a ride?"

Even though it would only take an extra minute for Grandpa to drop her off, there's no reason for him to drive her if she and I are going to the same destination. Still, that doesn't stop my first thought from being that she wants time alone with me to ask about the sleep out and everything else I haven't told her.

But since I have no credible reason for saying no, I agree.

We haven't done this—me driving with Mom in the passenger

seat—since I got my license, and it brings back not-so-fond memories of having my learner's permit. My body thrums with tension as I grip the steering wheel. I remind myself this isn't a driving lesson and relax my muscles.

"I'm so glad you did the show," she says.

I smile, pleased to be appreciated instead of grilled, but don't take my eyes off the road.

"I'm very proud of you."

A knot forms in my throat. The closest car is several subdivisions in the distance, so I allow my eyes to meet hers. "Thank you." It comes out as a whisper.

Her words echo in my mind as I pull into the garage and say goodnight, a lovely ending to an amazing day.

"WE WEREN'T BORN TO FOLLOW"

The next morning, Mac and I both volunteer at the animal shelter. Without hesitation, he takes Rusty out first. We've staggered our shifts so I can walk with him.

"You know the cards Paul made?" I ask as I pull my woolly scarf tighter around my neck. "What if we make passing them out a thing?"

"A thing?"

"To get people besides us to want to share them."

"How do we do that?"

I contemplate this while watching Rusty zigzag in front of us to sniff whatever he smells beneath the snow, turning his muzzle white. When he discovers a particularly tantalizing aroma, he stops, and we almost trip over him. But the dog has given me an idea.

"What about a sort of scavenger hunt?"

"And we'd be hunting for…?"

"Random acts of kindness—we find something nice to do and give a card."

"Example?"

"Like...put money in the tip jar at a coffee shop and hand a card to the barista."

Mac grins. "Or take supplies to an animal shelter with a card for the people who work there."

"The object of the game is to complete good deeds in order to raise awareness of the sleep out."

"And everybody wins."

Rusty strains on the leash, pulling Mac's arm to the side, as we stare at each other excitedly. We finally put our feet in motion, and despite my fear of frostbite, I tug off my glove and pull out my phone to make notes.

"Text folks to see if they want to meet to brainstorm after we're done here," Mac says.

I include Paul too in case we want to put something on the website.

At Starbucks, it takes some maneuvering to fit everyone. Besides the six of us, there's Logan, two guys Casey invited, Joss's friend Chloe, and Paul.

While others get their drinks, I transfer our ideas from my phone to my notebook. Mac pulls out the chair next to me and hands me a raspberry steamer. After the last person sits down, Joss waves her hands to quiet the group, then all eyes are on me.

"We need to promote the sleep out so we can raise as much money as possible." I hold up one of Paul's cards. "Anybody who wants to can take some of these cards and pass them out after performing a random act of kindness."

I tap our list with my pen. "So far, we've got: Leave money in the tip jar at a coffee shop, then hand a card to the barista. Donate supplies to an animal shelter and offer a card to someone who works there. Give someone a compliment and a card. Go to a drive-thru and pay it forward—the person at the window would get the card. And put a card inside a book you love and leave it somewhere for someone to take. We need more ideas."

"What about buying someone a present for no reason?" Chloe suggests. I write it down.

"You could donate to a food bank."

"Or fill empty meters."

"How would you handle the cards?" Mac asks Rory.

"Tape them on?"

"If you go out to eat, you could leave a big tip."

"Or write the server a nice note on the bill."

"Or compliment good service to management."

The ideas are coming faster than I can write. As they snowball, my pulse accelerates too.

Joss props her elbows on the table. "We could deliver thank-you cards."

"And put notes in people's mailboxes," Casey chimes in.

"Saying what?" his buddy asks.

"I don't know—that they have pretty Christmas decorations or something."

Onto the list it goes. The paper is filling up, along with my heart.

"What about baking? Everybody loves cookies." Logan looks at Rory, and they start pinballing ideas back and forth.

"Neighbors."

"The dance studio."

"A fire station."

"Police."

"Library."

"Hospital."

Joss tags onto their verbal volley and adds, "We should stick Post-its with happy messages on people's cars." She picks up her Frappuccino but immediately sets it down as another thought occurs to her. "And if you let someone in front of you in line, you hand them a card."

"Maybe people write a note to the mail carrier," Casey says.

"Or the trash guys."

"We can tape money to vending machines."

"And washers and dryers at the laundromat."

Arlo scoots his chair forward. "How about visiting a nursing home? The residents might not be able to donate, but the staff probably could."

I almost don't hear Paul over all the other voices, but when I catch, "Did you know," I look at him.

"...men have been opening doors for women since at least the 1700s? Possibly earlier, depending on which origin theory you subscribe to. You could hold doors for people and offer them a card when they walk through."

I flash an encouraging smile before putting it on the list.

"Should we make it a contest?" Mac's question subdues the chatter. "Give everyone who wants to participate a certain number of cards on Saturday and see who can get rid of them first?"

"What's in it for the winner?" I ask.

Joss claps her hands. "Let's make an '80s-themed gift basket!" She picks up her phone and starts typing. "Ooh! This site has all kinds of suggestions—movies...candy...toys and stuff."

I take the opportunity of flipping over the page to shake some feeling back in my hand, then split my attention between recording all the ideas that bombard me and talking to Paul. "If we put this list on the website, can it be separate from the fundraising part?"

He opens his laptop. "That page can be hidden. It won't be part of the main navigation; you'll have to know the URL."

"What will—"

"You just put a slash at the end and add whatever you want, like SleepOutForSoul/ScavengerHunt."

I jot everything down. When I look up from my notebook, I catch Paul staring at me.

"Did you know the keyboardist for Bon Jovi, David Bryan, writes musicals?"

"Really?"

"He won three Tony Awards for *Memphis*. And he wrote *The Toxic Avenger*, which was based on an '80s movie."

"I've seen that musical!"

I can't believe there's a Bon Jovi–musicals connection I didn't know about.

Mac leans toward me. "What if we put cards in the programs?"

"Can we do that?"

"Why not? Maybe we have two sets—one with both QR codes for students and one with just the fundraising link for everyone else."

Paul is busy typing, already building the new page. I wait for him to pause, then say, "I have a question for you."

"I'll have an answer for you."

"If you add the scavenger hunt URL and another QR code to a second set of cards, could they be ready by tonight?"

"Tell me how many you want, and you'll have them before the show."

♪

When I get home, Mom is in the kitchen. She points to her ear; I pause the *Memphis* soundtrack and pull out my earbuds.

"How was the shelter?"

"Good." An image of my kitty friend pops into my head. "There's this one cat, Josie...she always curls up in my lap."

Mom tilts her head. "Aww, she sounds sweet."

I consider asking about pet adoption but decide against it; I don't have time to get ready *and* argue.

An hour later, I head for the garage. Mom calls from the family room, "Break a leg! We'll see you after."

I pause by the door. "You're coming again?" I know Joss said her mom and stepdad come to every show, but her mom is in the parent booster group and seems to love theatre. I've never known Mom to be one for plays.

"Of course." She walks over and kisses the top of my head. "I would never miss seeing you perform."

Pleasantly surprised, I smile and slip out the door.

At 6:11, I'm in my costume, working on my makeup, when I get a text from Paul: **I'm here with the cards.**

Great! Come backstage.

I hurriedly apply lipstick before meeting him for a quick handoff. "Thank you so much!" I yell as I race down the hall and miss the end of Paul's "Did you know...?"

Mac is in the wings; I thrust the box into his hands. "You've got the other ones too, right?"

He pats his jacket, lifts the new box in a salute, and jumps off the stage, jogging up the auditorium aisle to hand the cards to the ushers. I bound back to the dressing room—my heart couldn't get any lighter.

At intermission, Mac tells me they passed out almost all the cards. We'll need more for tomorrow's show. As I take to the stage for act two, I'm walking on sunshine.

"WHO'S CRYING NOW"

In the Starbucks drive-thru, Mac asks, "So, what's the deal with you and that Paul kid?"

"What do you mean?"

He points his eyes at me. "Raina-Rae. He is clearly into you."

Paul Chen? *Into* me? "What? No way."

"No?" Mac raises his eyebrows.

"No," I say, with little conviction behind it. "What makes you think he is?"

"The way he looks at you, the fact that he's willing to do whatever you ask of him, like *that*." He snaps.

Heat suffuses my body. I stare at my lap and think about the expression on Paul's face when I caught him staring at me yesterday. "What should I do about it?"

Mac shrugs as he pulls forward and rolls down his window, letting in a blast of arctic air. "What do you want to do about it?"

"I have no idea—the question did not cross my mind before this conversation." *How can I be equally oblivious to when boys don't like me and when they do?*

When Paul texts to say he's arrived with the next batch of cards, my heart flutters. He's no longer the awkward guy who regularly spouts random facts; now he's *Paul*, the really smart guy who's been unbelievably helpful with this whole sleep out thing and who apparently has a crush on me.

Could I see myself with him? I study his face as we walk toward each other. He's not unattractive. It seems his smile is no match for Mac's, but to be fair, I haven't seen him smile all that much. Clear skin; his short hair is mussed in the front, which softens his square jaw and lean, bony body.

He doesn't raise his eyes until he's mere feet from me, and then I examine the bright, brown irises behind his glasses.

"Thank you for doing this. Again."

With a nod, he stuffs his hands in his pockets, then shifts from foot to foot, like he's about to go. I blurt out, "Did you know more than 5,000 boys auditioned to play Oliver in the movie musical?"

Paul's eyes lock on mine, and I hold my breath. The corners of his mouth turn up slowly. "Okay, good," he says and walks away.

I exhale. *Maybe the idea of me and Paul isn't inconceivable.*

We get another standing ovation after Sunday's performance, people cheering and whistling as we bow. I grin from ear to ear, until I think, *I might not see these people tomorrow,* and tears worm their way into the corners of my eyes.

Joss looks over and squeezes my hand; I'm not the only one getting emotional. The five of us turn and entwine our hands again as we walk offstage. Mac rushes up to us, and Casey and I break the chain to welcome him into the circle, then we all bow our heads together, arms on each other's backs.

No one says anything. I close my eyes. Mac grips me tight. When his fingers finally loosen, I open my eyes to a dozen hands wiping faces.

Jay lets us have our moment, then walks forward. Joss, still sniffling, goes to him for a hug; with his other hand, he claps Mac on the shoulder.

"I hope you all are proud of what you put out there on that stage. You moved people. You connected—to the audience, to each other, and I think to yourselves. Live theatre has that power over us. Theatre touches the soul, and it has been an honor to experience its magic with you."

Joss and I cry openly. Mac gives a loud sniff, and he and Rory both dig their palms into their eyes. Casey gives his face a quick swipe, and even Arlo's eyes are glassy. With a wavering voice, Jay says, "Now, go on, get out of here. Go party like teenagers."

Laughing through our tears, we break, dispersing into the lobby to greet our adoring fans. I talk with Mom and Grandpa for a bit, but then they take off, knowing I'm headed to the cast party at Joss's. I feel a twinge of disappointment when I don't see Paul.

The dressing room is empty, Joss's costume laid neatly on a chair. I take my time changing, try to psych myself up for what should be a fun night of celebration. But all I want to do is cry.

As much as I agonized over whether to audition and to accept the role, I can't imagine not having done the show. The idea of it not being a part of my life is unthinkable, and now it's over.

Even if I do another show, it will never be the six of us doing *It's a Wonderful Life* again. All that's left is memories.

For me—Dad won't even have that. Despite not thinking too much about him the past couple of days, tonight my emotions plunge me into a dark rabbit hole as I dwell on all the things in my life my father will miss—first this show, then maybe the musical next spring. Prom, high school graduation. If I get married, my father won't be there to walk me down the aisle; if I have kids, they won't know their grandfather.

My breaths are too shallow, too quick. I sit in a chair, fold into myself, and close my eyes. *I can't do this again.* I need to escape from my thoughts if I don't want to pass out alone in this tiny room.

As soon as I can stand, I bolt and run down the hall. When I swing through the doorway to the stage, I bump forcefully into Mac.

"Whoa, hey." He steadies me. "Where's the fire?"

"I'm...my dad...I can't...." Incapable of coherent thought, I shake my head and cry.

Mac wraps me in his arms. Once I stop sobbing, he takes my hand and leads me into the auditorium, past the last few people milling about, to the very back row. We sit quietly and watch Jay and Dave dismantle the set.

"I can't believe the show is over," I say.

"Sometimes I forget this is your first show, that you haven't gone through closing night before. Closing nights are hard."

"So, this is normal?" I ask.

"Yeah. When you spend every day with people, it's like you're a family, so it's sad when it ends."

My heart turns over itself. "Because you don't feel like a family anymore?"

"What?" Mac gapes at me like I've said something ridiculous. He throws his arm around my shoulders and pulls me close. "No. We'll always feel like a family. I just mean it's not the same when you don't spend three hours a day, five days a week with people, but you're not getting rid of us that easily." He grins, and my cardiac system relaxes a little.

I lean against his shoulder and say, "Why do things have to change? Nobody likes it."

"Devil's advocate: if things didn't change, you wouldn't be sitting here now."

Skeptical, I turn my wet eyes up to him.

"Hear me out. Did you do any shows last year?"

I shake my head.

"No, you were grieving. Totally understandable. But—don't think I'm saying you're not still grieving—then something changed, and you let me write your name on that sign-up sheet. You took a chance and auditioned, and here you are."

The logic is sound, just not comforting. "I want the bad things to change and the good things to stay the same."

"Oh, Raina-Rae, we all want that."

"I wish my dad could have seen me." A fresh wave of sadness chokes my voice.

"I know."

"He would have been happy," I manage to say.

"Damn right."

We sit in silence for a few minutes. Mac reaches into his back pocket for his phone, then pulls earbuds from his front pocket, hands one to me, and puts the other in his ear. A moment later, the soundtrack to *Fun Home* starts.

During the song, "Sometimes My Father Appeared to Enjoy Having Children...," I ask, "Have you thought any more about telling your parents?"

"Yes—thought about it."

"And?"

"And you're not the only one who doesn't like change."

"What are you afraid will change?"

He sighs. "I don't know.... The way they see me. How they treat me."

"Someone once told me that change can be a good thing."

"Sounds very wise," Mac says.

"Profound, even."

"Said by someone who must be very smart. And good-looking."

I raise an eyebrow at him. "And humble."

He kisses the side of my head. By the time the album ends, Jay and Dave are gone. We make our way onto the stage and turn on the ghost light one last time.

I skip the party. When I walk inside the house, Mom sets her book on the arm of the couch and flips back the blanket to make room for me. "How are you doing?" Her tone suggests my face belies the rushing rapids of emotion beneath the surface.

"Sad."

She nods and reaches for my hand. "I know how special this was."

"I'm not ready for it to be over."

"Me neither. The show was good for you, Rae. I can't tell you how happy it's made me to see you acting like yourself again."

Is that what I've been doing? The me from before Dad's accident seems like a completely different person, like someone I could never be again. But the me from the past year feels like a stranger too.

"I wish Dad could have seen it." My voice catches.

"Me too." Mom dabs at her eyes.

"What do I do now?"

"The show may be over, but you still have your friends. I've seen the way you are together; they're not going anywhere."

I so badly want to believe that.

"And you've got the sleep out to plan with them, right?" Mom says softly.

Damn her—she caught me with my guard down. I pull my hand away and sit up straighter.

"Rae, why haven't you told me about that? About all the amazing things you've done?"

Her being nice makes it harder. As more tears well up, I whisper, "Because it isn't enough."

"What do you mean?" Mom leans forward, her expression full of concern.

I search her eyes and will her to know so I don't have to say it, to relive it again, but the universe ignores my pleading. So, along with the tears, the truth spills out. "I heard the police. The night Dad died, I listened outside the living room. He was speeding to get to my concert, which means he died because of me!" I cover my face with my hands and yield to hiccuppy sobs.

Mom scoots closer and wraps her arms around me. After a moment, she takes my wrists and gently pulls down. She wipes my cheeks with her thumbs and stares into my eyes, as tears fall from her own. "Raina." Seemingly unable to say more, she rests her forehead against mine. With a deep breath, she pulls back. "Why didn't you tell me you knew?"

"I asked, and you lied!"

Her face crumples. Speaking from behind her own hand, she chokes out, "I lied because I knew you would blame yourself! I couldn't protect you from losing your father, but I thought I could at least protect you from that."

"But you didn't," I cry.

"I didn't know you knew! I wish you had told me."

"What would you have said then? It doesn't change anything."

She places her hand on her chest and swallows hard. "What happened was an accident. You hear me? Yes, your dad wanted to hear you sing. But that does *not* mean you caused his death. A deer jumped in front of him—the deer caused it. If that couple hadn't wanted to put an offer on a house, he wouldn't have had to stay late —they caused his death. The SUV rolled—the SUV I convinced him to buy. Maybe a sedan wouldn't have rolled; maybe *I* caused his death—" Interrupting herself, she points a finger at me, "—and you better believe that thought has crossed my mind. I've spent a year obsessing over all the *what if*s, and if I know anything to be true, sweetheart, it's that too many things went wrong that night for any one of them to be the sole reason he died."

Relief floods my soul. More tears pour forth, and I let my mother rock me in her arms like a baby.

"I'm sorry," she says above my head. "I shouldn't have lied. Neither of us did ourselves any favors by trying to get through this alone."

"I'm sorry too," I whisper back.

Wʜᴇɴ I ɢᴏ ᴜᴘ for bed, a Post-it note is stuck to my door. Mom wrote, *With all the generous, selfless, inspiring things you're doing, don't forget to be kind to yourself.*

"POUR SOME SUGAR ON ME"

I know we're doing the sleep out to help other people, but planning it makes *me* feel a whole lot better because it means I still see my friends.

After school on Monday, our group meets at Starbucks to talk about the prize basket and the game plan for Saturday.

"I ordered a bunch of movies on Amazon." Joss reads her list. "*Breakfast Club, Goonies, 16 Candles, Ferris Bueller's Day Off, Heathers,* and *Ghostbusters.* And I got Twister and a Rubik's Cube. What else should we put in?"

"Clothes or accessories?" I suggest.

"We don't know if a guy or girl will win," Mac counters.

"Should we do two prizes—one for each?"

"I like it." Joss scrolls through her phone. "Let's do leg warmers for the girl's...and slap bracelets.... Ooh, parachute pants for the guy's.... Big sunglasses...and hair color. Is that enough?"

"Eyeliner—for the girl and the guy." Rory sips his iced chai latte. "How about candy?"

"There's a bulk candy place not far from me that has a retro candy section," Joss says. "I'll stop on my way home."

Casey fingers one of the cards. "How many of these are we giving everybody?"

Questioning glances are traded around the table. "Twenty seems doable, right?" I say. Several people nod. "What about thirty?" Half-nods. "Is fifty too many?" Blank stares.

Arlo glances at the others. "Fifty seems like a lot."

"Maybe that's a good thing." Thinking about doing fifty nice things makes my heart feel zippy. "If people don't give away all their cards, that's okay, but if we challenge them, they'll give away more than if we make it easy."

Joss uses her fist like a gavel. "First one to get through fifty wins."

Her approval turns the tide—Casey breaks into a grin; Rory playfully punches Mac, who shakes his head but smiles. Even Arlo nods after a loud exhale.

Then we're quiet as we contemplate the magnitude of our magnanimity.

"Does anybody know how they're going to do fifty things in, what, ten hours?" Rory asks.

"Ten hours?" Mac raises his eyebrows. "What time are you getting up?"

"I don't know, eight? If that's too early, you can concede now," Rory teases.

"I prefer not to leave my bed before eleven, but I suppose I can make an exception for a good cause." Mac grimaces.

Joss looks pensive. "We shouldn't be allowed to win. If any of us finish first, let's not take a basket."

Mac puts up a hand. "So, I'm getting up early and I can't even compete?"

"Your prize is knowledge that you're helping the Soul Foundation." I lecture him with my eyes.

"Eh, that's what I wanted anyway."

"Does anybody want to help me bake cookies?" I ask. With assistance, maybe I can make something decent.

"In," Mac says.

"I'm not a good baker," Casey admits, "but I take direction well."

More heads nod, and Joss declares, "Friday night—culinary party at Rae's house."

♪

EVERY TIME we go to the animal shelter, it gets harder to leave Josie. I mope as we take Rusty for a walk.

Mac pokes me in the side. "You don't own the market on pet withdrawal, you know. I hate saying goodbye too."

"I know." We walk several steps in silence, the old, frozen snow crunching beneath our feet.

"Raina-Rae, I think it's time."

"For what?"

Mac gives me an impish grin. "To petition our elders for feline and canine adoption. My parents may be inclined to relent now that I've bared my soul."

At a dead stop, I study his face to see if he's saying what I think he is.

"Yes, I am officially un-closeted."

I punch him hard in the arm. "How were those not the first words you said to me?! How did it go?"

He shrugs. "Eh, my mom seemed okay. Gave me a hug. Dad didn't yell, so that's something."

There's got to be more to the story than that. "Come on, what did he say?" When Mac doesn't meet my eyes, I nudge him with my elbow. "No secrets."

While he adjusts the leash in his gloved hand, he sighs. "His first words were, 'No, you're not.' And I said, 'Yeah, Dad, I am.' And he said, 'Well, if that's what you want to do with your life,' like it's a choice, and like the whole of my existence is wrapped up in this one thing. So I said, 'I *was* planning on being a basketball star, but since that's out...,' which probably wasn't helpful, then my mom said, 'Boys...,' and we both shut up."

I reach for his free hand. "I'm sorry."

"It could have been worse. It's not like he wants to kick me out, and that's what some kids face." He pauses, then says, "Like that girl."

Neither of us says anything else, torn, I guess, between feeling grateful his dad doesn't want to disown him and being depressed that that's what we're considering a win.

Back in toasty Dinah, Mac asks, "Do you know what you're wearing Saturday?"

"No. Where do you find clothes from that long ago?"

"Do you think your mom kept anything from when she was our age?"

It's worth a shot; we ask her once we're home.

"I'm pretty sure I kept a box," she says. "I don't remember what's in it." She descends to the basement, then returns carrying a large box that gives me hope. "No judging," she says as we open it.

I lift out a blazer on top and marvel at the shoulder pads. "This is terribly awesome." The more we dig, the more shoulder pads we unearth.

"That was the fashion!" Mom tries to defend herself amid our giggles.

I set aside a couple pairs of high-waisted jeans to try on but skip a hat that's as wide as the box—not something I want to wear for twelve hours. There isn't much in the way of accessories, but I can probably score some on Amazon.

In my room, Mac waits while I create an ensemble. Neither of the jeans fit, but I pair a pink skirt over top of black leggings along with the blazer and get a thumbs-up from Mac.

"You should wear a Bon Jovi shirt under the blazer."

Of course. I return to the bathroom and change into the Slippery When Wet Tour shirt. It's big on me, but I gather the bottom and use a scrunchie to knot it at my side, then put the blazer back on.

"You look gnarly," Mac proclaims.

I go back to the pile of Dad's shirts and offer him the New Jersey Tour. "Do you want to wear this?"

He kneels next to me and gently takes the shirt. "I would be honored."

♪

By Friday afternoon, our outfits are assembled, the gift baskets are ready, and cards have been distributed. Jay even enlisted parents and some local businesses to supply us with water, pizza, and snacks. All that's left is making cookies, and with five helpers in the kitchen, I might not mess them up.

After a couple batches, we turn the operation into a well-oiled machine: Joss and Arlo mix, Mac and Rory scoop, and Casey and I wash dishes. We've got—*What else?*—the musical *Waitress*, about a baker, playing in the background.

Arlo rests a measuring cup on top of the flour container and says, "My grandma makes the best oatmeal cookies—she puts cinnamon chips in them."

"Like chocolate chips?" Rory scrapes down the sides of his bowl.

"Yeah, but cinnamon. Hershey's makes them."

Mac sets down the scoop he's using. "Well, now I want one."

"Do we get to eat any of these?" Casey eyes the racks of snickerdoodles cooling on the counter.

Joss wipes her hands. "We *should* make sure they're edible."

We all drop what we're doing and swarm to the cookies. Mom comes into the kitchen and teases, "I thought those were for tomorrow."

"Quality control," Mac says.

With a hand on my shoulder, Mom asks, "Do you think you'll have enough that I could take a dozen?"

"What for?"

"The police officers."

"We're already planning to take some to the station," Joss says.

Mom looks at me meaningfully. "These are for a couple officers in particular."

Officers Petty and Monroe. Mom told me more about the night they came, about the things I didn't see—like how Officer Petty took Mom's hand after she told her the news. And that when Mom collapsed onto the floor, Officer Petty sat next to her and held her until Grandpa came. Plus, Officer Monroe talked to Grandpa several times over the days following the accident to answer all his and Mom's questions.

I squeeze her hand. "We've got plenty."

"EYE OF THE TIGER"

–50 Acts of Kindness to go–

I wake up at seven, too excited to sleep, throw on a long-sleeved shirt, and wear a "Be kind" tee over it. In the kitchen, I straighten the bows on the crinkly cellophane around the plates of snickerdoodles and make sure the cards are taped on securely.

Mom comes in and points to the cookies I set aside for her. "I know you'll be busy today, but do you think you might have time to go to the station with me?" Her eyes plead for support.

"Of course. Do you want to come to the animal shelter?"

She nods as she turns on the coffee maker. "You can show me the cat you've fallen in love with."

Mac texts at eight; I'm impressed he actually got up early. **Care to make today interesting?**

What do you have in mind?

A bet: assuming our parents agree to the pets—(A big *if*, I think.)—**whoever gives away all their cards first gets to name them. I'm thinking Fiyero and Elphaba. You could call her Elphie for short. Cute, right?**

Well, now I have to convince Mom to adopt the cat. And as fun as *Wicked*-inspired names would be, I want something rock-themed, which means I have to win.

♪

THE SUN SLANTS over the yard, turning the frost on the grass to glitter. I bundle up; grab a stack of note cards, a pen, three gift bags, and a plate of cookies; and take my stand against the elements.

At the end of our driveway, I hang a note card containing a gift card from the knob of our mailbox for the mail carrier. One down, forty-nine to go.

In front of the house on the corner, I pull off a glove and write a quick note to compliment the giant wreaths hung from every window by enormous red velvet ribbons.

Over the next ten minutes, I deliver three more notes, the gift bags of activity kits for our neighbors with young kids, and snickerdoodles to an elderly woman in the cul-de-sac. When I get back home, my cheeks red and stinging, I've checked nine items off my list, and it's not even 8:30.

♪

—41 to go—

MOM REACHES into the back seat of the car for her two plates of cookies, and I pick up one for the library. We take it to the information desk. "Hi. I wanted to give you these to say thanks."

The librarian breaks into a huge smile. "That's so sweet." After she reads the card, she holds up a finger. "Would you wait a moment?"

I nod, and she leaves, only to return with another woman, who shakes my hand. "Thank you for the cookies. I'm Sara Greene; I run social media for the library. Would it be all right if we post about this? We can mention your website to encourage more people to donate."

"Sure, yes. That would be great." I get goose bumps as I imagine our kindness campaign spreading even further throughout the community.

We walk from the library to the police station. Mom pauses in front of the door, takes a deep breath, and steps forward.

An officer slides open a window in the wall. "What can I do for you?"

Mom stares at her but doesn't say anything. I glance back and forth between them, then finally say, "We brought cookies."

This seems to break the spell that has washed over my mother. She clears her throat. "Are Officers Petty and Monroe here?"

The woman seems hesitant, so Mom keeps talking, sort of. "They both came to my house...last year, my husband...they told me...I wanted to say thank you." She whispers the last phrase.

"One moment; I'll come around." The woman disappears, then emerges from a door off the side of the vestibule. "Would you prefer I give the cookies to the officers, or would you like to see them?" Her voice is gentle.

Mom looks down. "I'd like to see them."

Nodding, the woman puts a hand on Mom's shoulder. "Give me a minute, and I'll send them out."

Looking like she doesn't trust her legs to support her, Mom sinks into a chair. When the side door opens again, she pops up. Officer Monroe comes out first, followed by Officer Petty. Mom thrusts out the plates and waits until they take them, then covers her face with her hands. My heart beats faster.

No one says anything while Mom composes herself, digging in her purse for a tissue. "I'm so sorry."

"It's okay," Officer Petty says.

Once she recovers, Mom removes two envelopes from her purse and hands them to the officers. "I should have said thank you long before now, but I want you to know...how much I appreciate... the way you treated me that night."

Officer Petty sets her cookies and card on a table and folds Mom into a hug. When she pulls back, she keeps her hands on Mom's shoulders. "How are you doing?"

With a shaky breath, Mom nods. "Okay." She looks at me, then reaches out her hand for mine. "We take it day by day, but I think we're doing all right."

I give her a firm nod.

Officer Monroe holds up his plate. "This was very kind of you. It means more than you might imagine."

Everyone smiles as the officers go back to work and Mom and I turn toward the door. Mom blows her nose as we step into the cold.

"Want to get coffee?" I ask.

"That would be nice."

Although Mom pays for our drinks, I take a five from my wallet, paper clip a card to it, and drop it in the tip jar. I follow her to a table and pull a copy of *The House at Pooh Corner* from my purse.

Mom sips her vanilla latte, then examines the card before returning it to the book. "How did you learn about the foundation?"

"I saw it at the Rock and Roll Hall of Fame." My eyes widen. *Here it comes—*

"When were you there?"

In the moment after she asks, my mind rapidly processes the possible answers and likely ramifications. *No more secrets.* "On Dad's death-iversary, I skipped school and drove up."

Her mouth opens, but no words come out.

"I'm sorry."

She purses her lips, but then her eyebrows unknit, and she reaches for my hand. "Was it what you needed?"

I nod and squeeze her fingers. "It's what led to all this."

With her thumb, she caresses my skin. "Then I'm glad you went."

Next up is the animal shelter.

"Hi, Jerry." I set the cookies on the counter. "These are for the staff."

He picks up the plate. "You're too good to us, Rae."

"I'm not scheduled to volunteer today, but can we go in the cat room for a minute?"

"Take as long as you want."

Josie finds us immediately. Mom crouches beside her and rubs her whiskers. I sit cross-legged on the floor, and Mom does the same, an invitation for lap snuggles. The cat purrs, and Mom turns to me. "How do you not want to take them home?"

My heart pounds. "I do.... Not all of them, but this one.... She's my favorite."

"I can see why." Mom scratches under her chin. "Do you remember Grandpa's cats? This one reminds me of Mickey. He was so friendly."

I hesitate. "Did you ever have a cat?"

"Not once I moved out on my own."

"Why not?"

"You can't take a cat to college. And my first two apartments didn't allow pets. Then I met your dad." She shrugs like this answers everything.

"What about after you and Dad got together—did he not like cats?"

"Oh, he liked them just fine; they just didn't agree with him." When she sees my confusion, she scrunches her eyebrows. "He was allergic. You know that."

I do? "But he went to Grandpa's...."

"Never without allergy medicine."

How do I not remember this?

"You know, it might be nice to have a pet, and now there's no reason we can't have a cat."

Hope flutters in my heart. "Are you saying we can adopt her?"

"She seems to like us." Mom strokes her silky fur, then smiles at me.

We're adopting the cat!!!!! I text Mac once we're back in the car.

He responds, **That's awesome! Tell Audrey I say hi…. Audrey and Seymour.**

You mean Jack and Diane. It's got to be rock. And I've got to get moving.

♪

—37 to go—

AFTER MOM and I get home (sans cat until tomorrow), I go in the house just long enough to use the bathroom before hopping in my car and heading out again, making a quick stop at Panera.

I pull my sandwich out of the to-go bag and take a bite, then set it on the passenger seat. Before I leave, I take a pad of Post-its from my purse and sticky the windshields of other cars in the parking lot:

I hope you're having a great day!

Believe your dreams will come true.

Never forget you're amazing.

The world is lucky to have you in it.

Smile—it's contagious!

Be you, and be proud.

My phone buzzes. I plop in the driver's seat, take another bite, and check the text from Mac: **How many do you have left?**

31, I answer. **You?**

…

21.

21?? I toss my phone aside and put the car in reverse.

♪

228

—3 1 to go—

In Kroger, I hurriedly fill a basket with pantry staples, a bag of chocolates, and a bouquet of flowers. Of course, I pick the slowest checkout line, so as soon as I'm through, I book it to the bank and exchange a five-dollar bill for twenty quarters.

I play some old-school Bon Jovi and kick up the volume as I put all the delivery destinations in Google Maps, then hit a nursing home, laundromat, food bank, and hospital (nurses' station and four vending machines)—BOOM!

Your girl's got skillz.

♪

At the Starbucks window, I hold out my phone. "I'll pay for the car behind me too."

The barista smiles. "Okay, but the car ahead of you already paid for yours. This has been going on since this morning—you're the twenty-third person to pay it forward. That's a record for this store."

Is one of our people responsible? I show her a card. "Did you get one of these?"

"Yep. Good luck with your sleep out!"

Well, I'm another good deed away from beating Mac, but being part of the chain is worth the stop. And being the twenty-third person lifts my spirits, like Dad has my back. *He did see Bon Jovi in concert 23 times.*

I sip my steamer as I return to the library, where I put dollar bills in five kids' books and inspiring Post-its in five adult novels, then sneak my last four dollar bills into various nooks on the playground.

My heartbeat quickens knowing I have less than ten to go. But as I'm on my way to the community center, my phone dings with a group text from Mac: **Got a winner.**

Boy or girl? Joss writes.

Boy.

That's fine. Mac isn't done. And when I win, I'm naming our pets Tommy and Gina. *Bon Jovi all the way.*

—9 to go—

I PUT money in two more vending machines and tell the desk staff at the community center how much I loved their holiday dances when I was little. Then I get an individual text from Mac: **Done!**

Hells bells.

And my parents said yes to Rusty! Aka Nathan....

He's typing again, but I don't need him to tell me my cat's new name, and if I'm being honest, Adelaide is even better than what I had planned because *Guys and Dolls* is special to us both. **I approve.**

The dots stop, then a smiley face comes through.

With so few cards left, I take the time to finish, taping three along with gift cards at gas station pumps and buying three poinsettias to leave on neighbors' doorsteps. I also impulse buy a set of eight note cards with Times Square on the front.

Exhausted, I drive home and collapse on my bed, the first time I've relaxed all day. But there's no rest for the weary, so I muster the energy to sit up and grab the note cards and a pen.

Arlo,

I have the sense you're not entirely comfortable being onstage, in the spotlight. Don't let that stop you. You were amazing in the show, and your calm presence is a welcome addition to a group that can sometimes be a little crazy. You belong here.

Your friend,

Rae

Rory,

Your confidence is inspiring. You embrace who you are, and you're not afraid to take chances. I don't know anyone else so full of passion and joy; it's contagious, and I'm glad to be one of the people you've spread it to.

Warmly,

Rae

Casey,

I could not have asked for a better partner in my first show. As a scene mate, you were open and helpful, and as a friend, you were encouraging and upbeat. You have all the best qualities of George Bailey plus some original Casey magic.

Sincerely,

Rae (aka Mary)

Joss,

You welcomed me into your theatre world and helped me have fun again. You're the nicest person I know—the best kindness comrade in arms—and the friendship you've shown me means more than I can say.

xoxo,

Rae

Mac,

 I'm proud of you. It's not easy to let yourself be vulnerable. Thank you for sharing the real you—the whole you—with me. You are amazing (almost as amazing as you think you are), and I am grateful you came into my life.

 Love,

 Raina-Rae

I GIVE my hand a break and check the clock. Mac will be here in ten minutes.

Dear Grandpa,

 My whole life, I've cherished our time together. You instilled in me your love of movie musicals, cooked for me, and made me feel special. Since Dad died, you've been patient and supportive, giving me space when I needed it and a safe place to talk if I wanted to. Thank you.

 I love you,

 Raina

Dear Mom,

 I'm sorry I was distant after Dad died. I know you understand I was dealing with a lot, but I should have let you help me through it; we should have gotten through it together. You're wonderful, and I want to be there for you too.

 Love,

 Raina

One card left. Before my pen even hits the paper, my eyes sting. I write fast and make sure no tears spill onto the ink.

Dear Dad,

I miss you. I hate that you're gone. But I know you would want me to be happy, and I'm getting there. I'll never stop loving you. You'll always be in my heart, because I can't be me without you.

Your daughter,
Raina

"ROCK THE NIGHT"

–Before 7:00–

I stand before Mac bedecked in '80s glamour and await his appraisal.

"More eyeliner."

Once I give the top and bottom lash lines another coat, I make room for Mac in front of my mirror and hand over the tube. He applies it to himself, then dons his white jacket. We bend our heads together and smile at our reflections.

Downstairs, Mom squeals, "You look so good!" and starts taking pictures. After she's done, she pulls Mac in for a hug, then wraps her arms around me and whispers, "Your dad would be so proud of you."

I can't afford to let tears ruin my makeup, so I shake my head and say, "Gag me with a spoon."

We load up Dinah and hit the road. I turn to Mac and ask, "Can we make one stop on the way?"

I haven't been to the cemetery where my father is buried since the funeral. When we arrive, I wait a moment before pushing open the door. The wind gusts, and I pull my coat tighter around me.

The sound of my car door closing echoes, and Mac makes his way over.

"You don't have to come," I say because that's the polite thing to do. But inside, I beg him to ignore me.

He takes my hand. "Of course, I do."

So much for my eye makeup.

We use our phones as flashlights. Dad's plot is in the southeast corner. As we approach, my footsteps slow at the same rate my pulse accelerates. At the sight of his headstone, my breath catches in my throat.

Flowers—fresh flowers—decorate the grave, and I suspect Mom was here today. I crouch and rub a silky red rose petal between my fingers, then set my card next to the bouquet. Mac crouches next to me, and I lean my head on his shoulder.

I hold a tissue to my eyes and trace the letters—*Derek Andrew Ballester*—on the marker. The stone is rough and cold. My dad was so full of warmth, this incongruity feels wrong. But the message is right: *Loving husband and father.* He was that and so much more.

Before we go, I kiss my fingers and place them gently on the ground. *Rock those dreams, Daddy.*

Mac wraps his arms around me, and we stand smushed together in the cold, my tears freezing on my face, until I can stop squinching my eyes shut and take a breath. He holds me for several minutes, then takes my hand again as we walk silently toward Dinah.

Back on the road, I wipe away what I can of the mess I've made of my face, then reapply eyeliner at red lights. I touch up my Glamour Gloss and pucker my lips at Mac, who says, "Bitchin'."

♪

—7:oo—

Laden with sleeping bags and pillows, Mac and I make our way to the grassy area by the front entrance. Jay, dressed in a track suit, is setting up tables and stacking packs of bottled water. "More Than a Feeling" blares from speakers by the doors.

"What can we do?" I ask.

"I think we're in good shape: hot chocolate is on the way, pizza will be here at nine, the school is unlocked, and it's above freezing."

According to my watch, it's 33 degrees, but I love Jay's optimism. "Thanks for your help."

With a salute, he steps behind the table and pulls out paper cups.

Someone pounces on my back. Joss spins me around and screams, "Fifty thousand dollars!"

I laugh as she shakes me. "What?"

"Haven't you seen? We raised fifty thousand dollars!"

The blood drains from my head. "Are you serious?"

She yanks off her glove—revealing a fingerless lace glove that matches her frilly skirt and the bow in her crimped hair—whips out her phone and thrusts it in my face. Mac throws his arms around my neck, staring at the screen from behind me.

To stop the tears from spilling out, I jump up and down.

"You should make an announcement," Joss says.

We share the news with Jay, who claps his hands together and beams. "I shouldn't tell you this, but you all are my favorites."

Once it seems like the crowd is well assembled, Jay turns off the music and helps me onto one of the tables.

"Hi, everyone. Thanks for coming out tonight. It may be cold, but we've got the hottest party in town." Cheers go up around me.

"But the real reason we're here is to raise money to help make it so no one has to sleep outside. Thank you so much for your hard work today. I'm thrilled to announce that we absolutely rocked it for the Jon Bon Jovi Soul Foundation and their efforts to fight hunger and homelessness. Because of you, we raised over fifty thousand dollars!"

"Fifty thousand, nine hundred and eighty-seven!" Joss yells.

"Fifty thousand, nine hundred and eighty-seven! That's amazing." My voice catches. "You all should be really proud. I know I am." Before I lose my ability to speak, I say, "You guys are rad!" and jump off the table to resounding applause, only to be mobbed by Joss and Mac and more arms than I can identify from the darkness of the group hug.

–8:oo–

THE FASHION SHOW is a last-minute suggestion from Rory, so we figure it out as we go. People congregate on the grass; we designate the walkway up to school as the runway and name Rory the MC.

Casey walks along the line of participants with a pad of Post-its, jotting names and a few details about what everyone is wearing, then hands the notes to Rory.

First up is Laila Akers, who struts up and down the sidewalk as Rory describes her hot pink leggings, high-cut leotard, and striped leg warmers. At the doors, she whips her head around and holds a pout for a second before laughing.

"Next, we have Serena Gonzales in her denim overalls, rockin' the side ponytail. Work it, Serena!

"Now make some noise for these dudes sporting totally bodacious windbreakers! Give it up for Trent Jacobsen, Dan Thoms, and Heath Isaac."

I enjoy the procession of parachute pants, high-waisted jeans, blazers, and shoulder pads until it's my turn. Even though it feels like it's dropped ten degrees, I toss my coat on the ground and command the catwalk.

"Here's Rae Ballester, who set this whole thing in motion! I don't know which is bigger, her shoulder pads or her hair—or her heart. Way to go, Rae!"

A guy in my Spanish class points and says, "Cool shirt. That's vintage. How did you get it?"

"It was my dad's. He saw Bon Jovi in concert 23 times." I smile, knowing Mom would roll her eyes at me for saying it.

"Nice." He flashes me devil's horns before disappearing into the crowd.

♪

—9:00—

I SNEAK my five heartfelt cards into the appropriate bags, then line up for pizza. As I walk away with a plate of pepperoni, I run into Shelby.

"Hi, Rae."

"Shelby, hi."

"This is incredible, what you've done here."

"Thanks." I try to pick up a slice without getting sauce on my gloves.

"Your dad would be proud."

A bite of pizza gets stuck as it competes with the lump that forms in my throat. "I hope so."

"Are you kidding? As much as he loved Bon Jovi? How many times did he play 'Bad Medicine' during carpools? We all know every word."

I glance around somewhat nervously. "Are Maya and Carolyn here?"

"No. I mean, I don't know, maybe. I don't think so." Shelby shrugs. "We don't really hang out anymore."

"You don't?"

"Maya didn't even do choir this year."

"Huh."

She continues in a rush. "So, listen, I want you to know it was Maya's idea to take a break with you. Not that I'm blaming her, because I should have said no. She thought you needed tough love or something, and I didn't have a better idea...but I'm really sorry."

I look at the ground. "I didn't know what I needed."

"Of course. That's okay. I'm sorry we made you feel like it wasn't."

We're both quiet. After a moment, Shelby shifts from one foot to the other. "It's great to see you, you know, doing things again. You were amazing in the show."

"Oh, thanks. How's choir this year?"

"Good. I had a solo in the last concert."

"Congratulations. I'm sorry I missed it. I'll come to the next one," I promise.

"Or...you could be in it...." Shelby raises her eyebrows.

"Maybe," I say. And I mean it.

−10:00−

SOMEONE FINDS a broom for a game of limbo.

I easily shimmy under the bar on my first attempt. We go a few more rounds before I'm forced to stop, back up, and try again. I lean backward, almost losing my balance, but just make it under, the bar so close to my nose I go cross-eyed. But on my next turn, even with two restarts, it's a lost cause, and I drop to my knees.

The numbers dwindle until the only person I know still in the running is Logan. His dance training must have given him abs of steel and superhuman flexibility, because he makes it to the final three, along with two girls who are probably gymnasts or cheerleaders.

They have height on their side, but Logan makes it through again, and one of the girls falls. I yell, jumping up and down, as Logan runs forward and bends his body *Matrix*-style to clear the bar. Cheers explode all around.

But the last girl puts up a fight. She's more measured, tipping back and taking one shuffling step at a time until her nose passes under, and she raises her arms to more shouting.

Logan stretches his neck from side to side, then goes Neo again, his knees mere inches off the ground. Across from me, Rory pumps his fist in the air.

No change of strategy for the girl either. One step, two.... All but her head has made it under...chin...mouth...and...the tip of her nose touches the bar.

The crowd goes wild for Logan, who gives the girl a hug before getting mobbed by Rory.

While Logan basks in his victory, I snag some hot chocolate, then return and offer my congratulations. "I didn't know the human body could bend like that."

"Too bad they don't give scholarships for limbo," he says. "Might make up for all the money my parents have spent on dance."

I chuckle, while Rory hugs him tighter. With the cup beneath my chin, the steam warms my face, and I say, "It's not as good as money, but you can get PE credits, at least at RHS; I don't know about where you attend school."

Logan raises his eyebrows. "I go here."

Wait—what? When Rory said he asked out a guy from his dance studio, I assumed he meant someone from another school. Before I can explain, Logan says, "I was in your English class last year."

My brow furrows as I process what he's saying. Freshman English. *Of Mice and Men. Shit.*

"Oh...right." No use pretending I remember. "Last year was...I couldn't—"

"It's cool how affected you were by *Of Mice and Men.* I'll be honest, I wasn't that into it, but after seeing how much it moved you, I read it again, and now it's one of my favorites."

I contemplate what to say, my head spinning. Thankfully, Logan asks, "Have you read *One Flew Over the Cuckoo's Nest?*"

♪

—11:00—

A Skip-It tournament is happening on the sidewalk while a group of people toss a Koosh ball in the grass. One guy is timing another to see how fast he can solve a Rubik's Cube, but the '80s paraphernalia I've got my eye on is the slap bracelet.

"Rae?" Danielle Bache, from choir, joins me.

"Hi, Danielle."

A girl in charge of the bracelets hands two to me and I offer one to Danielle. I hold out my arm, and we take turns smacking each other's wrists.

"Hey, Rae?" she asks. *Smack.* "Did you write the note on my locker before Thanksgiving? About helping you learn music?"

I smile, despite the sting on my forearm. "Yeah."

She nods, then stops slapping and gives the bracelet to someone else. "That note meant a lot to me."

I pass off my bracelet too and follow her to a bench. She clasps her hands in her lap. "I've been having a tough time lately, just, I don't know, feeling sort of invisible?" Her eyes dart to mine. "Sometimes it feels like no one notices I'm here. But you noticed. Thank you for that."

My heart sings. "You're welcome."

Her voice drops, so low I can barely hear her. "My mom made an appointment for me to see a therapist. She told me about it over the holiday weekend, and I don't think I would have agreed to go if I hadn't just gotten your note."

A chill runs through me. I know all the kind things we've done have made people happy and hopefully given them a little burst of self-confidence. But knowing our kindness has helped someone when it really matters—now I've paid it forward successfully.

—12:00—

THE BREAKFAST CLUB is projected on the side of the gymnasium, the grass a sea of sleeping bags.

Halfway through the movie, Joss leans over. "Who do you think we are?" She nods at the screen. "Which one of us is Claire?"

"You, probably. I'm more like Allison."

"You're not a basket case."

I raise my eyebrows. "Of the two of us...."

She gives me a playful nudge and asks, "What about the guys? Rory's got to be Andy."

"And Casey's Brian."

"Who am I?" Casey props himself up on an elbow so he can see me over Arlo and Joss.

"Brian, if we were each a character in *Breakfast Club*."

Casey tilts his head. "Who's John Bender?" We look from Arlo to Mac.

Having a sixth sense for attention, Mac sits up. "What are you talking about?"

Joss smirks. "Of the six of us, you're most like John."

"The criminal?" With his hand over his heart, Mac mocks offense.

"You both have charisma." I defend the selection.

"The guy threatens to urinate on the floor. I would never do something so crass."

"Well...." Joss grins, and Mac rolls his eyes at her.

"Who would Arlo be?" Rory has taken an interest.

"We'll have to double cast," Mac says.

Joss stares intently as she asks, "Who are you, Arlo?"

He holds her gaze. "I'm not from *Breakfast Club*.... I'm Lloyd from *Say Anything*."

Ohmigod, is he about to do what I think he is? I smile and look at Joss to see if she understands the reference, this classic romantic movie moment.

Whether she knows the film or not, her expression is full of happy anticipation as Arlo gets on his knees. He turns out his phone to show John Cusack raising a boom box above his head and says, "I like you, Joss. You're nice and funny...and beautiful."

Arlo sits, pulls his knees up to his chest, and studies the ground. My heart thumps as I wait to see what Joss will do. I remember her saying she likes a guy who's willing to be vulnerable—Arlo definitely checked that box.

True to her word, Joss leans over, kisses his cheek, and scoots closer. He puts his arm around her and exhales for probably the first time in three minutes.

—1:00—

AFTER THE MOVIE ENDS, we burrow into our sleeping bags. I pull my hat down as low as it will go and tuck Dad's basement blanket around my face. My cheeks are so numb, the fleecy softness barely registers. I roll toward Mac, whose eyes are the only part of him that's visible.

"Top five kindest things someone has ever done for you—go," he says.

Challenge accepted. "One: Wyatt Gardner helping me find my bus on the first day of kindergarten. Two: hmm...I had a friend in elementary school who had the coolest toy cat that flipped and did tricks." I haven't thought about Ava Henson in years, but I spent hours playing with that cat. "She gave it to me because she knew how much I loved it.

"Three: the sympathy and support people showed us after my dad died." Because the days, weeks, and months after his accident felt like a black hole, it's easy to forget the kindness. "They sent flowers and cards and dropped off more food than we could eat."

Mac's blink is so long I wonder if he's falling asleep, but then he opens his eyes, so I continue. "Four: the woman who showed me Bon Jovi's stuff at the Rock and Roll Hall of Fame. She told me to pay it forward, and I don't think we'd be here without her."

"And five: you signing me up to audition."

His eyes crinkle, so I know he's smiling.

"Your turn."

He pulls his sleeping bag down just enough that his words aren't muffled. "Jay and Rob taking me to *The Lion King*. The director of summer camp before eighth grade teaching me about all the things you can do in the theatre if you don't want to be onstage. My mom finding a woman on Etsy to make my shoes."

So, that's where they came from.

"I guess my dad letting me quit basketball. And you—the way you reacted to me sharing my secret at Starbucks."

We grin at each other before ducking under our blankets.

—2:00—

It's damn near impossible to fall asleep when you're freezing. I'm scrunched as far down in my sleeping bag as I can be. It's tucked around my head, pinched tight to block out even the smallest draft of frigid air. My blanket is draped over me, a second layer of defense against the cold. If I stay completely still, surrounded by the tiny bit of warmth my body is producing, I'm not utterly miserable, but as soon as I move a muscle, shivers run from my scalp to my toes, and any headway I've made in my attempt to drift off is for naught.

The face of the girl at the homeless shelter haunts me. How many nights has she spent like this? *Not like this*, I remind myself. She doesn't have a sleeping bag, a blanket, a heated building to escape to if she can't take it anymore, the reassurance that tomorrow night and the next night and the night after that, she'll be in a warm bed.

I'm unbelievably grateful we raised as much money as we did. But if there are still people—kids—living on the streets in the Midwest in winter, we haven't done enough.

—3:00—

I DREAM I'm in the ocean, surfing, which I've never done and have no desire to try. A giant wave rises above me, and I'm terrified of it crashing down on my body.

Just as it's about to hit, my eyes pop open and I see it, the wave obscuring the sky. But then it slowly descends, and Mac's face appears above the blanket as he pulls it back up over me.

—4:00—

SAYING I wake up is misleading because I'm not sure you could call what I was doing sleeping. Regardless, I stop tossing and turning and open my eyes. While it's by no means warm inside my sleeping bag, it's less warm outside it, so I resist getting up to use the bathroom for a good five minutes.

Eventually, I concede there's no hope of even pseudo sleep until I satisfy this biological urge, so I quickly slide myself out of the bag.

Once I'm done, I stand inside the front doors struggling to motivate myself to go through them. *Like pulling off a Band-Aid.* I yank open a door and shiver my way toward my spot, my breath making little puffs as I walk. Not far from my makeshift bed, someone is sitting up, a blanket obscuring all but the top of their head. *Paul.*

He looks up as I pass, and I wave over the three prostrate bodies between us. His gloved hand emerges. At the foot of my sleeping bag, I hesitate, then grab my blanket and turn around.

"Want some company?" I wrap the blanket around my shoulders. Paul nods, and I clumsily plop down, tucking the fleece under my chin to keep the air off my throat. "Couldn't sleep?"

"I'm not the outdoorsy type."

"Then it means more that you're here."

Neither of us says anything. The clouds dissipated sometime while I sort of slept; stars now sprinkle the sky.

Paul pulls his blanket tighter. "Did you know that every year, 2.5 million children experience homelessness?"

This is the most sobering fact Paul has shared with me, and it makes my chest hurt.

"The world needs more people like you, who care." He glances at me, and I'm overcome with pride.

"That might be the sweetest thing anyone has ever said to me."

When our eyes meet, Paul holds my gaze for several seconds before looking down and asking, "Why the Soul Foundation?"

"Bon Jovi was my dad's favorite band."

"Was?"

Directly above us is the brightest star I can see. If I stare hard enough, it twinkles. "He died last year."

"I'm sorry.... Did you know Jon Bon Jovi's grandfather was a mortician?"

I shift my bundle toward him. "As a matter of fact, I did."

He tries to figure out if I'm messing with him, then nods.

"Why do you do that?" I ask quietly.

His head dips as he looks at the ground. "Do what?"

"The questions."

"It's easier."

"How?"

"Did you—" Catching himself, he blushes, barely visible in the limited light coming from the school. "The average conversation operates at 150 words per minute. I'm not interesting enough for that many words. But facts are interesting."

Although that's debatable, I don't argue. "Okay. But I bet you're interesting too."

He looks at me doubtfully.

"Come on, tell me something you do or something you like."

It's quiet for so long I think he's not going to answer, but finally, he says, "I build robots. I've won four competitions."

"See, that's cool. You should talk about that."

"People don't think robots are cool."

I frown at him. "You won't know what people think is cool if you don't give them a chance. Do these robots fight each other?"

"Sometimes."

"Are the battles like gladiator showdowns, with fights to the death?"

The corners of his mouth turn up. "I guess you could say that."

"And crazy, cheering fans, and violence and dismemberment?"

Now he genuinely smiles. "Yes, actually."

"Then how can you say that's not cool? I, for one, would be thrilled to see such a spectacle." Tiny butterflies awake in my stomach as I cheekily invite myself to one of his competitions.

His mouth opens like he's going to speak, then he presses his lips together.

"What?" I lean toward him. "Say it."

He turns his head, but I move my face closer to his, the puffs from our breathing mingling in the space between us. "Don't overthink it," I press. "You had a thought you almost let yourself say, but your brain interfered. Tell me what—"

"I wish I could ask you out."

My heart thumps, and I'm suddenly not freezing. Paul wants desperately to look away, I can see it in his eyes, but he holds steady. Tilting my head up, I nod at the stars. "Then make a wish."

He stares at the sky and takes a deep breath. "Raina, would you go on a date with me?"

"Yes. I can't imagine anything more interesting."

—5:00—

Now I can't sleep for a new reason. I will Mac to wake up so I can tell him what happened, even though he'll be smug and say he was right.

Every time he moves, I expect him to open his eyes; after the third time he doesn't, I consider "accidentally" bumping him. But the next time my eyelids flutter, I find him looking at me.

I scoot as close to him as my sleeping bag will allow and whisper, "Paul asked me out."

Despite being horizontal, he manages to tilt his head back in a silent laugh. "Good for you."

All my excitement is swiftly replaced by nerves. "I haven't been on a date before," I confess. "I've never kissed a guy, besides you."

Mac gives me a wry smile. "Something tells me Paul hasn't kissed anyone either."

At least neither of us will know if we're doing it wrong.

—6:00—

AT 6:13, I stop trying to sleep and climb out of my sleeping bag. Others start to stir. Jay works behind the tables and sets out bottles of orange juice in the still-dark. He waves as I approach and takes a sip from a travel mug. "Good morning."

"Morning." I point to the cup. "Did that stay warm all night?"

He looks around, then leans closer. "Don't tell, but my husband stopped by to bring me fresh coffee."

I lock my lips with a pretend key. Jay offers me an OJ bottle. *I should have written Jay a note.* "Thank you again—for helping with this, and everything else, and for putting me in the show. It...I think it changed my life."

Jay puts one hand in his pocket and takes another sip of coffee, looking out at the scene coming to life before us. "When I was a child, my younger sister was diagnosed with a very rare form of cancer. She spent nearly two years in the hospital before she passed. Her days were so full of hardship, I did anything I could to make her smile. I put on increasingly elaborate plays, bringing costumes and props to her hospital room and writing scripts that included the few things she could do from bed so she could participate.

"After she died, our house was filled with sorrow. My father was angry; my mother was broken. I was an eight-year-old boy, and that's all I knew. It wasn't until high school that I rediscovered theatre and had an outlet for my pain. I imagine you can relate to that."

Swallowing the lump in my throat, I say, "So, you knew?"

"I knew of your loss, but that's not why I cast you. You're talented. I did, however, hope theatre might offer you a lifeline." Jay puts an arm around my shoulders and gives me a squeeze, and I lean into his embrace.

♪

−7:00−

I PRACTICALLY RUN toward Dinah and the warmth that awaits, but when I get to the car, I pause with my frozen fingers on the door handle. I take in the parking lot, the school lawn behind it; everyone around us is smiling and laughing, and my heart swells. Spending a single night outside within the safety of school grounds is a far cry from the experience of being homeless. But it makes it harder to take for granted how fortunate we are. Winter is definitely the right time to have a sleep out if—no, when—we do it again.

"I WANNA KNOW WHAT LOVE IS"

I enlist Mac to help me get ready for my date with Paul. "What should I wear?" Butterflies make themselves at home in my midsection as I slide open my closet door.

"Where are you going?" Mac asks as he sits on my bed.

"I don't know."

He raises his eyebrows. "You don't know? This should be...interesting."

Smiling at his word choice, I hold up a couple options.

Mac tilts his head, studying them. "Not the sweater—too everyday. What would you wear with the shirt?"

The lavender, ruffly camisole might look good with my gray cropped jacket and pinstriped leggings. I show Mac the whole ensemble, and he directs, "Try it on."

Once I've changed, I spread my palms and await Mac's verdict: "Hot."

My face flushes. He continues, "And it works for a variety of date destinations—not too fancy, not too casual."

While I zip up my boots, he rifles through my jewelry box, then holds out a silver choker. I lean close to the mirror to fasten the chain and finish with dangly, faux-diamond earrings. Mac presses his head against mine, holds out his phone, and snaps a selfie.

The doorbell rings, and my stomach tumbles over itself. Both Mac and Mom hover in the foyer while I let Paul in. As soon as he steps inside, Adelaide, presumably feeling left out, rubs against his legs. "Hi." I gesture to my entourage. "Excuse them all."

Mom steps forward. "Nice to meet you, Paul."

Paul offers his hand. "It's nice to meet you, Mrs. Ballester."

"You know Mac." I push him in the chest as he tries to shake Paul's hand. Mom is just as incorrigible, flashing me a thumbs-up, which I shoo away before Paul notices.

"Okay, we're going now." I bend down to stroke Adelaide's silky fur before opening the door.

"Have fun!" Mom calls.

Mac goes out first. Then Paul steps onto the porch and looks at me over his shoulder. "Did you—" He stops himself. "Cats can make over 100 vocal sounds."

"Have you counted?" I tease.

As I'm locking the door, Mac puts an arm around Paul's shoulders. "If you break her heart, I'll destroy your robots."

Paul laughs nervously.

"He's kidding," I say. But I smile at Mac because I know he's not.

WE PULL into the parking lot at Tibbett's Grille, and Paul asks, "Is this okay?"

"Sure."

I step through the door he holds and am greeted by a sign on the hostess stand: Trivia night. *Of course.*

Once we're seated, I say, "I don't think I'm going to be much help."

Paul looks up from his menu. "You might be surprised."

The waitress comes over, all smiles. "Hi, Paul. Who's your friend?"

"Hi, Angie. This is Raina."

I give a little wave.

She takes our drink orders and leaves.

"I guess you come here often?"

"They do trivia every week."

"Is that why you know so much?"

"No. It's fun because I know so much." He straightens his silverware. "And they're nice to me here."

A voice comes over the speakers. "Okay, everybody. We'll start in a few minutes. You all should have slips of paper and pencils. If you need more, let your server know. For the new faces joining us tonight, the game will consist of twenty questions that appear on the TVs. Write your answer and hold up the paper; someone will grab it. Five points if you get it right. After two minutes, four answer choices will appear on screen. Three points if you choose correctly."

Jeff, the guy on the mic, waves as he walks past, and several other people nod when they catch Paul's eye. It's endearing to see him in his element.

The TV screens go blank as Jeff says, "First question: what band's second album was named after the Ray Bradbury novel *Fahrenheit 451*?"

Mid-sip of my Coke, I nearly choke, and my eyes jump to Paul's. "That's Bon Jovi!" I yell.

Laughing, he says, "Shhh...," and writes it down.

After he hands the piece of paper to Angie, he looks at me. "Why did they name it after that book?"

"The album is called *7800 Fahrenheit*. Books burn at 451 degrees and most rocks start to melt at 7800."

"How interesting." He grins, and I decide smiles are attractive on just about everyone.

Once the multiple-choice answers disappear from the screen,

Angie takes our orders. Then Jeff says, "Okay, question number 2: what is the stage name of the actress who was born 'Frances Ethel Gumm'?"

When I look excitedly at Paul, he's staring at me expectantly, trying to keep a straight face, but the corners of his mouth turn up. "Is this rigged?" I ask.

"What's the answer?"

Hurrying out of my side of the booth, I slide in next to him and whisper, "Judy Garland." He holds up the paper, and I ask again, "Is it?"

"I've been coming here for years; I asked Jeff for a favor."

"But that's not fair to everyone else."

"The winner gets a gift card. Jeff will give it to the team that comes in second. If anything, this is fairer to everyone else—no one has beaten me since April twelfth of last year."

I reach across him and pull a pile of papers toward me. "Then let's crush it."

Paul hands me the pencil, and his smile widens.

"Next question: what movie was the first to feature the song 'White Christmas'?"

It's a trick question. I ask Paul, "Do you know?"

"The obvious answer is *White Christmas*, but that feels too easy."

I write the answer and show him the slip of paper—*Holiday Inn*, filmed twelve years before *White Christmas*—then hold it up.

"I get Bon Jovi," Paul says as he shifts to face me, "but how do you know so much about musicals?"

"My grandpa. We've watched movie musicals together since I was little."

"What's your favorite?"

I used to think it was *Meet Me in St. Louis* since that was the first. But tonight, I'm thinking of a love story. "*Brigadoon*."

"What's it about?"

"Maybe we'll watch it sometime," I say, and he smiles again. *I could get used to that smile.*

♪

"AFTER THIS QUESTION, we'll take a twenty-minute break," Jeff says. "I want to give a shout-out to our waitstaff—make sure you tip them well! Question ten: what actor was originally intended for the role of George Bailey in the film *It's a Wonderful Life?*"

I know why Paul included *It's a Wonderful Life*, but I don't know much about it other than what's in the script. "I'm not sure."

We wait for the answer choices: Clark Gable, Cary Grant, Humphrey Bogart, and Kirk Douglas. When I don't offer a suggestion, Paul says, "I think it's Cary Grant."

The timer counts down until that's the only answer left on screen. I give him a high five; his hand is warm.

Our eyes lock, and his mouth twitches. "I didn't say it earlier, with Mac and your mom there, but you look very pretty tonight—not just tonight, I just mean that tonight you do look pretty, which you always do, but I thought I should say—I wanted to say...." He trails off and stares at the table.

I lean forward until he looks at me. "Thank you."

He takes a deep breath but doesn't smile. "I'm bad at this."

"Did you know 83 percent of girls appreciate a guy who will admit he's as nervous as she is?"

After a second, he says, "Did you make that up?"

"Does it matter, if I'm one of the 83 percent?"

"But guys are supposed to be confident and cool, and I'm neither of those things."

"Some girls want a guy who's smart and kind and honest."

The corners of his mouth turn up at the compliment, only to drop again. "Will you tell me if I do something wrong?" His eyes are earnest. "I don't want you to act like it's okay but secretly be laughing at me."

"I promise. I'm done with secrets."

♪

WHEN JEFF ANNOUNCES the last question, my heart sinks. I don't want the night to end.

"What Broadway musical features music by Bon Jovi keyboardist David Bryan?"

Paul and I look at each other immediately. He points to my paper, and I quickly write, *Memphis*. Angie collects our answer, while Paul pushes away his plate and rests his arms on the table. "We were only two points away from a perfect game—we make a good team."

I grin. "When the questions are rigged in our favor."

We pay our bill—and leave a generous tip for Angie—and walk toward the front, passing the bar. Jeff hands three guys gift cards and winks at us.

Neither of us says much during the drive, and I wonder if his thoughts are spinning as frantically as mine. Is he expecting us to kiss? If I don't get out right away, will that force him to make a move when maybe he's not ready? Is it better to ask what he wants, or would that ruin the mood?

By the time Paul parks in the driveway, my heart is pounding. "I had a lot of fun tonight," I say.

"Me too."

The longer we stare at each other, the more awkward it gets. I turn to open the door, but he says, "Did you know that in Naples, Italy, in 1562, kissing was banned under punishment of death."

Smiling, I take my fingers off the handle. "I'm glad we don't live then."

We both lean forward, and I close my eyes. When our lips touch, a rush of adrenaline runs through my body. He presses softly, or maybe I do, I'm not sure. His skin is warm against mine, and I want to caress his cheek but am afraid of doing too much too soon, so I hold back. Then it's over.

I open my eyes and find Paul staring at me, inches away. His eyes ask if it was okay; for an answer, I kiss him again. He relaxes into it, reaching under my hair to place his hand on my neck, and I melt into a happy puddle.

ENCORE

"I'LL BE THERE FOR YOU"

I stand in the wings and stare at the empty risers. It's been almost a year and a half since I stood on one.

Mrs. Whaley puts a hand on my shoulder. "Are you okay?"

I give a little nod.

We line up and wait for our cue. At Mrs. Whaley's signal, Shelby takes my hand and leads me into the front row.

The curtain opens, and we sing.

When Mrs. Whaley offered me a solo, I didn't say yes right away. Choir was one thing, but another solo? Mac is the reason I decided to do it, although he doesn't know that. I came across the list of cast albums he gave me back in November and listened to *Miss Saigon.* In the middle of weeping, I thought about Dad. Like Kim for her son, he would have done anything for me. And he would be disappointed to know there were things I wasn't doing because of him.

My solo is in the third song. Shelby keeps her fingers entwined with mine until I give her a squeeze, step off the end of the riser, and take my place before the stand mic.

I fill my lungs with air, contract my diaphragm, and release my breath on the wings of a beautiful melody that ascends and dips and makes me feel like a balloon, my heart expanding until my feet leave the ground and I float, light and calm, through the sky.

Obviously, I wish Dad were in the audience, but in this moment, I'm singing for me. For the first few bars, I exert the control Mrs. Whaley taught me, keeping my voice soft and even. But as the tempo increases, I give the sound room to play. Opening my mouth wide, I belt the final note.

As I step back into place, applause bursts forth. I can't help but smile as Shelby leans into me.

After the concert, we swim through the sea of bodies in the lobby to find our families. Mom and Grandpa are talking with Shelby's parents, and when we arrive, hugs are exchanged all around.

"You were incredible!" Mom cries.

Grandpa winks. "You stole the show."

"It was so good to see you up there again," Shelby's mom says.

"Nice going, kid." Her dad squeezes my shoulder.

I soak in the compliments before spotting more waiting fans, then step behind the adults to join my friends.

"You were ah-mazing!" Joss releases Arlo's hand in order to wrap her arms around me. "I knew you could sing, but I didn't know you were *that* good. You are auditioning for *Millie*, right?"

The posters for the spring musical, *Thoroughly Modern Millie*, went up yesterday. "Of course."

In typical fashion, Mac intrudes on our conversation by picking me up off my feet. "Flawless. But I wouldn't expect anything less."

He makes way for Rory and Logan, and Casey and Paul stop talking about their robots for this Saturday's competition while Casey gives me a hug.

Paul takes my hand and pulls me in for a kiss. "You keep surprising me."

"You're going places, Raina-Rae." Mac's eyes widen, but I just smile. The name has grown on me.

"Frank Sinatra has 'The best is yet to come' engraved on his tombstone." Paul swings my hand between us. "I think this is just the beginning for you."

♪

WHEN WE GET HOME, Mom holds out an envelope with a ribbon tied around it.

"What's this?"

"A gift." She rests her elbows on the island and leans across the counter. "I'm so proud of you. And Dad would have been too."

I reach into the envelope and pull out two pieces of paper—tickets. "Bon Jovi?!"

Mom beams. "They're going to be performing here in two weeks! I know you wanted to go with your dad, but I thought—I was hoping you'd still be excited to see them in concert. You can take Paul, or Mac or Joss—whoever you want."

Wrapping my arms around her neck, I scream, "Thank you!" too loudly.

"You're welcome," she says, laughing.

"Best gift ever!" I cry as I pull out my phone. But after a second of scrolling through my text threads, I stop and look up. "Would you go?"

"What?" she asks.

"I choose you. Will you go with me?"

She puts a hand on her heart, then gives me a teary hug.

♪

I'M APPLYING mascara when Mom knocks on my door and pokes her head in. "Do you have a shirt I can wear?"

I wave her forward, then open my dresser drawer and lift out the stack of Bon Jovi shirts, minus the one I'm wearing. "Take your pick."

Once we're both ready, we look each other up and down. She's wearing more eyeliner than I've ever seen her wear, and with the leather jacket she's got on over the tour shirt, it looks perfect.

"You look great," we say at the same time and laugh.

At the arena, we follow throngs of people inside, packed so tightly together it feels like we're moving as one. On the back of some guy's T-shirt, I read the cities and dates from the This House Is Not for Sale Tour. A woman with bright red hair has a giant Bon Jovi tattoo on her arm, the sword with angel wings piercing the heart. Electricity crackles in the air, excitement radiating off 20,000 fans. I'm so distracted that Mom has to push me gently when it's our turn to get our purses checked.

As soon as we're funneled into the open, we get lured in by the merchandise. I shout at Mom, "We have to get a shirt, right?"

She nods and points. "I like that one. What do you think?"

"Mm...*I* like it, but I think this one is more *Dad*." The house on the shirt would have made him think of our home, of us.

"You're right."

"What size?" the man behind the table asks.

We look at each other. "Large?" I say, and Mom nods at the seller. He might never wear it, but this shirt is still for Dad.

Our next diversion is food. Armed with a soft pretzel, popcorn, and two Cokes, we find section 107 and walk into the arena. Lights dazzle the darkness—electronic billboards flash from every corner and running text on virtual displays encircles us.

Mom sets her purse on the floor and tosses a handful of popcorn in her mouth. "This is my seventeenth concert."

I set my Coke in the cup holder and raise my eyebrows. "What?"

"You didn't think Dad went to all those shows alone, did you?"

"But you rolled your eyes every time he talked about it."

"Yeah—just because I've seen them that many times doesn't mean I need to tell everyone."

"Why didn't you see all 23 with him?" I take a bite of pretzel, the salt heavy on my tongue.

"I saw every concert after we met. Even the one when I was nine months pregnant. Technically, this is your second concert."

How did I not know this?

"I think I have pictures. I'll show you when we get home."

After a few more minutes, the lights dim, and the band runs onstage. Mom and I and thousands of other fans jump to our feet, and the roar that goes up is so deafening, I have to cover my ears. Jon raises his hand in greeting, and my breath catches. I don't know how much Mom paid for these seats, but they're close enough it's like he's staring right at me.

We stay on our feet as the band starts playing—"When We Were Beautiful," which is one of my favorites. I asked Dad once if he liked the older or newer songs better. He said it depended on his mood. For running, organizing the garage, or dancing around the kitchen, he preferred the older. But some of the newer music was more cathartic when he was feeling mellow or a little down.

They launch into "Bad Medicine" next. In sync with everyone around us, we jump up and down, pumping our fists in the air and hollering so loudly my voice will be hoarse tomorrow.

Halfway through "All About Lovin' You," Mom wipes away the tears streaming down her cheeks. I forgot; this was their song— the first one they danced to at their wedding. I put my arm around her, and she leans her head against mine.

She gets time to recover since the next three songs—"Wanted Dead or Alive," "You Give Love a Bad Name," and "Lay Your Hands on Me"—aren't particularly emotional, just fun.

The people in front of us sit for "Superman Tonight," and I don't mind getting off my feet for a few minutes. But when Jon says "Born to Be My Baby" will be the last song, we jump up again.

Even though everyone knows there will be an encore, we scream our love at the stage. Jon introduces the band, and then they sing, barely audible over our yelling.

At the end, the audience erupts into thunderous applause. Shouting over the din of the crowd, Jon thanks the fans before the band starts playing "I'll Be There for You." Although I wouldn't have thought it possible, the decibel level in the arena skyrockets.

Mom grips my hand, and I smile at her through my tears. After Dad died, I felt like I had to face the world alone. But I was wrong. Mom was waiting in the wings the whole time, even though I didn't realize it. And now she, and Grandpa, aren't the only ones I can count on: Shelby. Jay. Casey, Rory, and Arlo. Joss, who inspires me with her kindness to help others heal the way she helped me. Paul, with his endless supply of knowledge and the courage to learn the joys of being in a relationship together. Mac, the soul mate I didn't know I needed.

And Dad—through memories and music, he'll always be there for me.

BONUS MATERIAL:

RAE & JOSS'S REVERSE BURN BOOK

Kathryn Morel is nice, even when it's not cool to be.

Allie Nagy doesn't let me drive when I'm drunk.

Skye Lassiter gives great manicures.

I had to give up my cat because of my brother's allergies, and Lacey Middleton took her.

Every day, Alyssa Rapp gives me a ride.

Jenna Meech is my favorite person to spend time with.

Lilly Oscar doesn't talk about people behind their backs.

Aaliyah Bach is the bravest girl I know. She knows why.

Tess Farrell said my bangs looked good even though I know they didn't.

Giselle Weinraub is like a sister to me.

Sophie Juracek doesn't cheat, even when Nolan Cahill asks her to.

IT DOESN'T MATTER TO NATALIE TEPLEY THAT I HAVE WAY LESS MONEY THAN HER.

Autumn Haddox is smarter than anyone gives her credit for.

Naomi Hacke will make a kick-ass lawyer because she's wicked smart and cunning.

Peyton Osland is the heart of the varsity basketball team.

McKenna Szasz invites me on her family's summer vacations.

Trinity Nguyen doesn't hide how **smart** she is even if its not popular.

Val Emmanuel said no when Colby Davenport asked her out because she knew I liked him too.

Sydney Pace is nice to my little sister and doesn't mind when she tags along.

Kara Wafford is full of grace.

Laila Akers is the most optimistic person I know.

Even though I'm dating the guy we both like, Taylor Diorio is still my friend.

Nora Taft didn't make fun of me when I was scared of the dark in second grade.

I'm glad my parents made me and my brother leave Seattle because I met Jade Kahley.

After my Mom split, Alina Byers taught me how to French braid my hair.

Anahi James lets me use her discount at H&M.

Hazel Poplin never makes me feel like a third wheel when I'm with her and her girlfriend.

FATIMA KARIM HAS A BEAUTIFUL SOUL.

Mara Daniels should be first chair in band but is humble and kind enough to tell me I deserve it.

Seeing Evie Abernathy every morning makes me smile.

I ♥ Olivia Hoopes.

I wish I were as funny as Destiny Scherer.

No one is more joyful than Piper Ruiz.

Ingrid Segovia genuinely means it when she asks you how you're doing.

Navaeh Jones is going to conquer the world with her brains, talent, and attitude.

Quinn Lyttle is an awesome leader, on and off the field.

Reagan Armel bakes the absolute best cupcakes.

Elena Reyes asked if she could be my friend in first grade, and we've been besties ever since.

The Kindness Domino Effect

Just like a domino, an act of kindness can set off a chain of events.

Scan the QR code above or visit www.kindnessdominoeffect.com to learn how you can be a part of the movement, and use the hashtag #kindnessdominoeffect if you set a kindness domino in motion.

ACKNOWLEDGMENTS

Kindness can be transformative, and I am immensely grateful to these amazingly kind people, without whom this book, and I, would not be the same:

Michael Dolan—your phone call fulfilled a dream nearly 20 years in the making, and I cannot thank you enough. During our first conversation, you described Winding Road Stories as a family, and I am so happy to be a part of it. My heartfelt gratitude to you, as well as the rest of the staff and my fellow authors at WRDS.

Vanessa Lanang—from the moment you asked if I had a beat sheet, I knew we spoke the same language. Working with you has been nothing but wonderful. You entertained my questions and ideas with openness and enthusiasm while injecting humor into the publishing process, and your insights, suggestions, and edits turned this book into my greatest hope for what it could be.

Rejenne Pavon—I could not be more pleased with the cover. It captures all the key elements of the story and thrills me every time I look at it.

Playbill Inc.—taking the quiz, "Which Broadway Writing Team Are You and Your BFF?" by Logan Culwell-Block on Playbill.com as Rae and Mac was great fun; thank you for letting me include it in this novel.

Steven Hill—much appreciation for guiding me through permissions, answering my many questions, and granting me peace of mind.

Joe Landry—you wrote a *wonderful* play that I had a blast stage managing in a community theatre production years ago, so to get to include it in this story is an honor, and to have developed a friendship with you is a delightful bonus I never expected.

The writing partners, theatre groups, colleagues, and friends who have given me so much support, encouragement, laughter, and love over the years—in particular, Melanie Amato; Don "Diesel" Davis; Veronica Karingada; Will and Riley King; Al and Gloria Marcinonis; Lynn McConnell; Laura Wall; and Steve and Betsy Wonderly. To Susan Albert, for being one of the sunniest people I know and for sharing her artistic talents with me on multiple occasions; to Julie King, for being my theatre friend who turned into my everything friend and who remains my BFF more than two decades later; and to Kelli Rex, for being my books' biggest fangirl and an all-around lovely human.

My family—

My grandparents, Audrey Dodson, who swore she could pick my voice out of a 100-person choir, and Dale Dodson, who always believed this would happen. My aunts, Sue Fillers, who shared her love of theatre and life lessons on positivity, and Pat Smith, whose advice on publicity was invaluable and whose pride in me warms my heart. And my mother- and father-in-law, Diane and Jon Wilkoff, who would do anything for the people they love.

My parents, Tom and Denise Stout, whose life goal for me was to be happy and who share my every joy tenfold. You epitomize the definition of unconditional love.

My daughter, Elise: since even before you were born, one of my favorite moments of any day has been reading stories with you. You impress and inspire me, and I am ecstatic to be your mama.

My husband, Shawn, for doing whatever was necessary to help this passion of mine fit into our lives. Mostly, thank you for being there for me to share all of my words.

Finally, to all the kindness champions out there—even the smallest act of kindness can have a tremendous effect. Let's change the world....

ABOUT THE AUTHOR

Brieanna Wilkoff (she/her) believes wholeheartedly in the power of kindness, the importance of theatre, and the awesomeness of '80s rock. She married her husband onstage at the oldest surviving theatre in central Ohio, and their first dance was to Bon Jovi's "Thank You for Loving Me." Her favorite musical is a three-way tie between *Les Mis*, *Wicked*, and *Hamilton*.

I'll Be There for You is Brieanna's debut young adult novel. It was inspired by her family's commitment to kindness, including performing 100 kind acts in a single day. Brieanna lives in Westerville, Ohio, with her husband, daughter, and dog. You can visit her online at brieannawilkoff.com or follow her on Twitter @BrieannaWilkoff or Instagram @brieanna_wilkoff.